WEREling
DARK MOON

The place:
A luxury apartment in Docklands, London. HQ of Charron Industrial Inc.—a global empire dedicated to fighting the powers of the Netherworld

The time:
Spring. Five months after fourteen-year-old Trey Laporte discovered he was a werewolf

The characters:
Lucien Charron—vampire
Alexa Charron—daughter of above; sorceress
Trey Laporte—ex-ordinary teenager; last hereditary werewolf
Tom O'Callahan—human. Tough guy and enforcer

The bad guy:
Caliban—evil vampire brother of Lucien Charron; bloodthirsty beast, intent on destruction

The mission:
Read on . . .

Bloodthirsty books by Steve Feasey

Wereling

Wereling: Dark Moon

Look out for

Wereling: Blood Wolf

Dark Moon

A WEREling NOVEL

STEVE FEASEY

FEIWEL AND FRIENDS
NEW YORK

A FEIWEL AND FRIENDS BOOK
An Imprint of Macmillan

DARK MOON. Copyright © 2009 by Steve Feasey. All rights reserved. Printed in
December 2010 in the United States of America by R. R. Donnelley & Sons
Company, Harrisonburg, Virginia. For information, address Feiwel and Friends,
175 Fifth Avenue, New York, N.Y. 10010.

A CIP catalogue record for this book is available from the British Library.

ISBN: 978-0-312-64643-1

Originally published in the United Kingdom as *Changeling: Dark Moon* by
Macmillan Children's Books, a division of Macmillan Publishers Limited

First published in the United States by Feiwel and Friends, an imprint of Macmillan

Feiwel and Friends logo designed by Filomena Tuosto

First U.S. Edition: 2011

10 9 8 7 6 5 4 3 2 1

www.feiwelandfriends.com

For my mum.
Thank you for all the love.

1

The vampire Lucien Charron lay motionless on the high-sided bed. The room, one of many in the luxurious apartment, had been specially converted to house the bed and the various bits of medical equipment linked to the unmoving figure. As a result, the space was stark and clinical. The penthouse nestled at the top of a building in the region of London known as Docklands. Once a derelict and neglected part of the city, money had flooded into the area a couple of decades back, and now Docklands boasted some of the most expensive riverside properties in the capital. But even these fabulous glass-and-chrome edifices looked bleak and dreary in the gray early morning daylight that washed over the cityscape today, and the same light spilled through the window of Lucien's room, making the interior all the more harsh and unwelcoming.

White sheets had been stretched smooth over Lucien's body, tucked in around the edges, tracing the hills and valleys of his body to create a miniature landscape of virginal snow. The covers would stay like this, intact and unspoiled, as he lay unmoving beneath them. It would be easy to think that the pale, still creature was indeed dead—the skin was the color of gray pumice stone, and that essence of *being*, which you instinctively feel when sharing a room with someone, had all but vanished. The vast array of machines and monitors blinking and beeping from the other side of the bed were the only things to suggest that the vampire still defied the inevitable end that the doctors anticipated.

Lucien had woken only once in the five months that he had been in this state—a few weeks after he had saved his daughter's life from his evil vampiric brother, Caliban. Even then, he had regained consciousness for only a matter of moments—asking questions as to his daughter's safety and Caliban's defeat. Upon hearing the news of their success, he had sunk back into the darkness, diving back down into a coma from which it was unclear if he would ever return.

The doctor glanced up from his chart to his patient, and recorded the data that again signified no change in Lucien's condition. He returned the clipboard to its position at the bottom of the bed, and turned to the three people waiting just inside the door who were staring back at him with eyes full of hope and worry.

"There is no improvement, I'm afraid," he said. "As I explained last week, the lung seems to have made an almost full recovery following the surgery, and the wound where the stake was driven through his chest and back has also healed better than we had any right to hope for. But this bite wound . . ." He shook his head and glanced down at the dressing that covered the offending injury. "It defies all attempts that we have made to treat it. The localized infection that we have been fighting since we first saw it is, I am afraid, getting worse."

The wound was a result of Lucien "misting" between his daughter and Caliban at the very moment his evil brother had attempted to kill her. The huge fangs that were meant for her young neck had instead buried themselves into Lucien's shoulder. Lucien had survived only because the young werewolf, Trey Laporte, had attacked Caliban and forced him to release his brother.

The damage to Lucien's shoulder refused to heal. Like all wounds inflicted on nether-creatures by their own kind, it would not mend in the extraordinarily quick fashion that "normal" wounds would. The rejuvenating powers of vampires and other beings from the Netherworld made them almost impervious to injuries caused by humans and animals from the human plane. But the wounds inflicted by their own kind were subject to different healing processes, and were more often than not deadly. Lucien had been injured by nether-creatures before, but this wound, and the resulting sickness it had caused, was unlike anything that his physicians had encountered before.

The doctor peeled back the dressing to reveal a raw, infected lesion beneath. The bite marks where the teeth had punctured the flesh were still wet, refusing even to scab over, and an acrid-smelling pus still oozed from the angry red craters, despite the huge doses of antibiotics that the doctors had administered. The skin surrounding the puncture wounds looked pinched; a purple lividity discolored the flesh, making it look sore and tender even after all this time. And it smelled. It reeked of the rot that attacked the body—a parasitic infection that was all too eager to consume its host.

"The sepsis that continues to seep into Lucien's blood from this wound is not responding to any of our treatments. I'm afraid that he appears to be losing the fight that he has waged for so long. The situation is very bad. If we can't find a new way to stop this infection, then we will lose Lucien."

Three pale and strained faces stared back at him. A mean-looking man with a scarred face, a tall, lean teenage boy, and a fine-featured girl with jet-black hair all searched the doctor's face for some sign of hope.

"How long does my father have?" Alexa asked in a small voice.

"It is too hard to say, Miss Charron. To be honest, we're amazed that he is still alive, so it is beyond me to predict how long he might be able to continue fighting. We really have run out of options. We will use any and all palliative care at our disposal to keep your father as comfortable as possible, but you should prepare yourself for the worst."

The tall Irishman, Tom, stepped forward into the silence that followed and shook Dr. Tremaine by the hand. "Thank you, Howard. We appreciate how hard you and your team are working." He gently guided the doctor to the door and followed him out, leaving Trey and Alexa behind.

"Are you OK?" Trey asked when the silence in the room became too much to bear.

"No, not really," Alexa replied, trying to summon up a brave smile.

"Is there anything I can do?" he said, feeling utterly helpless as he looked between his friend and his guardian on the bed.

"No. But thanks, Trey. I think that I'd like to be alone with my dad if that's OK."

Trey nodded and left the room, closing the door behind him. On the other side he sank back against it, closing his eyes and trying to absorb everything that the doctor had just said. He sighed and opened his eyes again, briefly taking in the opulence of the apartment that he now lived in—the fine furnishings, the artwork and tapestries that lined the walls, the vast array of technological gadgets and equipment that filled the luxury penthouse. It would not have looked out of place on a TV show about the houses of the rich and famous. But the apartment was only a tiny part of the empire that Lucien Charron had built up through the years, an empire that was dedicated to destroying the evil forces of the Netherworld and to protecting the human race from those creatures within it that would do them harm. It was a business that needed Lucien at its head to function, and Trey didn't want to imagine what would happen if his guardian was not around to lead the fight. Tom and Alexa had been running things, keeping on top of everything as best they could, but Trey suspected that they had only been able to do so because Caliban had been so very quiet. Too quiet. They hadn't heard from the evil Netherworld lord since they had returned from Amsterdam five months ago. The lack of contact with the vampire lord had led Trey to hope that he might have perished as a consequence of his own injury—Trey had bitten off Caliban's hand in the battle to rescue Alexa—but he knew better. Vampires were hard to kill; Lucien was living proof of that. No, Caliban's silence was deliberate, and that could only be a bad thing—whatever it was that he was planning, it was something big. And they needed to hear from the vampire; Lucien's survival depended on them doing so and finding out where he was.

Trey nodded to himself and strode toward the elevator set in the wall to his left, heading for the research rooms on the floor below.

Moving to her father's side so that she could hold his hand, Alexa fought to stop the tears from falling. She leaned forward and whispered to the prone figure on the bed, "Don't you listen to them. There *is* something that can be done for you. Trey, Tom, and I are still working on it. So you . . . you just hang on in there, OK? Do you hear me? You just keep on fighting for a little while longer."

She reached out and ran her hand across his bald, smooth head, the way that she had done since she was a little girl, sitting on his lap and listening to stories about the things he had seen during his incredibly long existence. As far back as she could remember, he had always been bald, and she found it impossible to imagine him with hair. She leaned forward and kissed his cool cheek, before placing the hand that she had been holding back on top of the covers.

She left the room and wasn't surprised to see Tom waiting just outside for her. She nodded to him and smiled sadly. They had only one option left. They were going to have to steal Mynor's Globe—an ancient object with incredible powers to heal nether-creatures.

The globe had played a key role in the early Demon Wars. Much coveted for its ability to bring wounded individuals back to health, the globe itself was the cause of many conflicts between rival demon lords. But it had been lost, supposedly forever, on some muddied, bloodied battlefield, and largely forgotten about until Caliban and the sorceress Gwendolin had somehow managed to locate it. Even then, the globe was assumed to be useless to the pair; it was difficult to use, and its powers had proved to be beyond the ken of even Gwendolin. But Alexa's mother was nothing if not relentless in her thirst for knowledge. She'd tracked down a demon that had taught her the secrets of the globe—a demon that Alexa had subsequently located and quizzed—and now the globe was functioning again, and it might be the only thing capable of saving Lucien.

The look that passed between Alexa and the Irishman said it all. They had no choice—they were going to have to enter the Netherworld to try to steal the globe from right under the nose of Gwendolin.

If they failed, Alexa's father would die.

2

"Ah, here he is," Tom said in his broad Irish accent as Trey plodded into the kitchen the following morning. "I was debating whether to wake you from your much-needed beauty sleep and get you to face the world—it being your birthday and all—but, knowing how you like to lie in for obscene lengths of time, I figured that I'd wait it out, and that you'd rise of your own accord when the sound of your belly growling became louder than that of your snoring."

Trey squinted, screwing up his face against the strong light that flooded in through the floor-to-ceiling windows that made up one entire wall of the kitchen. He nodded in the direction of Alexa, who was standing at the kitchen table, a small pile of gifts and sealed envelopes arranged in the center. They had hung a banner up in the middle of the room—HAPPY 15TH BIRTHDAY picked out in silver and blue on a black background.

"How did you know that it was my birthday?" he said, sitting down opposite her at the table and helping himself to orange juice. "I didn't tell anyone."

"Are you kidding?" Alexa said. "You think that because you tried to keep it secret that we wouldn't find out?"

"So how did you know?"

"It's logged in Dad's calendar. Tom has access to all my father's computer files, and guess what popped up as an alert three days ago? Fancy not telling anyone it's your birthday! How lame are you, Trey?"

"I've just never really been one for birthdays, I suppose. In the care home they'd give you a card signed by all the staff and kids, a cake, and an extra few quid in your allowance that week. So it was never really a big deal."

"Well, now it's a big deal," Tom said, moving toward him. "Here, that's from me." He indicated the largest present on the table and nodded at Trey in a way that suggested that he was to open it first. Trey looked up at the tall, fierce-looking Irishman and picked up the gift, hefting it in his hands as if trying to guess by weight alone what it could be. He looked down at the package—it was long, just over three feet in length, and quite heavy.

"Oh for God's sake! Are you going to open the bloody thing or sit there and gawk at it all day?" Tom came and sat down next to him, the look of anticipation on his features made somehow horrific by the ugly, puckered scar tissue that dominated the side of his face nearest to Trey.

Looking up at Tom's excited expression, it was almost impossible for Trey to reconcile the person in front of him now with the man he knew to be Lucien's right-hand man—his enforcer. Tom was as hard as nails—a warrior who was always by Lucien's side in the toughest of situations, armed to the teeth with an arsenal of guns and explosives—but here he was behaving like a kid on Christmas morning.

Trey let out a short breath of exasperation and pulled at the red ribbon that was tied around the paper. He tore at the paper, frowning down at the long, zippered canvas bag in his hands. Unzipping it along its full length, he pulled the two sides apart, revealing the weapon inside. He quickly closed it again, as if the thing were in danger of leaping out of its own accord, and looked up at the Irishman.

"It's a rifle," he said, looking at the older man in horror.

"Well spotted," Tom replied. "A Marlin Model Sixty, to be precise. And"—he reached into his back pocket and pulled out an envelope that he handed to Trey—"I bought you a year's membership to the Marylebone Rifle and Pistol Club. You can come down with me later on, and we can have a little go with it, eh? I'll have to be with you at first, but after a few months you can go alone and practice when you like."

Trey opened the carry case again and stared in disbelief at the wood and metal gun nestling inside the canvas lining. Then he closed the zip, aware that Tom was leaning forward over him waiting for his reaction to the gift, so he obligingly donned a big, dumb smile and nodded his appreciation.

"Fantastic, Tom, thank you so much. But I really don't—"

"I saw how you liked the guns and things that we took with us on our little sortie over to Holland to rescue the lovely Alexa here. So when I found out that it was your birthday, I thought it'd be just the thing. You'll love it."

Trey couldn't even imagine picking up a gun, and was stupefied to think that his friend had actually gone out and bought him one. He placed the gun bag on the floor next to his chair and nodded his appreciation again. He hoped that Tom had not picked up on his dismay. The Irishman had never treated Trey with anything but kindness and respect, and the teenager felt a debt of gratitude to the man for everything that he had done for him since Lucien had taken him in as his ward. In addition, Trey was still more than a little nervous about Tom; there was a hard and ruthless aspect to the man that simmered just below the surface, which Trey hoped to carry on avoiding for as long as possible.

"Just humor him, Trey. He's been so excited about the whole thing since he thought up the idea. I tried to talk him out of it, but he wouldn't listen." Alexa spoke directly into his mind, using the telepathy spell that she employed in situations like this. He glanced over and saw her smiling back at him in amusement.

"This is from me," she said, stepping forward and holding out a much smaller gift that looked as if it had been wrapped by an expert in origami.

Trey took the package from her and carefully tore the paper away. It was a book. It appeared to be bound in some kind of skin that was rough to the touch, like very fine sandpaper. He went to open it, but Alexa stopped him with a gesture of her hand.

"I'd probably wait to open it," she said.

"Why?" Trey asked, looking over at her suspiciously.

"It's a book of spells. *Most* of which are perfectly safe," she added quickly, holding a hand up to stop his objections, "but some of them have a habit of catching you by surprise if you are not quite ready for them. It'll be better if we go through them together to start with."

Trey wanted to go back to bed. He suddenly felt that the signed card and chocolate cake that he had been given for his last three birthdays back at the care home were infinitely preferable to the gifts he had been given this morning. Tom had bought him a lethal weapon, and now Alexa appeared to have given him a book that was likely to kill him if he opened it unsupervised.

"Thanks," he said. "Thank you both very much. It's very . . . kind of you."

"There's one more thing," Alexa said. "Obviously he isn't able to give it to you himself, but I know that my father would have wanted you to have this."

She handed Trey another present. He looked down at it and then back up at her, a quizzical look on his face.

Alexa smiled at him sadly. "It's OK. You can open that one quite safely."

Inside was a silver photo frame. His mother and father were standing in front of a large lake with a dense and lush forest in the background. They were laughing straight into the lens of the camera, as if the photographer had just cracked some great joke that they'd enjoyed. There was another man in the picture, standing beside his father. Trey had never seen him before.

He kept his eyes on the photograph, breathing deeply to get his emotions under control. It must have been warm by the lake on the day that the photo was taken; his father's shirt buttons were undone at the top, and Trey could just about make out the chain around his neck. His fingers snaked toward his own chest, and he fiddled with the silver amulet through his T-shirt. The amulet had been his father's, and Lucien had given it to Trey when they had first met at the care home. Eventually he looked up, nodding his thanks to Alexa.

"Who's the other guy in the photo?" he asked with a gesture of his head in the direction of the photo frame, which was still in his lap.

"I don't know. My dad will, he'll . . ." Alexa's voice trailed away.

"Come on, Trey," Tom said loudly, breaking the uncomfortable silence that followed. "Mrs. Magilton has cooked you up some of those blueberry pancakes that you like so much, and I'll make you a nice cup of tea. And after that, we'll grab that peashooter of yours and I'll take you down to the shooting range for a lesson."

"Mr. Allen is coming today. I'll have to be in for him," Trey said quickly, looking for any excuse not to have to go to shoot the gun.

Mr. Allen was Trey's tutor. He was a strange little man with a beard that he let grow into an unruly mess beneath his chin. It hung down almost to his waist and gave him an odd, dwarfish appearance. He had been hired when it was decided that it was safer for Alexa and Trey to be home-tutored rather than attend school—something that Alexa

14

had vehemently fought against, but she'd had to acquiesce when Tom reminded her of the dangers that they had already faced following her abduction.

"Ah now, there'll be no lessons today," Tom said with a wink. "I've sorted the whole thing out. You've got a day off for your birthday. So wipe that miserable look off yer face and follow me. Blueberry pancakes and rifle shooting—perfect."

3

The shooting range was not far from Docklands, and Trey, trying to think of anything he could to delay the trip as much as possible, suggested that they go on foot.

"I don't really like the idea of walking around London carrying a rifle," Tom had said, and arranged for one of his men to take them by car instead. "Besides, the quicker we get there, the more shooting you'll be able to do."

Trey looked over at Alexa, who had sat smirking at him from the sofa throughout this exchange. "I suppose you think this is hilarious," he hissed at her when Tom had left the room for a moment.

"Look, just go along with him and see how you get on. Who knows? You might love it."

Trey shook his head and looked across at the rifle case that Tom had placed by the elevator. "I don't believe this," he muttered, and stomped off to find his jacket.

In the back of the car on the way over, Trey had tried to think up as many different ways as possible to let Tom know that he had no intention of firing the gun. He was scared witless of the things. As they pulled up outside the gun club Trey was about to say something, when he noticed the Irishman's face—excitement was etched into every feature at the prospect of what lay ahead, and Trey resigned himself to going along with his friend for one afternoon at least. He smiled back, hoping that his face portrayed the right amount of enthusiasm and none of the deep-seated anxiety that he really felt.

They entered through a small door, descending the steps into a foyer where Tom swiped a card into a slot by the door and entered a code on a keypad. A buzzing sound, like an angry wasp trapped in a tin can, signaled that the door was open, and they entered a short, poorly lit corridor. At the end of the passage, next to a giant cork board that held various notices and league tables for the club, they were met by a smiling middle-aged man, who introduced himself as David Rampton, the club secretary.

"Pleased to meet you, Trey," Mr. Rampton said, shaking him by the hand. "I'll show you around our facilities here and then we'll go through the safety talk. After that, I'll leave you in the more-than-capable hands of Tom here, and you can have a go with your wonderful new present. I'm sure that you will enjoy it here at the Marylebone, and congratulations on your birthday."

After an extremely long, painstaking safety lecture, Tom and Trey went down to the range, picking up some ammunition on the way. The range was empty, and Tom explained that this was his favorite time to come to shoot, when the bays were not full of people and you could take your time to get things right. They entered one of the central bays, placing their coats and bags under the small table toward the rear.

17

The walls on either side were high enough to block out any views, and Trey glanced down the range spread out in front of them. Tom unzipped the bag containing the rifle and placed it on the table between them. He explained the workings of the rifle again, going through the checks with Trey, making him perform the same procedures over and over until his hands began to ache. After an hour of this, Tom clapped him on the back and reached over for the ammunition box.

"Right, young Trey," he said, placing the box on the shelf, "do you think you're ready to have a go?"

Trey sighed. He was uncomfortable handling the gun when it was unloaded, but the thought of having live ammunition in the clip and firing it simply terrified him. "I don't know, Tom—it's all a bit scary."

"You're right," Tom replied. "It is scary, and it should be. These things are made for one reason and one reason alone. To kill. They really serve no other purpose. Yet more people are killed with knives every week than with guns. Guns don't kill people—people do." He looked over at Trey with a warm smile. "I know you're not one of those eejits that treat these things like a toy. But if you give it a go, and you listen to what I tell you to do, I'm certain that you'll enjoy the experience."

"OK." Trey nodded.

Tom loaded ten cartridges into a small hole near the stock of the gun, inserting the tube and locking it in place with a turn of his thumb. He handed the gun to Trey. "Pull back on the lever like we practiced and you're ready to go."

Trey looked over at Tom, who nodded in encouragement.

He held the gun up to his shoulder, the barrel pointing down the range. Tom reached up and flicked the switch that sent the target away from them on the mechanized pulley system that was fitted to each bay and stopped it at the ten-meter mark.

"Right, nice and close to start with. We'll send it right back later, once you've got the hang of things." He moved over to Trey and placed the ear protectors and safety glasses on his head. He gently took the boy's shoulders and maneuvered him into a firing position, nudging his feet into place with his own.

"Rack it up like we practiced, Trey. Take the safety off, aim down the sights, and gently squeeze the trigger," he said, before pulling the ear protectors right down over Trey's ears and giving him a big, cheesy thumbs-up.

Trey was sweating profusely as he aimed the rifle at the target; a little rivulet of perspiration ran down his cheek, detouring around his mouth before picking up speed again and sliding down his chin. He thumbed the safety switch and tried to take aim along the rear and front sights, his hands shaking so horribly that the end of the gun bounced around, making it difficult to fix on the large black-and-white target ahead. Taking a deep breath, he steadied himself and gently squeezed the trigger.

The explosion was loud—even with the ear protectors— and the gun snapped back into his shoulder. He had expected it to recoil more than it did and was even more surprised at the complete lack of smoke. He shivered, the adrenaline that

19

was coursing through his veins making his heart thump against his ribs as the thrill of the power that he had just controlled truly dawned on him. He sensed Tom step in behind him and he remembered what they had practiced beforehand. He thumbed the safety back, checked the chamber to ensure that there was no ammunition, and placed the gun—barrel still pointing down the range—back onto the table.

Tom placed a hand on his shoulder, and Trey removed the ear protectors and turned around.

"How was that?" Tom asked.

"Fantastic!" Trey said, grinning back at him.

"I'm very impressed by the way you made that gun safe again at the end there. It's easy to forget those things when you're all hyped up." He put his hand on Trey's shoulder and grinned one of his lopsided smiles at him. "Ready for some more?" he asked.

"Definitely," Trey replied, reaching out for the weapon again.

4

Trey had increased the target distance to the full twenty-five meters of the range and was now intent on increasing his accuracy as he fired round after round at the paper target mounted on the board in the distance. Every six shots he would press the button on the control panel to initiate the pulley system, peering intently at the large paper-and-board target as it slid back toward him on the overhead wires. He checked his shots, noting how many had found the black central area and how many had slipped into the white concentric rings on the outside—or missed entirely. When he had done this, and compared the scores with his previous best, he would replace the target with a fresh one and send it back down the range.

The shooting gallery was still empty. Tom stayed behind Trey, helping him to load the rifle and encouraging him when he had shot particularly well. It wasn't long before Trey had used up the entire box of cartridges. His arms ached and his right shoulder felt bruised from the recoil of the rifle. He placed the gun down on the table to rub the muscles in his forearms that felt tight and were starting to cramp.

"Had enough for one day?" Tom asked.

Trey grinned back at him. "That was fantastic, Tom. Thanks so much. I honestly didn't think that I was going to enjoy it at all, but it really is very addictive, isn't it?"

"I'm glad that it was fun. You're actually quite a good shot, you know. I'm impressed with how well you picked it up. If you keep coming, we'll get you entered into a competition for your age group. Now, I'll take this," he said, picking up the gun and checking that it was not loaded, "and put it in the gun store with mine. Next time we come, we'll get you your own space in there." He turned to leave, adding, "Will you be OK here on your own for a couple of minutes? There is something that I want to talk to David about, and then I'll be right back."

"Sure, Tom," Trey said. "I need to check that last target anyway, so I'll have a look at it while you're gone."

Tom nodded and left by a door at the back of the range, taking Trey's gun with him.

The teenager turned and opened a bottle of water, relishing the feel of the cool liquid on his parched throat. Sniffing at his hands, he noted how strongly they smelled of an acrid residue from the gun, and he grinned again at the feeling that he had experienced immediately following that first shot—the rifle kicking backward as it sent the deadly projectile hurtling toward its destination at impossible speed.

He glanced up at the target at the far end of the range and was about to start the machinery that would pull it toward him when he stopped, his finger hovering over the small green button. He frowned, squinting from behind the

22

yellow lenses of the safety glasses at the concentric circles of black and white. He was about to dismiss the notion as a simple trick of the light when it *flexed* again, the shapes that made up the target twisting on the paper, the black center bulging and squirming as if trying to pull itself free of the white surface. It had grown. The target appeared to have almost doubled in size, and it continued to grow as the printed outlines writhed and distorted upon it.

Trey's heart knocked into his ribs, and he was vaguely aware that he had let the plastic bottle that he had been holding slip from his fingers, spilling water all over his feet and onto the dusty concrete floor. He wanted to shout out, make somebody aware of the unnatural happenings, but all he could manage was a small croaking sound that got wedged in his throat.

The target had grown again. Now at least a meter in length and still distending in every direction, it had begun to take on a distinct shape. The contours of a humanoid figure were clearly visible now, the head and shoulders stretching the surface outward as if trying to push through from the other side, and Trey thought that he could almost make out the vague outline of a face peering at him. A hand suddenly shot forward, its fingers splayed as it groped for a handhold on the now rubberlike membrane of the paper—except Trey had stopped thinking of it as such; he now believed it to be some kind of skin between this world and that from which the creature was trying to break free. Trey saw the target pucker as the creature succeeded in getting a good grip and briefly wondered how on earth the thing, which had doubled in size once more, was still being held by the small retaining clips at the top of the apparatus.

Trey glanced behind him at the door, praying that Tom would appear. His heart was thumping in his chest, and his mind raced through a thousand different thoughts, stopping at none as he fought to figure out what he should do. He wanted to turn and run away, but his legs stubbornly refused to move, his feet anchored to the floor. He stood and gawked as the creature's other hand shot out toward him, stretching the membrane almost the length of the arm so that it wrapped around the limb, revealing it in perfect detail. This hand was not the one that had originally been attached to that arm. It was a grotesque prosthetic substitute—the fingers replaced by long, hinged talons that appeared to flex by means of a series of metal rods that ran back into the flesh of the wrist behind them. There was a sudden tearing sound, and a talon ripped through the membrane. It slashed at the air in Trey's direction before pulling back in an attempt to rip a bigger hole in the skin between the two worlds and allow the whole of the creature through.

Trey knew that he was looking at a portal between this realm and the Netherworld, and there was no doubt as to what or who was trying to break through from the other side.

Caliban had found him.

Caliban, the vampire responsible for the destruction of everything that Trey had ever held dear. Caliban, the reason

24

that Lucien was lying in a coma, fighting for his life. Caliban, who would stop at nothing in his quest to subjugate the human race and turn them into little more than cattle to be fed upon at will.

There was a harsh screech, the motor on the retrieval system suddenly sparked into life, and the entire thing started to advance down the long alley toward the teenager.

Trey stabbed at the stop button on the control panel, but the thing continued to rumble inexorably toward him, swinging slowly from the wires that carried it overhead. He began to turn his head to look for Tom, knowing he would not be there, when the vampire's face suddenly reared out at him, forcing itself against the membrane and stretching it out in his direction until Trey thought that it must rupture and free the hideous death face behind it.

Trey could clearly make out the fangs protruding from the upper jaw, and he imagined those exquisitely sharp and deadly barbs tearing and rending at his flesh as soon as Caliban managed to break free of the portal. With the target no more than ten feet away Trey did the only thing that he could: He morphed into a werewolf and attacked.

The change was almost bearable now. The excruciating agony that had accompanied his early changes was now a brief explosion of white-hot pain as his cellular makeup mutated—his bones thickened and elongated, and the muscles attached to them hypertrophied, the myofibrils within them multiplying ten-fold as he transformed into the huge, hulking man-wolf. Thick coarse hair erupted from unseen pores, and huge black claws and fangs burst forth from his fingers and mouth. His clothes and shoes tore at the seams and fell like rags to the floor around him.

Trey leaped at the grotesque figure in front of him, springing forward on huge, muscular legs. A great bellowing roar escaped his jaws as he ripped and tore at the bulging figure of the vampire. He had little doubt that something was wrong with the portal and that his best chance was to attack the vampire now and stop him from breaking through the viscous shield. Trey's huge jaws opened wide and he clamped his teeth around the crown of the vampire's bulbous head. With one wolf-hand, Trey grabbed the metal claw, pushing it back away from him. His other hand grabbed the top of the target and he shifted his immense weight downward, trying to wrestle the entire thing to the ground where he could attack more freely. The insubstantial wire and metal tubing that made up the overhead apparatus finally gave way and it crashed to the floor, creating a huge noise as the devastated machinery collapsed into the firing range. As he fell backward, Trey's jaws suddenly closed around nothing, snapping together in the empty air, and at the same instant the grip that he had had on the vampire was also lost.

Trey leaped to his feet and looked about him frantically, expecting the vampire to mist back at any second and attack him with taloned hands and fanged mouth. But the attack never came. There was no sign of Caliban. The air still rang with the metallic clamor of the broken equipment. But the vampire was not there. It was as if he had never been there. Trey had managed to drive him back to where he had come from. He looked at the ground, which was littered with the wood, metal, and wires of what had once been the target retrieval machinery. In the center of the mess were the ripped and broken pieces of the small wooden board and black-and-white target.

Tom burst in through the door at the back of the range, staring in horror as the seven-foot werewolf turned around to look at him.

"Change back, Trey. Quickly!" Tom said, looking through the door he had just come through.

Trey morphed back again just as David Rampton appeared.

The club secretary looked aghast at the sight of the boy standing naked in the firing range, surrounded by destroyed equipment.

"My God, what . . . what have you done?" he said. His voice was high and strained, accompanying the dark crimson color that had flooded his face.

Trey looked at him and then back down at the wreckage around him. "Er, there was a problem with the equipment. It got jammed and I lost my temper with it. I'm . . . truly sorry, Mr. Rampton. I'll pay for the damage . . . sorry."

"You bloody hooligan. What on earth do you think you are playing at?" He stopped for a moment, his eyes registering the incredible sight in front of him. "And why in God's name aren't you wearing any clothes?"

Trey grabbed his jacket, which was hanging on the back of a chair in the bay, and wrapped it around him as best he could to cover his nakedness. He could not think of a single excuse for why he would have been standing stark naked in the middle of a firing range.

"I got hot," he said, looking away and shaking his head at the absurdity of his answer.

Tom came to his rescue, his calm voice cutting though the silence in which David Rampton seethed and fumed and struggled for the words to express his fury. "He has some problems, David. He's been through some bad times recently, which have caused him some . . . emotional difficulties. I thought that bringing him down here might help him to get his head right again, you know, the discipline of shooting and all. Please accept our apologies for all of this, and as Trey said, we'll pay for everything."

David Rampton looked over at Tom as if noticing him for the first time. "Too bloody right you will. This equipment costs a small fortune. *And* you will also have to compensate the club for this bay having to be closed during the repairs. I will have to terminate both of your memberships with immediate effect. People like you, young man," he said, jabbing an angry finger in Trey's direction, "are simply not welcome at a club like this." He turned to look at the Irishman again. "You can pick your things up in the week, Tom. Right now, I'd like you both to leave."

Tom started to say something, but stopped, nodding

instead. "OK, David. We'll go right away. Come on, Trey; let's get out of here."

Trey walked toward him, stepping over the tangle of wires at his feet. He nodded his apologies again to the older man and allowed himself to be ushered out.

5

"What happened?" Tom said, as the car that had come to collect them pulled away.

"Caliban happened," Trey replied. "One second I was looking down at the target at the end of the range, the next thing I know, he's emerging out of some kind of portal, trying to get to me. I didn't have any choice. I'm sorry."

Tom looked at him, shaking his head slowly. "You have nothing to be sorry about, Trey. I shouldn't have left you on your own like that."

Trey looked out of the window at the high-rise buildings that made up London's financial district. Lunchtime was coming to an end and the office workers were all making their way back to their desks, walking along the streets slowly and trying to soak up as much of the sunshine as they could. Normality filled their lives, and Trey was bitterly jealous of them all. He doubted that he would ever feel anything close to normal again.

"I wanted to believe he might have given up," Trey said, shaking his head at his own foolishness. "We haven't seen or heard of him in all this time. You said yourself that he'd dropped off the radar and couldn't be found. So I hoped . . ." The teenager tipped his head back and closed his eyes, picturing the scene at the shooting range again in his head. "This is how it's always going to be, isn't it? Me always looking over my shoulder, waiting for the next time he attacks."

Tom was silent for a while. He looked over at the young man sitting next to him, and when he spoke it was in a soft voice that Trey had to strain to hear. "Yes, Trey, I think that you'll always have to be on your guard. Caliban doesn't really do 'giving up.' That is, until we can stop him for good. But you won't be on your own." The Irishman reached over and gave the boy's shoulder a gentle squeeze. "You have Alexa and me to watch your back, and we'll all find a way to get Lucien well again soon. If we get Lucien back, we *will* be able to stop Caliban." It was the Irishman's turn to look out of the window, and Trey turned his head to study him.

"I don't think today's attack was planned," the Irishman continued. "Caliban has been up to something, something that he is desperate to keep hidden from us. That's why we haven't been able to find him. But he's been keeping an eye on us, and I think the opportunity to get at you today was too much for him to resist. From what you describe, it sounds like they rushed the creation of the portal—either that or he was too impatient to wait for it to form properly and he got stuck. You were lucky, although I don't suppose you feel it right now."

Tom punched Trey gently on the arm. "You might want to put these clothes on." He indicated a small pile of clothing that he'd asked the driver to bring with him from the apartment. Turning in his seat, he stared out of his window, humming to himself and giving the boy a small degree of privacy.

They sat in silence for the remainder of the journey, eventually pulling up next to the entrance of the huge building that was home to Charron Industrial Inc. as well as being the London home of Lucien and his family.

Trey stood on the pavement looking up at the former warehouse. The building didn't look like much from the outside, but it contained a small army of demons, djinn, and other nether-creatures dedicated to directing their powers—earthly and magical—to protecting this realm from the Netherworld. They were protecting him too. These creatures that he had come to regard as the closest thing he had to a family were also shielding him from Caliban. The vampire wanted the boy dead. Trey was a danger to him—the last hereditary werewolf. Caliban believed in an ancient legend that foretold that a full-blood werewolf would bring down a vampire ruler. As a growing force in the Netherworld, building his power base, Caliban wasn't planning on letting a werewolf get in his way.

Tom coughed politely, bringing Trey's thoughts around. "Are we going in or are you going to stand there all day gawking up at nothing?"

Trey nodded and followed his friend through the door into the small foyer at the front of the building. They walked past an ordinary-looking security guard who Trey knew was actually a demon and stepped into the elevator. It started its ascent, and as it slowed, Tom looked over at Trey, a strange, unreadable expression on his face.

"Be nice," he said mysteriously. He gave Trey a stern look before turning toward the doors as they slid apart.

"SURPRISE!" A great cheer went up as they entered the apartment and party poppers went off, dumping paper twists on their heads. Trey's nerves were so frazzled that for a split second he thought he was under attack again and almost morphed right there and then.

"Happy birthday, Trey," Alexa said, and kissed him on the cheek.

She was wearing a short black dress, and her long hair was piled up in a style that Trey thought looked too old for her. Nevertheless she looked stunning, and he blushed as she kissed him.

"We know that you 'don't do birthdays,' Trey," Alexa said, holding out a bottle of soda for him, "but we decided that we would like to hold a little party for you. It was Tom's idea really, but I'll take full credit for setting it up."

There were some people from the office downstairs that Trey had made friends with, and Stephanie, Alexa's best friend, was there. Mrs. Magilton, the housekeeper, waved at him, a silver party hat at a jaunty angle on her head. Trey was pleasantly surprised to see Jens van der Zande in the crowd, the tall Dutchman towering over everyone else in the room. He stepped forward and shook Trey warmly by the hand. Jens had been with them in Amsterdam when they had rescued

Alexa from Caliban, and Trey was genuinely pleased to see him.

"Many happy returns, Trey," the tall Dutchman said, almost managing to break his stern, chiseled features into a smile. "I didn't know what to get, so I brought this for you." He handed Trey a rectangular package about a foot in length. "I thought that you might like it. A memento of your last visit with us."

"Thank you, Jens—you shouldn't have," Trey said, unwrapping the paper.

Inside was a glass case that held what looked to Trey like a gray mummified hand resting on bright purple silk.

"What is it?" Trey asked, staring down at it in horror.

"Don't you know?" the Dutchman said, raising an eyebrow at Trey.

"Oh, Jens, please tell me this isn't—"

"Yes, it's his hand. Caliban's. The one that you bit off."

Trey was about to say something that he was sure he would regret later on, when Tom rushed over and clamped his hand around his shoulders, steering him away from the Dutchman. "Come on, fella," he said. "Let's be getting you and your *delightful* new gift into the kitchen. Alexa has organized the caterers, and I for one could do with a large, strong drink right now."

Trey allowed himself to be firmly pushed in the direction of the kitchen as the party started in earnest behind him.

He threw the glass case with the hand in it onto one of the

34

kitchen worktops, stepping back from it as if expecting the thing inside to suddenly come to life and crawl toward him.

Tom picked up the macabre gift, peering in at the severed limb before glancing back over to Trey and shaking his head, a wry smile on his face.

"Don't ask," he said as Trey started to speak. "I have no idea what he was thinking either." The Irishman looked at the door before continuing, shaking his head sadly as he spoke. "I'm really sorry, boy. I'd planned to celebrate your birthday with you tonight, but I'm going to have to skip the party. This sudden appearance by Caliban is what we've been waiting for, and I need to get downstairs to do some work."

Trey nodded. "It's OK. Do you want me to come down and help?"

Tom grinned back at him. "You don't get out of it that easy. Get yourself back in there and try to enjoy yourself. See if you can forget what happened today, for now at least. Alexa's worked hard to set this all up. We'll all meet up at six a.m. sharp to discuss anything that I might discover." He walked past Trey and out through the kitchen door, leaving the teenager alone.

Trey looked at his reflection in the large sliding windows, wondering how he was supposed to go back into the other room and join a party after everything that had happened to him. He turned, glancing again at the hand in the case, and resolved to take it down to the incinerator first thing in the morning and have it disposed of. He only wished that the appendage's former owner could be so easily destroyed.

He took a deep breath, held it for a second, and then, plastering a cheesy grin on his face, he too left the kitchen, to join his friends in celebrating his birthday.

6

Trey stood on the balcony outside the kitchen looking out over the Thames that snaked its way past Docklands on its way out to sea. The water was high now and a breeze blew up from the water, tousling his hair and carrying a briny, metallic smell that he liked.

The party had slowly broken up as the few people who had attended drifted away throughout the evening. Guests had come up to him at various points to say good night and wish him happy birthday. He'd thanked them for coming and for their cards and presents before seeing them to the elevator. When they'd all left he'd come out here to get some fresh air. During the party he'd surprised himself by actually managing to heed Tom's advice and somehow forget the earlier events of the day, but now that he was alone again they crashed back in on him and sent his mood spiraling downward. Alexa had indeed done a great job organizing everything and making sure that everyone he had befriended in the last few months had been invited.

This is my family now, he thought. *These are people that care about me.* He considered how lucky he was to have the one thing that he had wanted for so many years. *But why did it have to come at such a terrible price?*

He sighed again and looked down at the contents of the same bottle that he'd been handed upon entering the party. The soda was warm and flat, having been nursed in his hand all evening. He emptied the remains out over the balcony, turned, and went back inside.

Entering the apartment he was surprised to find Tom sitting in the kitchen, reading a paperback novel by some thriller writer—the book's glossy cover had the silhouette of a gun sight's crosshairs centered on the outline of a Nazi SS badge.

"How's it going?" Trey asked.

"Not great. I'm just having a quick break and then I'm back off downstairs. I'm convinced that this morning's unexpected reappearance by you-know-who is the signal that he's up to his old tricks again. I just need some small clue as to where he's hiding. The office is quietest at this time of night so I can get more done."

Trey knew that there was another reason that Tom liked to work so late—there was a traitor somewhere in their midst. They knew that Caliban had an informant inside Lucien's organization, someone who had put all of their lives at risk, and Tom had taken steps to make sure that either he, or someone who he trusted, was in the office at all times.

This was one of the many offices that Lucien Charron had set up around the world, and it was manned by a vast array of people (and creatures) who specialized in various aspects of magecraft, demon lore, the occult, and other things that Trey still had no idea about. It was like an incident room at times and he would sometimes visit and marvel at the level of activity that kept the place buzzing with excitement.

Most of the staff were demons, but to Trey's eyes they looked as human as he did. The human *shell* that they wore in this world to disguise their true appearance was impossible to differentiate from the real thing. *Unless you too were a nether-creature.* Then you could see through this mantle and spy the true being beneath. It was like looking through a shimmering gauze curtain at a figure that lay just behind. Trey could see demon form only when he was fully morphed into his werewolf state. Nosy and frustrated at this, one day he had locked himself in a meeting room and, after transforming, had peeked out from behind the venetian blinds to see who was who and what was what. He was surprised to discover how many of his guesses as to who was human and who was not were wrong, and equally taken aback at the huge range of nether-creatures on display.

Some were humanoid in form but with grotesque faces, features ranging from multifaceted eyes, beaks, large razor-lined mouths, and even one that appeared to have a number of snakelike tentacles that hung down the front of its dark green face, the demon's eyes mounted at the tips of these appendages. Some were utterly alien in appearance. Trey was surprised to discover that Nathan, whose desk Trey had sat at having long chats about football, was actually a giant sluglike creature. His "head"—nothing more than an extension of his black glistening body—was topped by two huge bulbous eyes that seemed capable of looking in any direction.

Below these was a perfectly round mouth that opened and closed like some ghastly sphincter, showing a series of perfectly triangular teeth. As Trey watched from the meeting room, Nathan laughed at a comment made by someone across the room from him, coming back with a quick retort of his own. Trey could see the human mantle that the demon wore on the outside sitting in his chair with his legs crossed, but *through this* he could see the giant gastropod, its body covered in mucus, and that hideous mouth opening and closing as it communicated. After the initial shock, Trey merely made a mental shoulder shrug and continued to spy out the other members of the office. What did it matter? Nathan was a slug-thing, Trey was a werewolf, Lucien a vampire.

It occurred to him how quickly he had become used to these things. It was just another *layer of weird* that he had been forced to accept as his old, normal life had been peeled away piece by piece to be replaced by this supernatural one that he was now a part of.

He'd asked Alexa if the demons that worked for her father could see the huge seven-foot werewolf—the nether-creature he was able to transform into—when he spoke with them in his human form.

"It doesn't work like that," she had told him. "In the same way that you, as a human, are unable to see into the Netherworld, the nether-creatures when they look at you see only the human Trey. But when you morph, they can see both elements of your makeup—the werewolf and something of the human form within."

He'd nodded when he'd heard this, but didn't ask her the question that was really bothering him—why did everybody seem so uncomfortable around him when he was in his werewolf state? Demons and humans alike had that same nervous look about them that he had seen on the faces of people when they had spoken to Lucien, suspicion mixed with a liberal dose of fear. As if the thing in front of them was apt to turn on them and attack without provocation, like a dog that suddenly takes it into its mind for no good reason to bite the child that it grew up with.

Trey walked into the living area, debating whether or not he wanted to put the television on. He picked up the remote control and stared at it. A shrill giggle came from behind Alexa's door, and he half turned to look in that direction. Stephanie was staying over tonight, and she and Alexa were no doubt deep in conversation about "girly" things—whatever they might be. He felt troubled and restless but didn't want to bother Alexa right now. Instead he turned, knocked softly once, and then entered Lucien's room, closing the door quietly behind him. Leaving the lights off, he lowered himself into the chair by the side of the bed. The LEDs from the various machines that monitored Lucien day and night emitted an eerie glow into the murk, and he cast his eyes over the still figure on the mattress before reaching across to pat the hand that lay on top of the covers, the skin soft and cold to the touch.

"I hope you don't mind me coming in, Lucien. It's just that I find it easier to get things off my chest to you. Alexa and Tom are up to their necks in trying to find Caliban and Gwendolin so that we can get this Mynor's Globe to make you well again, and every time I try to help I can tell that all I'm really doing is getting in their way." He turned his head and smiled as he caught the muffled sound of music coming at him across the apartment from behind Alexa's bedroom door.

"Tonight is the first night in months that Alexa has let her hair down," he said, turning back to the figure of Lucien. "She's been in the research room every night, and when she isn't there she's in here with you. You're all she's got." He paused, closed his eyes, and allowed the silence of the room to wash over him.

"It isn't the same without you around, Lucien. We're like a ship without a captain." One of the machines made a beep and Trey glanced up at it. "I'm all mixed up. I could really do with you right now." He looked back at his guardian. "Thank you for my birthday present. It's a nice picture of them both—they look really happy in it."

He stood up, looking down at the figure, the head of their little clan, and allowed the sadness to consume him.

"Keep strong. We'll find a way to get you back soon."

7

The Necrotroph looked around the office, its eyes skimming over the desks, quickly taking in the personnel that were still working at this late hour. The human, Tom, had left the office, announcing that he was having a break, and the demon considered how long it might take to do what it needed to. It waited for five minutes, watching them slowly count off from the clock on its desktop. Then, deciding that the Irishman had gone upstairs, it stood up, picked its cup off the table, and walked over to the research room that the man had vacated, glancing back over its shoulder as it slipped inside and closed the door behind it. It stood on the other side, taking in the scene.

The table surface was invisible beneath the mess of papers, maps, and used mugs strewn across it. Some of these papers appeared to be ancient texts, no doubt taken from the vast archive of work that the vampire, Charron, had gathered over the years. Others were computer printouts, and it was toward these that the demon walked, reaching out for the nearest one. It checked over its shoulder again before returning its attention to the paperwork. The table of data showed nothing more interesting than the use, for the last few weeks, of a particular spell, and the demon pushed the paper away, positioning it in exactly the same place that it had been beforehand. It was looking for notes of some kind, anything that might suggest what the Irishman, the vampire's brat daughter, and recently, even the werewolf boy might be looking for. Some clue as to what they were up to—any information that it could pass on to its master, Caliban.

It moved a map detailing some region of the Netherworld and smiled as the corner of a hardback notebook revealed itself. It reached out and was about to pull it across the table when a voice stopped it in its tracks.

"What are you doing in here?" It was unmistakably the Irishman, Tom O'Callahan. "I've specifically asked that nobody come into this room when I'm using it. Even if I pop out for a break. That's why the sign on the door says 'occupied.'"

Luckily the demon's back was to the door, blocking off any view of what its hands had been doing, and it withdrew them to its sides, one brushing across the map to return it to its original position, the other hooking up the handle of the cup that it had placed on the table in front of it. It turned toward the door, a smile on its face.

Tom looked at the woman standing before him, taking in the embarrassed flush that filled her cheeks and the way that her fingers fidgeted around the cup in her hands. She'd worked with them for a very long time now and he knew her to be a loyal and honest worker. A bit of a nosy busybody, but a good person for all that.

"I just popped in to see if you wanted a cup of tea or

coffee. You're working so very hard at the moment that I thought you could do with a nice hot drink." She watched as his eyes flicked toward the table. "I was just looking on the table for your cup. I didn't touch anything though, I swear."

There was a silence as the Irishman studied her face, his eyes never blinking as he took in her every feature.

"No, thank you, Ruth," he said eventually, apparently satisfied with what he had seen. "I've just had a cuppa upstairs." He stood to one side, signaling for her to leave the room, before continuing in a hard voice. "And, as I say, I'd appreciate it if you didn't come in here when the room's in use." He held a hand up to stop her protestations.

The deep red hue flushed through the woman's cheeks again, and she bustled past him, murmuring her apologies over again as she did so.

Tom watched her settle back into the seat at her desk, returning her attention to the monitor in front of her. He closed the door and stood just inside the room, studying the papers on the table and trying to determine if anything was out of place. After a moment he shook his head and returned to his seat, admonishing himself for being so paranoid. He blamed it on his tiredness. Ruth was one of their most trusted employees. He had known her for so many years—had known her and her husband before she had come to work for Lucien. He would have a chat with her tomorrow and apologize for being so brusque.

* * *

The demon eventually felt that it was safe to look up from its desk. It glanced over at the figure of the Irishman, who was now poring over the maps and papers again. It let out a little sigh of relief and inwardly cursed itself for being so sloppy. It would not do to be careless like that again. It would have to wait, bide its time, and find some other way to discover what they were up to.

8

"Put this one on again—I love this band." Steph knelt up on Alexa's bed and pointed to one of the titles on the LCD screen, the empty soda bottle that she still clutched knocking against the plastic housing. Each room in the apartment was equipped with a multifunction panel from which you could control the room's lighting and temperature as well as audio, video, and telecoms. Stephanie was trawling through the huge list of songs that were stored on a central server, stopping and adding them to a playlist that was already far too long for them to get through in one evening.

Alexa looked over at her friend and smiled. She hadn't seen her in ages. After Lucien's injury, the threat to her life was increased, and since Tom had insisted on her being home-tutored, her contact with her school friends had utterly stopped. The fact that Alexa's father had suddenly opted to remove her from school didn't come as too much of a surprise to Alexa's school friends. Everybody at the school thought Lucien was strange and mysterious, always locking himself away whenever they came to visit, and never attending school events, sending the big Irishman instead. Many theories about who and what Alexa's dad might be had spread through the school; some of them were bizarre, others

47

just plain mean. One theory had Lucien down as a madman recluse—some kind of Howard Hughes figure—another had him as a drug trafficker or criminal mastermind. Alexa never did anything to quash the gossip, knowing that the rumors could never be as shocking as the real truth about her father.

"Play it then, pest."

Steph grinned back and pressed the touch screen with the pad of a finger hidden beneath a long bright pink fingernail. Music filled the room from the hidden speakers in the walls and ceiling, and Alexa picked up a remote control to turn down the volume a little.

"Don't, Lex!" Steph said.

"It's getting late and it's not fair to everyone else," Alexa said, smiling back at her friend. "Besides, I didn't ask you over tonight to listen to music all evening. I want to know the gossip, what's going on that I don't know about." She shuffled over on her knees to get closer to Stephanie. "Come on, spill the beans. What don't I know that I should or, even better, shouldn't?"

"Not a lot really," Steph said. "Most of it you know already."

"Oh, come off it. There must be *some* juicy goss."

Steph flashed a wicked smile back at her. "Well, there might be a couple of little snippets that I've picked up here and there. You know Emma Myers? She's supposed to be going out with Jake Chalmers, but, and here's the big but, Jake Chalmers is already going out with Tracey King. And when Tracey finds out, I would not like to be in Emma Myers's shoes. She'll kill her."

"Jake Chalmers? He's ugly, for heaven's sake! What on earth does either of them see in him?"

"He's got a car. I think that might have something to do with it. Besides, he's not that ugly."

"Stephanie Ellis, book yourself an appointment with an optician because you need glasses in a hurry. Jake Chalmers is the pits."

Steph raised an eyebrow and looked over at her friend, shaking her head. "I'm assuming that there is still no man in your life? When was the last time you went out with anyone?"

"It's been a while."

"*A while!* That has to be the understatement of the year. You need to get out and about a bit more, Lex. You live like a nun." She smiled at her friend, and then a look that Alexa knew all too well crossed her face. "Has *he* got a girlfriend?" she asked with a gesture of her head toward the closed door behind her.

"Who?"

"The sexy Irishman," she said, rolling her eyes. "Who do you think? Trey!"

"No. He's been through a lot recently, and I think the last thing he needs right now is a girlfriend. Why?"

"Because he's cute, that's why."

"Yeah, whatever," Alexa said, turning her back on Steph to change songs.

"So you're not interested in him then?" Steph asked.

"Because I was thinking of asking him out on a date. Maybe go to the movies or something. There's a horror movie on at the multiplex at the moment, something about a group of school kids that get trapped in a bus in the middle of nowhere, and how they get picked off one by one by a group of homicidal inbreds. There is nothing like a good horror flick in the dark to get a guy in the mood."

Alexa's mind was instantly cast back to the moment, five months earlier, when she had witnessed Trey as a huge, seven-foot-tall, black-and-gray werewolf biting down through the arm of a vampire, severing the limb just above the wrist and saving her father's life. He had attacked with a fury that was difficult to reconcile with the shy, quiet fifteen-year-old who Stephanie was referring to as "cute."

Steph, you have no idea, Alexa thought, smiling back at her friend.

"Would you be bothered?" Stephanie asked. She had that mischievous look about her again and Alexa knew that she was fishing.

"Me? No. Why should I be bothered?"

"Oh, come on, Lex. I've seen the way he looks at you sometimes. And you aren't exactly doing anything to put him off, are you? Batting your eyelashes and playing with your hair every time the two of you talk. I just assumed that you were, you know, keen on him too."

"Don't be so lame, Steph," Alexa said with a shake of her head. "He's not my type. He's too young, for one thing. We're just good friends. Besides, we live together. I hardly think that my dad would be over the moon at the thought of his daughter going out with the boy that he has taken under his charge."

Alexa stopped then. The mention of her father had suddenly brought everything back to her and she thought about him lying on the other side of the apartment surrounded by machines and drips and needles while she laughed and joked with her friend following a party. And yet she had enjoyed herself tonight. Perhaps more than she liked to admit. She had felt herself let go a little this evening, and for the first time in months she had laughed out loud and banished some of the sadness and worry that she had harbored inside her for so long.

Steph picked up on the change in her friend's mood. "How is your dad?" she asked.

"No better, but thanks for asking." She nodded her head at her friend's empty bottle, quickly changing the subject. "Do you fancy another drink?"

Stephanie shook her head. "No, thanks, I'm fine." The smile crept back over her face and she looked at Alexa from beneath eyebrows that had been shaped recently at some salon or another. "So you don't mind then? Me asking Trey out."

Alexa looked across at her friend. She and Steph had been friends from the first day that they had started high school together, and she knew her to be a caring, kind, and loving person. But she also knew what a complete shark Steph was when it came to guys. She'd had countless boyfriends in the time that they'd been at the school. Something inside Alexa balked at the idea of her going out with Trey, and from the way that Stephanie was looking back at her now, she guessed that her face had revealed some of this. What was it she was feeling? Jealousy? Surely not.

This is madness, she thought. *I don't have any feelings for Trey.*

She frowned slightly, trying again to pinpoint exactly the emotion that her friend's question had created within her.

It really isn't any of my business, she told herself. If Steph liked Trey, and he chose to take her up on her offer of a date, what difference was it to her?

"No, I don't mind. Go for it," she said.

"Great," Steph replied. "I get the feeling that young Trey could do with a woman to teach him a thing or two. Hand me those bottles. I'll take them out to the kitchen and see if he's hanging around outside."

Alexa watched her friend start to move toward the door and was suddenly acutely aware that she really *did* mind if Steph went out with Trey. She felt cross at herself for allowing these unwelcome feelings to spring forward so unexpectedly and wondered where they had come from. She needed some time to think things through, to figure out why it should make any difference to her who Trey might or might not choose to go out with. She watched as Stephanie approached the door.

Alexa closed her eyes, tilting her head backward slowly, and took a deep breath.

52

"N'gart astollamon ashath . . . ," she spoke in a flat monotone.

"Alexa, what are you doing?" Steph asked. She'd stopped with her hand on the door handle, looking back at her friend with a combination of bewilderment and amusement. The voice that had come from Alexa's mouth was not a sound that she could ever have imagined hearing from her best friend. It was a dry and ancient sound, and as Alexa continued to intone the ominous-sounding words she felt something akin to panic rising up within her.

" . . . Elnieth ralleth n'gor, allemn agrath shallerith."

"Lex, pack it in now. It's not funny . . ."

Alexa kept her eyes shut for a few seconds more, filling her consciousness with the appropriate thoughts and feelings that were necessary to make the spell work. Something seemed to push gently inside her, a mental nudge that signaled to her that the incantation had been successful.

She opened her eyes and smiled back at her friend.

"Oh, come on, Lex. I've seen the way he looks at you sometimes. And you aren't exactly doing anything to put him off, are you? Batting your eyelashes and playing with your hair every time the two of you talk. I just assumed that you were, you know, keen on him too." Stephanie repeated the words that she had said moments before, her expression and intonation identical in every way.

Alexa nodded shyly and glanced down at her lap. "I suppose he is pretty cute," she said. "And maybe I do like him a little bit."

"Well, that's settled then," Steph said, frowning at the bottles in her hand and sitting back down on the bed. "I was going to ask him out tonight, but I guess I'll have to find some other poor victim to work my womanly charms on, eh?" She winked at her friend, a wide, genuine smile on her face.

Alexa watched as the smile faded, the frown deepening on Steph's features until her face was a mask of consternation.

"Oh, weird," Steph said, wrinkling her nose.

"What?"

"I just had one of those déjà vu episodes. You know, where you think that you've lived through a moment before. They always freak me out. Do you ever get those?"

"Yes," Alexa replied, kneeling up and pressing the screen to pause the music. "They freak me out too. But they're just a trick of the mind. What music do you want on next?" she asked, turning her back so that her friend wouldn't see the broad smile that had crept over her face.

9

Trey had gone to bed a little before midnight, closing the door on the muffled sounds of the two girls, who were still busy gossiping and giggling in hushed tones. He removed his clothing and climbed into bed, too tired to take a shower or even brush his teeth. He resolved to redeem himself in the morning by grooming himself properly, but right now he just wanted to sleep.

He turned onto his side and reached out to switch off the lamp on his bedside table.

When he turned back, the vampire was there.

Caliban stood by Trey's bed, leering down at him with a look of pure hatred. Trey strangled the scream that rose out of him and instinctively grabbed at the lamp. He swung it in a tight arc, aiming to smash the heavy metal base into the creature's head. His aim was true, but the lamp simply passed straight through the vampire's features, emerging on the other side without slowing. Trey was up on his knees now and he gawked at the thing in his hand; the power cord had snapped free from the base but otherwise the lamp was utterly intact.

Caliban glowered down at the boy. "You delude yourself, Mr. Laporte," he said. "Do you think for one second that were I really here you would still be breathing?" The vampire opened his mouth and revealed those teeth to the boy again, the lips curling back over them to form a hideous smile. "No, Trey, if I were able to bypass my brother's defenses this easily I would have welcomed the chance to try out my newly acquired appendage on your tender young throat." He held up the mechanical hand that had been grafted into his flesh and flexed the knifelike fingers, turning them in front of his face and staring at them with a morbid fascination. "It was such a shame that we didn't get a chance to speak earlier, down at the gun club. Face to face."

Trey could now see that the figure in front of him was hardly solid at all and that the room behind was clearly visible through it.

"But there will soon be time enough for us to become properly acquainted. My brother is losing his battle for survival, and soon the protection that you have been afforded under him will be gone. And *then* we will meet in the flesh, Mr. Laporte. Then I will show you the true meaning of pain and agony and torture—you *and* the others that have sought to thwart me for so long. There is very little sand left in my brother's hourglass, and when the final grain has fallen I shall simply walk into his world and wreak havoc on those that sided with him against me."

The vampire tilted his head to one side, the sunken yellow eyes tracing Trey's features.

Trey blinked his eyes shut for a second, hoping that when he opened them again the phantom would be gone.

"You look like him, you know," the vampire said.

The sound that came out of Trey was little more than a whisper. "Who?"

"Your father." An ugly sneer formed on the nether-creature's face, mocking the boy. "I'll let you in on a secret, Trey. Just before I removed his head from his shoulders, your father begged me to kill him. Such was his exquisite suffering that he lay at my feet and pleaded with me to end his torment. Eventually, when I became bored with him, I obliged." The vampire's eyes flashed menacingly, and Trey flinched under their despicable gaze. "Soon you too shall beg for an end to the misery you will experience at my hands, Trey. Although I think that I will take longer with you. Yes, I think that I shall enjoy watching you squirm and beg like your pathetic coward of a father."

Trey threw himself out of the bed toward the foul crea-ture. He reached out with clawed fingers to grab at the vam-pire but instead passed clean through the apparition, crashing into the chest of drawers on the other side and knocking a tumbler to the floor, where it shattered, bejeweling the car-pet with tiny glass daggers. He forced himself to his feet, ignoring the pain as a number of the glass shards bit into the soles of his feet. He spun around, anticipating some kind of attack.

The vampire's laughter filled the room, but there was no longer any sign of Caliban.

Trey sank to the floor, a harsh, ragged sob escaping his lips. He hung his head and gently pulled his feet toward him, staring down at them as if they belonged to somebody else.

57

Blood pooled, growing into heavy droplets before snaking down his soles as tiny rivulets to deposit their crimson contents on the floor. Tears welled up in his eyes and he blinked, allowing them to fall and join their ruby cousins sinking into the carpet. His heart rate was gradually returning to its normal speed and he slowly brought his nerves under control.

The sound of a knock on his door made him jump and hit his head on the wooden drawers behind him. His nerves were shot to pieces.

"Trey?" Alexa's voice was muffled. "Are you all right, Trey? Steph and I thought that we heard a crash."

Trey looked from the wreckage that had been the tumbler to the bloody mess on the carpet.

"Trey?"

He started to say something but stopped himself, remembering the good time that she appeared to have had this evening. This was the first time in a long while that she had let her hair down, and he wouldn't screw that up for her by talking about apparitions, regardless of how much he wanted to. No, he could wait. Wait and talk to Tom about it first thing in the morning, before the briefing.

"I'm fine, thanks," he said, trying to keep his voice steady. "I was messing about and accidentally knocked a glass onto the floor and it smashed."

"Do you need a hand clearing it up?" It was Steph's voice this time.

"No. No, thanks. It's all done."

"OK. As long as you're all right. Good night, Trey."

"Night, Alexa. Night, Steph."

He sensed them still hovering outside his room and he held his breath, willing them to leave, until he heard the sound of her door closing against the music that was still spilling out from her room. Then he puffed out his cheeks and tilted his head back so that he was staring up at the ceiling, still trying to bring himself under control. It hadn't been real. He'd tell Tom about what had happened, but it hadn't been real and there was no need to bother him now. The vampire was just trying to scare him. He'd done a great job.

He picked the tiny glass shards out of his feet, collecting them together in a small pile and inspecting the cuts. He knew how quickly he healed and that by the morning there would be nothing to suggest that he'd cut himself at all. He grabbed a shirt that had fallen out of his laundry basket, tore it in two, and used the pieces to wrap his feet, hoping to limit any more sullying of the carpet. He'd have to let Mrs. Magilton know about the blood so that she could get the carpet cleaned. He could almost hear her already, going into histrionics at the sight of the mess that he had made in the room.

When he was done he picked up all of the broken pieces and placed them on his sideboard. The photo of his mother and father was on the wooden top, and he stared at it for a long while, thinking about the terrible things that Caliban had said.

He was so glad to have a picture of his parents again.

Recently he'd tried to conjure their faces, desperate not to let the memory of them fade. But he'd struggled, castigating himself for beginning to forget them. His only previous photograph of them had been destroyed in a fire at the care home where he'd lived before coming to live with Lucien— the fire had been started by Caliban's people and was meant to kill him—but now he could see their faces again and couldn't help but wish that they were with him, helping him to get through all of this.

He sighed and walked to the bathroom, stepped into the shower cubicle and turned the tap on to full and allowed the hot needles of water to wash over him. When he was done he reentered the bedroom, glancing at the mess of covers that had fallen from his bed. He bent down and picked them up, piling them on top of each other on the mattress. He walked around the bed and sat at the desk, reaching across and sliding a book toward him—he doubted if he would get much sleep tonight.

A hot, springtime sun skewered its way through a gap in the curtains, causing Trey to grumble and flinch as it came to rest on his face. He had finally fallen asleep in the chair and he grunted at the sharp pains that sprang up in his legs and back as he rose from his crumpled sleeping position. He pulled his feet up to inspect them and was unsurprised to find that they were now unmarked. He quickly showered and dressed, glancing at his watch and wondering if he could still grab Tom before the morning meeting. He left his room and quickly crossed the apartment to the kitchen, hoping to grab something that he could eat while searching for the Irishman.

On the kitchen table were the remnants of someone's breakfast—the vestiges of a still-lukewarm coffee and a plate of toast crumbs told Trey that Alexa was already up. She'd left one of her old books facedown next to the plate. The ancient brown leather cover had worn away at the corners, and the animal hide was turning back on itself like a small tongue licking at the surface.

Trey grabbed an apple from the fruit bowl, and holding it in his mouth, he wiped his hands and reached over to pick up the book, glancing at the text on the page where she had left it open.

It was written in a language that he did not recognize and he tilted the book with one hand, as if reading the text at a different angle would somehow make it decipherable. He flicked through some of the pages, hoping that they might reveal something to suggest what the book was about. The paper was incredibly thin and reminded him of the pages of a Bible that he had leafed through in his grandmother's house as a small boy.

Trey's hand stopped at a page that caught his interest. The words on this page were much larger and bolder than in the rest of the book. He frowned at the text, trying to work out what language it could be. He shook his head. Taking the apple from his mouth, he started to sound out the words phonetically, stopping and going back to the start of each line and saying it out loud once he thought he knew how they should be said. The words had an odd resonance and Trey was vaguely aware that somehow they *wanted* to be read, as if they had been locked away within the confines of the pages for too long and now desired nothing more than for someone to once more make the sounds that their letters formed. Inside his mind a warning Klaxon went off and he instinctively knew that he should stop what he was doing and put the book down. But those words wanted to be heard. They whispered to him, urging him to continue. And as he said them aloud he could feel the power in them grow.

He was halfway through the passage when Alexa came rushing into the kitchen screaming at him to stop. She hurled herself across the table to grab the book out of his hands, slamming it shut and glaring at him with thinly disguised contempt.

"What the bloody hell do you think you are doing, Trey?" she said, her face having taken on an unpleasant red hue.

"I was just reading from that book. Don't have a fit, Alexa."

"Do you have any idea what type of incantation you were just speaking aloud then? You were halfway through a summoning, Trey. And if you had managed to get to the end, a bloody great demon, the like of which I hope to never lay eyes on, would have suddenly been let loose upon this earth. Now I don't know about you, but I am really not overly keen on the idea of having a twenty-foot demon whose name translates as *The Disemboweler* summoned into the kitchen of my house." She brandished the book in his face. "This thing hasn't been seen for over five hundred years so I can't say for sure what might happen, but I'm guessing with a name like Mr. Disemboweler he isn't going to be the type of fellow that you invite around for a cup of tea and a slice of Battenburg cake!"

"Well, if the book's that sodding dangerous, what the hell are you doing leaving it around, you halfwit?" Trey shouted back at her.

They glared at each other across the table, neither willing to be the first to back down, when suddenly Trey's face cracked into a broad smile. The giggles started next and were quickly transformed into gales of laughter.

"What's so funny?" Alexa asked, crossing her arms.

"I was just imagining this gigantic demon sitting down at the table with a cup of tea and a slice of Mrs. Magilton's Battenburg cake. I can hear her now: 'If you so much as drop one of those crumbs on my floor, I'll have *your* guts for garters, Disemboweler or no Disemboweler.'"

Alexa struggled to keep the stern expression on her face, but then she too cracked up.

"Please, Trey," she said once their laughter had dissipated, "be careful around these old books. Many of them have tremendous power and shouldn't be opened by anybody who doesn't know what they are doing."

"You gave me one of *these old books* for my birthday," he pointed out.

"And told you to open it only when I am with you."

The phone rang in the kitchen. The ring tone indicated that it was an internal call from the office. Alexa picked up the receiver and listened to the person on the other end of the line. The mood in the room changed instantly, and Trey could see the tension in Alexa's features. She thanked the person, hung up, and looked over at Trey with what he thought looked like excitement mixed with apprehension.

"There's been a breakthrough. Charles thinks that he's located Leroth and my mother, and he wants me to go down to have a chat."

"Charles?" Trey said, feigning ignorance. "Oh, you mean Lord Farquar."

"Don't start all that again, Trey. He's actually very nice, if you take the time to get to know him."

Trey had bumped into Charles Henstall on a number of occasions while they had all been trying to locate Alexa's mother. The older boy had looked down his nose at Trey each time, and Trey had taken to referring to him by the nickname.

"Let's go." Alexa was halfway out the door when Trey stopped her.

"Alexa, there's something that I need to tell you about last night. When you came to my door. I—"

"If you're worried about the stupid glass, don't be." She glanced again at the phone on the wall, eager to be on her way. "What?" she said, when she looked back at his frowning face.

"Caliban. He was in my room. Well, he wasn't *physically* in my room, but he paid me a visit and—"

"Oh, Trey," she said. "Why on earth didn't you say something?"

Trey shook his head and looked down at the table. "I didn't want to spoil your evening," he mumbled. "Besides, like I said, he wasn't really there—just some projection of him . . . magic or something."

"Come on, we need to tell the others and find out what Charles has discovered." She took him by the elbow and pulled him out of the kitchen, across the lounge, and toward the elevator.

"What is it?" Tom asked as he entered the door of the research area. He looked tired and was still wearing the same clothes that he'd been in the evening before. Trey took one look at him and guessed that his friend had had almost as good a night's rest as his own. "This had better be good, to call off our planned meeting."

Alexa and Charles were hunched over the table looking at the screen of a notebook computer that had been set up on it. The tension in the room was palpable. Trey sat a little apart from the other two and stood up as Tom entered, looking over at the Irishman with relief.

"We think that we've found Gwendolin . . . my mother," Alexa said without turning her attention from the screen.

"I still don't understand why it's taken so long," Trey said.

"The Tower of Leroth, where Gwendolin resides," Charles

65

said, also opting not to turn from the data displayed on the laptop, "is not a static location. In fact, it isn't really a *location* at all. It's a portal between two worlds, this one and the Netherworld."

Trey guessed that Charles was about eighteen years old, maybe slightly younger, but he spoke in a way that suggested he was much older. His tone and manner suggested a privileged upbringing coupled with a good education. There was something about him that rubbed Trey the wrong way.

"Could you explain that again in English, please, Charles," Trey said. "I'm not too hot on gobbledygook."

Charles glanced at him before straightening up and addressing everyone in the room. "As you already know, Trey, Leroth can exist in both planes at once and has the ability to change the location at which it creates the bridge between them. Unlike other smaller portals that can be opened between the worlds, which are tiny in comparison, it occupies a vast area and can be disguised to blend in with its surroundings." He raised an eyebrow as if checking that Trey was taking all of this in before turning back to smile at Alexa.

"Caliban and Gwendolin use Leroth to stop us from countering a great deal of their activities. Gwendolin is a very powerful sorceress. She is able to wreak havoc through the use of her dark magic, but we have people within our organization who are capable of neutralizing *most* of the damage that she would create, but only *if* we can locate where the spells are being cast from. Once we know the location, we can implement anti-spells and counter-magic.

So she uses the shifting properties of Leroth to thwart us moving in and out of this plane, changing location at every opportunity."

Trey was only half listening to all of this. He had begun to wonder whether Charles might not be human, whether he might be another one of the nether-creatures that he had spied in the office that time. He made a note to check him out the next time he got an opportunity to morph in the meeting room. A large part of him dearly hoped that beneath that suave and smarmy outward appearance was some bizarre, unnatural monster—perhaps some giant sluglike creature like Nathan.

"No, Trey, I am completely human," Charles said, turning to look at him now and smiling at the expression of shock that crossed Trey's features. "No trace of gastropod or any other mollusk, I'm afraid. Neither can I shape-shift into some half-man, *half-dog* creature . . . thank heavens." From the look of things, he was enjoying the complete bewilderment on Trey's face. He went to turn away before adding, "I'm sorry, that was rather rude of me. I didn't mean to intrude into your thoughts. It's just that you were looking at me in such a bemused and . . . *vacant* way that I was unclear as to whether you were taking *any* of this in, so I thought I'd . . . take a peek. I hope you don't mind?"

Trey's forehead creased into an angry frown. He had sensed *something* happening inside his mind, a probing force, some smooth-bodied worm had entered his head and had begun squirming its way around. He suddenly felt horribly *violated.* A wave of anger broke through him and he leaned forward, staring into Charles's face, until their noses were almost touching.

"Charles, I don't know who or what you are, and quite frankly I don't give a toss, but if you ever 'take a peek' into my mind again like that, I'd be happy to show you exactly what kind of *half-man, half-dog* creature I can turn into. And maybe then I'll take a peek inside your head by ripping your skull off and sifting through the contents on the floor by hand." The words flooded out of him too quickly and too angrily, and the silence that filled the room as a result was complete and uncomfortable. Trey turned to look at Tom and Alexa and flushed with embarrassment when he saw the look of annoyance on their faces.

"When you two rutting stags have quite finished trying to establish your alpha-male credentials," Alexa said, "perhaps you'd like to join us in the meeting room next door to discuss what we need to do next." She closed the lid on the laptop, picked it up, and walked out of the room in the direction of the meeting rooms that lined the left-hand side of the offices. Tom shook his head at the two of them and followed her out.

Trey looked over at Charles and forced a smile. "After you, Charles," he said.

10

"So what does all that tell us?" Trey asked, nodding his head toward the large screen at the end of the meeting room. The same tables of data that they had all been looking at on the laptop were now showing on the huge six-foot display.

"We run daily reports on levels of magic that might be being used at any one time in the world," Alexa said. "A team of people in our organization tune into this sort of thing and they are extremely sensitive to any form of magecraft that may be employed, anywhere, at any time. Different forms of magic have different signatures, and these can, by the right people, be recognized and traced. If the team considers the magic to be a harmful form, they report it and then set about detecting the geographical source so that we can counter it as quickly as possible." She looked up at the data on the screen before continuing.

"Some forms of magic—the darkest and most malevolent kind—flag up that a big-hitter is at work, and they don't come much bigger than Caliban and Gwendolin. This morning a huge signal was detected—intense, but so short that we couldn't identify what kind of magic was being used. We think that someone was preparing something—a trial run perhaps. While they couldn't detect what kind of sorcery was being used, Charles and his team managed to trace the source to Iceland. About twenty miles outside Reykjavik, to be precise." She stopped and looked at Trey. "That and Caliban's appearance to Trey last night suggest that they have come out of hiding and are now hell-bent on achieving whatever it is that they are up to."

"Last night?" Tom said.

"I had a late-night visit," Trey said with a shrug.

Tom looked at Alexa. "Caliban also tried to get to Trey at the shooting range yesterday."

Alexa stared at Trey, the anger clear to see on her face. "You know, some communication around here might really help. Help everyone to know what is going on."

"We'll discuss this later," Tom said, before turning to Charles. "Do we have any idea what they're up to in Iceland?"

"Not yet," Charles replied. "We only just had enough time to triangulate their location. We hope to be able to work our way around their masking spells and get a grasp on exactly what they are doing within the next few hours. Then we'll start to counter their magic with our own and—"

"No. Don't do that," said Alexa.

"Why ever not?" Charles responded. He looked at her from across the room, his dark and intelligent eyes narrowing as he tried to fathom out what might be going on. "As I said, it shouldn't take us too long to discover what types of magic they are using."

"Charles, it is vitally important that you do not do anything at this time. Continue to monitor exactly what is going on in Iceland, and keep Tom and me informed, but do not start any counter-magic procedures without our specific say-so."

"I'm sorry, Alexa, but I don't understand. If something is going on, I think that my team should be informed. If Lucien was around he would—"

"Please do not presume to tell me what my father would and would not do under the circumstances." Alexa's eyes hardened.

"This is not acceptable, Alexa. I have to insist that—"

Trey could see the salmon pink color creeping up from the base of Alexa's throat. It was always a precursor for one of the angry outbursts that he had been on the receiving end of so many times in the last few months.

"Charles, while my father is indisposed, Tom and I are in charge of operations here. I appreciate that I am asking a great deal, and if it turns out that I would be risking lives by pursuing this course of action for any length of time I would immediately ask you to start your work to eliminate that danger. Tom and I are in agreement on this, so for now I need you to sit on this information for a while." Her face softened again and she gave Charles a look that made Trey want to punch him on the nose. "Will you do that for me, Charles? Please? I need your help on this one."

Trey looked over at Tom sitting across the table from him and grinned. From the look on the Irishman's face, it was

71

obvious that he had not discussed any of this with Alexa and was none too pleased with her using his name in this way. Tom looked back at Trey with a withering glare and Trey suddenly lost all interest in studying him any further.

"Now, Charles," Alexa purred, "if you would be so kind as to leave us for a few moments, Tom, Trey, and I need to discuss things in private."

Charles looked decidedly unhappy about being dismissed in this way. He stood up, pulling at the hem of his jacket as he did so. He glanced toward Tom as if hoping that the Irishman would intercede on his behalf, but when he was met with one of Tom's unreadable looks his eyes strayed toward Trey, who was grinning up at him, enjoying the sight of him being humbled in this way. Trey gave him a little wink, waving the tips of his fingers at him until Charles turned on his heel and marched out of the room.

As Trey turned back to the table the dumb smile that he was wearing withered and died before the angry looks that both Alexa and Tom were giving him. The pink flush was back at Alexa's throat again, and he guessed who might be next in line for the treatment.

"Do you think that you could please try not to completely alienate the very people that are trying to *help* us, Trey?" she hissed through clenched teeth. "You could at least *try* to act your age and not be so confrontational all the time."

"Me? What about *him*? Looking down his nose at me the whole time, making snide comments. He read my thoughts,

72

you know. He sneaked inside my head, using some magic or something, and read my thoughts. If that isn't inviting confrontation, then I don't know what is."

"All right already," said Tom, cutting in before Alexa could respond. "Let's all just calm down a little and try to screw our heads on." He blew out a frustrated breath. "Alexa, would you like to explain what your thinking in all this is, please? I should of course know, seeing as how you have *discussed all this with me already*, but I appear to have forgotten that conversation with you. It must be my age."

"It's simple, Tom, and don't for one second try to kid me that you haven't already worked it out." She smiled at him apologetically before continuing. "If we start to go at this thing with anti-spells and counter-magic, any element of surprise that we may have on our side will be gone. If they know that we know where they are, they'll simply shut up shop as soon as possible and disappear again."

"But we don't know what they're up to, Alexa."

"Tom, I understand your concerns, and as I've just said, if what they are doing over there looks as if it is going to put anyone in danger, I will immediately reverse the decision and let our people do what they have to in order to stop them. But this is what we have been looking for all these months, and I think we should use it to our advantage if we can."

Tom held her gaze for a few moments before slowly nodding his head. "OK," he said. "What's the plan?"

"A small team of us leave for Reykjavik as soon as

possible. We gain access to the Tower of Leroth, and if we can do so without getting caught we take Mynor's Globe from Gwendolin and return with it to heal my father."

Tom looked at her with a look of bemused disbelief on his face.

"Just like that?" he said, shrugging.

"Well, I'm sure it needs a bit of flesh on its bones, but that's the basic plan, yes."

"Who does this small team consist of?" Trey asked.

"You, me, Tom, and Charles."

"Charles?!" Trey said, standing up from his chair. "What in God's name would you want that great stuffed shirt coming along for?"

"Charles is probably the best sorcerer that we have. His father was an incredibly important part of our organization, and Charles looks set to follow in his footsteps." She looked toward the door through which the young man had exited before continuing in a low voice. "He hasn't had it all easy, Trey. He was brought up in an almost monastic environment surrounded by sorcery mentors from around the world. He's very good at what he does, and as we'll be going up against one of the most powerful witches that has ever existed, I think we should take along as much firepower as we can." She smiled a smile that Trey didn't like the look of. "But you'll have a chance to get better acquainted with each other before we leave. I need you to work with him on something."

"What?" Trey said, lowering himself back into his seat.

"Get some tips on how to win friends and influence people so that I can charm Caliban into submission? No, thanks."

"No. You need to learn the thought-transfer spell that is in the book I gave you for your birthday."

"And what would I need to know that for?"

"Do you remember how it was when you faced Caliban and his demons before? How frustrating it was for you not to be able to communicate with Tom or my father when you came to rescue me? As a werewolf you are completely unable to talk to those around you, but if you could learn that spell, and learn it quickly, you'd be able to 'talk' with us when you needed to."

"Why can't *you* teach it to me?"

"Like I said, Trey, Charles is probably the best mage that we have in our employ. I'm good, but nowhere near as good as him. If I tried to teach you the spell, it would probably take us a week. If Charles does it, I believe you could learn it in a day or two. We don't have a week. We might not even have two days."

Trey looked over at Tom for support, but the Irishman simply performed one of his winces followed by a little half-shrug of the shoulders. "Time is against us," he said.

Trey leaned so that his head hung over the back of the chair. He puffed out his cheeks and exhaled a long sigh. "Fine, I'll learn the stupid spell with him. But I cannot and will not pretend that I like him. The guy's an utter loser." He looked back at them. "What are you two going to be doing?"

"We're going to be putting some of that flesh on the

75

bones of Alexa's brilliant plan and getting ready to go," Tom said, standing up. His eyes had a hard, flinty look to them now and his mouth was fixed in a thin-lipped slash. It was a look that Trey knew all too well from their previous encounter with Lucien's evil brother. It was Tom's going-to-war face.

Trey stood up and was about to leave the room when Tom stopped him with a hand on his arm. "And you . . . ," he said, "you are to tell me of *anything* else that happens to you that is out of the ordinary. No matter how small you think it is, how real or unreal. Do you understand me?"

Trey nodded.

"Good," Tom said, removing his hand. "Let's go to work."

11

"Again," Charles barked.

Trey glared at him, hoping that the look would be enough to make Charles back off.

Charles looked back at him implacably. He blinked slowly. "Again," he repeated.

"*Lethren agorn shu alak hiroth*," Trey intoned for what must have been the hundredth time. In his mind he formed the message that he wanted to transmit to the man on the other side of the table: *Charles, you are a tool.*

He raised an eyebrow, inquiring if anything had come through.

"Again," Charles said.

"Bloody hell!" Trey said, letting his forehead drop down onto the table in front of him. "We've been at this for four hours. What am I doing wrong? It's five bloody words. It can't be that difficult to get this to work. Am I still mispronouncing *alak*?"

Charles steepled his fingers in front of his face and looked over the top of them at Trey. He had loosened his necktie and undone his collar button about two hours ago, but these were the only concessions that he seemed willing to make against the stifling heat that filled the meeting room the two of them occupied. An hour or so earlier Trey had set the air-conditioning to high, but it appeared to be on the blink, because if anything the room was getting hotter as the afternoon wore on.

Charles sighed and glanced at his wristwatch. "How many more times do I need to tell you, Trey? There is nothing wrong with your pronunciation. You got that perfectly right after the first hour—much to my surprise. It's your mind-set that isn't right. With this particular spell your mind preparations must be right before it will work. So, if you please. *Again.*"

"You're loving this, aren't you?" Trey said, lifting his chin up and staring across at Charles from under his eyebrows.

Charles snorted with derision. "If you think that I am enjoying sitting in a room with *you*, trying to teach *elementary* magic like this, you really do have too high an opinion of yourself. I am only doing this because Alexa asked me to. You can bet your soul that I have a thousand and one better things that I would rather be doing than be cooped up in here with *you*. I should be readying myself for our forthcoming little excursion to Iceland and making sure that I'm properly prepared." He let out a sigh and removed a handkerchief from his inside pocket, touching it to his forehead. "So, if you *please*, Mr. Laporte, clear your head—that really should not be difficult for you—imagine that your thoughts are like a fluid that you are able to push out from your mind into the world outside your body, a fluid that you can direct into the minds of others, *and repeat the incantation.*"

78

"Why is it so sodding hot in here?" Trey asked, looking around again at the thermostat on the wall. He considered getting up and checking it for a fourth time but knew that it would be to no avail.

"It's the magic." Charles sighed. "Whenever a spell is cast, or in this case *trying* to be cast, a huge amount of energy is created as a tiny portal is opened between this world and the Netherworld. It's this energy that allows us to trace the magic of others and counteract it. Different forms of magic produce different forms of energy. It just so happens that this spell, and others like it, produce heat. Now, please, *do* stop bitching and moaning about the temperature and repeat the incantation."

"Sod off."

Charles looked over at the teenager, an unpleasant look in his stare.

"I know you don't care for me very much, Trey Laporte, and to be perfectly honest I really am not overly keen on you, but I have been asked to teach this spell to you so that you can use it on our forthcoming mission, and I will spend all day and night in here if I need to in order to achieve that end. So prepare yourself as we have discussed, *and repeat the bloody incantation!*"

"Like I said, sod off." Trey got up and moved over to the thermostat, banging it with the palm of his hand.

"The heat is really bothering you, is it?" Charles asked with a sneer. "Well, let's see if we can't cool you down a little."

There was something in the way that Charles had said this that made Trey frown and look back over his shoulder at him. Charles's stare was particularly unfriendly—even for him—and as Trey watched, Charles's eyes suddenly snapped back in their sockets, the pupils rotating upward impossibly quickly so that the twin globes that gazed sightlessly back at Trey were now completely white. The sorcerer sucked in a great breath, tilting his head back slightly as he did so. Then he slowly stood and raised both hands in front of him, palms out, as if gently pushing against some invisible wall.

"Nashgrun alacnarog!" He enunciated the consonants with a hard edge to his voice, and to Trey's ears the words sounded vaguely Welsh.

There was a split second when nothing happened, and then the first chill burst of air hit Trey full in the chest, taking his breath away. He watched as a tiny vortex of swirling and dancing icy particles seemed to form just in front of Charles's upturned hands, before flying out at incredible force to hit Trey fully in the face and neck. He blinked his eyes against the stinging crystals and turned his head to one side, only to have his ear filled with the frozen matter. The wind increased in intensity, and fine, penetrating snow sought out the gaps in his clothing, making him gasp as it instantly turned to ice water against his skin. He backed away but there was nowhere to go, as hard, sharp ice crystals stung his face and eyes, forcing him backward until his back met the resistance of the office wall. The freezing wind continued to gather strength, and his teeth chattered noisily. The demented wood-pecker attacking the china cup inside his head was the only sound he could hear over the howling gale.

"Stop it, you madman!" Trey shouted over the noise, but it was clear that the sorcerer could not, or would not, heed him.

Trey looked down at his hands and noted how they had already turned a dirty gray-blue color, the blood deserting the extremities and retreating into the depths of his inner body. His foot caught against something and he fell backward, painfully catching his elbow on the baseboard. The cold was unbearable now, and he tried to curl himself into a tiny ball, huddling down and drawing his knees up to his chin as the snow gathered around him.

"I said stop it, you lunatic!" Trey bellowed. A small part of his mind could not help but wonder why nobody had come in to see what all the noise was about. Surely someone working in the office outside had heard this roaring wind and seen the swirling snow and ice that was rapidly filling the room.

"*Lethren agorn shu alak hiroth,*" Trey said through his chattering teeth. *Stop it, Charles.* He formed the thought as clearly as he could and concentrated on forcing it into the head of the other man. "*Lethren agorn shu alak hiroth.*" Trey formed the words of the incantation in his mind in the way that Charles had told him to.

STOP, CHARLES. STOP! he screamed inside his own head. He closed his eyes and forced the words out from his own mind into that of the man still standing statuelike on the other side of the room.

The wind stopped as suddenly as it had started. Trey opened his eyes again and looked about him. He shook his head in disbelief. There was no sign of the great drifts of snow and ice that had covered him seconds before. He held his hand up in front of his face and frowned at the regular pink color of the skin. He touched his bare forearm to confirm what he already knew—that it was a perfectly normal temperature.

Getting back up onto his feet from the floor he looked over at Charles, who was standing with his arms crossed, smiling at him from the other side of the table.

"Very good," he said. "That came through as clear as a bell."

"What the hell just happened?" Trey asked, shakily taking his seat again and looking about the room as though he was still unable to believe the images being sent between his eyes and brain.

"An illusion. A mirage, if you will. You said that you were hot, so I hooked into the part of your brain that wanted you to cool down and simply amplified that desire a little . . . well, rather a lot actually."

Trey looked at Charles afresh. He didn't like the guy's manner, and he doubted that they would ever be sharing a taxi back from a club together, but he had to admire his abilities. He puffed out his cheeks and cracked a smile. "Well, at least I managed to get that bloody spell to work at last," he said.

"Actually you had it perfectly about an hour ago. I just

wanted to see if you could perform it under pressure. Well done—you learn very fast, Trey." He stood up to leave the room. "Keep practicing, and pretty soon you should be able to invoke the spell whenever you want. You won't even need to say the words aloud."

Trey imagined what he must look like through Charles's eyes, sitting there with his mouth hanging open like a fish hooked out of the river by an artful angler.

"Charles," he said with a little shake of his head, "you are a complete and utter loser."

The young sorcerer stopped in the doorway and looked back at him.

"Well, that's one step up from being called a tool, I suppose." He nodded and left, closing the door of the room behind him.

12

The numerous bags that Trey was carrying managed to wedge themselves between his legs and the open doorway of the kitchen, forcing him to turn sideways and shuffle in like some crablike beast of burden. Once inside he unceremoniously dumped his cargo, allowing the bags to fall into two untidy islands of colored paper and plastic—a higgledy-piggledy mess of shop names and logos. He wandered over to the fridge, pulled open the door, and peered into the starkly lit interior, not at all sure what he wanted, but feeling the need to look anyway. It seemed to him that he spent a good portion of his days gazing into the refrigerator not knowing what it was that he hoped to find there. Eventually he grabbed a can of iced tea and, pulling the ring on top, went to sit at the table.

He looked across again at the piles of shopping bags on the floor and smiled derisively. They were nearly all Alexa's, and he wondered again at how anybody could gain so much pleasure from buying clothes that she really didn't need. But he knew that it was one of her ways of coping with what was happening so he'd gone along with her today, agreeing to the suggestions that she made for kit and clothes that they might need in Iceland.

"Where's Tom?" Alexa asked as she entered with her own set of shopping bags, all jostling for position around her knees.

The telephone rang as if in response to Trey's shrug, and Alexa snatched up the receiver.

She listened briefly to the voice on the other end before answering, "OK, we'll be right down." She replaced the handset in its cradle and turned toward the table, tiny lines creasing her normally smooth forehead.

"What now?" Trey sipped the cold drink from the can and looked back at her.

"That was Tom. He wants us to go downstairs again. They think they've found something a little odd. He sounded pretty worked up."

Tom momentarily looked up from behind one of the small partitioned booths that divided the open-plan office on the first floor of the building. He beckoned them over before returning his gaze to whatever was being displayed on the monitor screen perched on top of the wooden desk. A man Trey knew simply as Martin—some kind of data-analyst-computer-geek type—was leaning over the desk, pointing out something to Tom, who puffed out his cheeks and shook his head in response.

"Tom." Trey nodded at the Irishman and was concerned at the anxious look on his friend's face. "What's the problem?"

"We're not completely sure," Tom said, and ushered the

two of them forward so that they could get a look at the screen. "But I'm certain that it's going to have some influence on our trying to get ahold of Mynor's Globe."

The screen showed a graph. The dot-to-dot line of data tacked along quite steadily across the bottom of the graph to begin with, and then about halfway along the x-axis it leaped suddenly, creating a jagged incline like a steep and dangerous rock face.

Trey turned slightly to face the Irishman. "Never was much good at math, I'm afraid. What is it?"

"Me neither," Tom replied. "This graph shows the energy signature for a particular form of magic. The energy signature represented here happens to be quite unique so it's easy for us to keep track of it. As it happens, the magic shown on the graph is considered to be a benign form so we don't usually worry too much about it. However, as we are about to attempt to try to obtain the object that creates this particular energy signature, we—"

"It's Mynor's Globe," Alexa interrupted. "The graph is showing the usage of the globe over the last three months." She stopped and shook her head. "Why is there such a huge and sudden increase, Tom?"

"That's just what we were wondering. We've looked back on our records and these little jumps and dips here are the usual pattern," Tom said, pointing at the left side of the graph. "The globe is generally used sparingly and sporadically. Gwendolin is known for the destruction and chaos that she surrounds herself with, not for her compassion and healing, so it might be that she only ever uses the globe if one of her minions gets injured, or maybe she just uses it on herself occasionally. But this massive rise is simply unprecedented. Yesterday they began to use the globe in a way that we've never seen before. Whatever is going on in Iceland, it centers around the use of Mynor's Globe. And that for us is nothing short of a bloody disaster."

Trey frowned over at him. "Why does it make a difference? Our plan was to go over and try to take it from them, wasn't it? How does this change things?"

"We were planning an operation that relied on us getting in and out of the country undetected. We hoped that we would be able to steal the globe without them noticing that it was gone until it was too late and we were far away. I, for one, really do not want to even consider the idea of going up against Caliban *and* Gwendolin on their home turf. Especially without Lucien around. But if they are using the globe as regularly as this data suggests, it will be impossible to get it away without them noticing."

"It doesn't make any sense," Alexa said. "The globe only has one use—to heal and restore. Why would they be using it so much so suddenly?"

"Perhaps Caliban has seen the error of his ways and decided to turn over a new leaf," Trey said. "He might be using it to heal demon lepers as we speak." He had been trying to lighten the mood, but judging from the baleful looks that he was getting from Tom and Alexa he guessed that his attempt was not particularly welcome. "Sorry . . ."

87

"There's another possibility," Charles said. He had crept up silently. In his right hand he was carrying an old scroll that looked as if it might disintegrate completely if he decided to brandish it any more violently than he was already doing. "I've been looking for this since discovering that we were going to try to find the globe. It was misplaced in the library." He held the rolled-up parchment out to Alexa and pushed a stray strand of hair away from his eyes with his other hand.

"What is it, Charles?" she asked, taking it from him and smoothing it out.

"I think it might be the answer to what Gwendolin is doing with the globe. Every mage knows how the globe was used in the Demon Wars to heal creatures of the Netherworld. But there is also an ancient story about how it was misused. That scroll," he said, nodding his head in Alexa's direction, "describes the power that the globe had when it was used in conjunction with another lost artifact—a staff that had been owned by the demon lord Skaleb the Unforgiving."

"That's just a load of old crap!" Alexa snorted. "It's the kind of thing that we get told when we are young."

"Yes? And *who* told you about it, Alexa?" he asked.

"My mother, but—"

"Whoa, hold your horses, you two," Tom said, raising his hands and looking between them. "Would somebody please like to explain to Trey and me exactly what it is that you are babbling on about?"

Charles glanced at Alexa and received a little shrug of her shoulders followed by a nod.

"I think that Gwendolin has somehow found this staff and united it with Mynor's Globe," he said. "The manuscript in Alexa's hand is a copy of the one that my father alluded to, and while it is scant in detail, it does describe the power that the globe might now have if my fears are correct." Charles looked around at the group of people, his eyes moving quickly across all of their faces. Trey noticed how his usual cocky, arrogant look was now replaced by a nervous, almost frightened expression. "If I am right, and I have the most horrible feeling that I am, Gwendolin now has the power to bring the dead back to life, and she is using that power as we speak to try to raise an army of revenants."

There was a silence as they all let this last statement sink in. The rest of the office continued working as normal, unaware of the drama that was unfolding among the small group in their midst. Tom was the first to speak. "Are you telling me that Caliban has the power to create and control an army of friggin' zombies?" he said through his teeth.

Charles met the Irishman's eyes and nodded. "I believe so, yes."

"Great. Just bloody great!" Tom spat. He quickly looked around the office and then turned his attention back to Martin, who had been silent throughout. "How many other people besides you and the four of us know about this?" he asked him.

Martin Tipsbury was a small, rodent-featured man with

wild, curly hair that looked as if it was trying to escape from his head. With his neatly pressed trousers and corduroy jacket he reminded Trey of an eccentric physics teacher that he had once had.

"N-nobody, Tom. I called you as soon as I found it." He peered over his glasses, blinking rapidly at the people around him.

"Good lad. And thank you for that. I know how things can slip out in this place." He put his arm over Martin's shoulders conspiratorially. "When was the last time you had a vacation, Martin?"

"I went on a hiking trip with my walking group last February—why?"

"I'm putting you on vacation leave, Martin. Effective immediately." He gently steered the man away from his work station before clamping his arm around his shoulders again and walking him over toward one of the meeting rooms. "I'm going to ask you to wait in this room and stay there until my colleague Mr. Ellington from security arrives. He will take you to the airport and escort you to the company villa in the Seychelles—you can pick up some clothes and your passport on the way. You'll be staying there as our guest until we call you back. Don't worry about money; all your costs and expenses will be covered by the company."

"But, my daughter . . . she can't just take time out of school . . . Besides, I—"

"She'll love it there—it is one of the most beautiful places on earth."

90

The look on Martin Tipsbury's face was not that of a man who has just been told that he's been given an all-expenses-paid trip to a tropical paradise. Instead he looked as if Tom had just informed him that he had only a fortnight to live.

"M-Mr. O'Callahan," he stammered, "it's a very kind gesture, but I really don't see how I can just up and go away like this. I have work to finish, and as I said, my daughter's schooling is of the utmost importance at the moment—she has her college entrance exams next year."

"We can sort out a tutor for your daughter while you are out there. We'll find out what she might miss at school and cover it all. I'm sure that she'd jump at the chance of some private tutoring while sitting on a white sandy beach. Lucien entertains some of his most important clients at the villa, and it is about as sumptuous a place as you could possibly imagine." Tom opened the door to the meeting room and clapped his hand on Martin's back, gently shoving the flustered little man into the room and quietly closing the door behind him. He was on the phone to security as soon as he'd turned his back on the room and had finished the call by the time he got back to Charles, Trey, and Alexa.

"What was all that about?" Charles asked.

"Just making sure that we keep a lid on this," Tom said, nodding toward the monitor screen. "We still have a rat in this organization and I don't want news of this discovery getting back to Caliban and his goons." He looked around the room to see who might be watching. Nobody was.

"Alexa, I'd like you to get rid of that data and look into removing any sign that these files have been accessed from our network. Can you do that?"

"Sure, Tom."

"Good. Then I propose that we all meet upstairs in two hours to discuss exactly what we are going to do about this mess. I'll have Mrs. Magilton cook us a meal and we can sit together and come up with a plan. Right now though, I'll have to wait for security and make sure poor Martin Tipsbury and his daughter get away safely." He nodded to them all, his lopsided smile now back on his face, before striding off in the direction of the meeting room and the bemused-looking Martin Tipsbury.

13

The Necrotroph looked over the top of the low, fabric-covered divide that separated it from its nearest coworker, and watched as the four of them nodded in agreement to whatever it was that the vile Irish human had suggested. Its fingers hovered over the keyboard on the desk, but it paid no attention to the manuscript that it was supposed to be editing. Instead its eyes greedily took in the scene in front of it, darting among the four people gathered together on the other side of the office and the lone figure of Martin Tipsbury, who was pacing nervously in the meeting room where the Irishman had placed him.

The demon needed to discover why Martin had been put in that room, and it needed to find out what the four of them were talking about and report back to its master. It sensed that this meeting was about something important—something *very* important. It could see this from the expressions on their faces, and from the way that they kept looking around them to check that nobody was observing. They were extremely nervous, and this merely added to the delicious feeling of anticipation that was building inside it at the thought of unearthing their secrets and reporting them back to Caliban.

He would reward the demon handsomely for the information, if it was as important as it suspected.

The Necrotroph suppressed the urge to wander over to their side of the office to see if it could, in passing, glean some small clue as to what they were discussing. It would not be wise to bring any suspicion upon itself at this time— the Irishman was being extra careful since the kidnapping of Lucien's daughter from under his nose, and the demon had been warned not to jeopardize its position within the company unless it was absolutely necessary.

Its eyes flicked back toward the pathetic creature still pacing back and forth within the confines of the meeting room. A small shudder of excitement rippled through the demon as it started to formulate a plan. In allowing itself this brief moment it dropped its guard for a split second, giving the former owner of this body the tiniest sliver of control again. Memories and emotions that belonged to the woman called Ruth—the one-time owner of this human carcass—surfaced momentarily. The Necrotroph had imagined that the host body's original inhabitant was utterly crushed by now, and this unexpected reemergence was irksome. However, it was little more than a minor irritation; the demon quickly took complete charge of its host again, shutting down any areas of the brain that might have been responsible for this glitch. It silently chided itself for allowing even this temporary slip, and reminded itself of where it was and the dangers it faced if it was ever discovered.

The demon considered what was to be done next and felt

something akin to regret that it would soon have to leave the body that it had inhabited for so long. It had grown comfortable inside this host, and while it relished the prospect of another possession (it tired of these pathetic creatures so very quickly), it knew that the dangers in transferring between hosts without the proper preparations were not inconsiderable. The Necrotroph cared nothing for the fact that, as a result of this impending transference, the current host would be rendered either dead or insane—in its long life it had moved between countless organisms, using all their skills and knowledge before discarding them to move on to another, more useful, body. But it knew that to be successful in its plans it would have to possess at least two people in a short space of time, and that was fraught with difficulties.

The office worker on the other side of the partition looked up as Ruth Glenister let out a small gasp, reached down and clutched her abdomen as a knifing pain shot through her stomach.

"Everything all right, Ruth?" Brian asked.

Ruth Glenister let out a deep sigh. "To be honest, Brian, I'll be glad when today is over," she said with a frown. "I'm really not feeling myself, you know."

14

"Why are we eating in here?" Trey asked Tom, looking at the table that had been laid out for dinner in the dining room. "We eat all our meals in the kitchen."

"Because, young Trey, I thought that it would be nice for the four of us to sit around as a group and talk like adults over a nice meal." Tom lit the candles in the center of the table and stood back, checking that everything was in place.

Trey shook his head. In the six months that he had lived here, he couldn't remember eating in this room more than a couple of times—Mrs. Magilton's birthday dinner and Christmas. He reached forward and straightened a knife that had been knocked askew at one of the place settings.

"Besides," Tom continued, " 'The cat's tail is in the hot ashes,' as my dear old mother would say, and I want us all to bond a little before we throw ourselves into the fire along with it."

"Tom, I love you to bits, but sometimes I don't have a clue what you are banging on about."

"Are you going to get changed before we eat?" Tom asked.

"Why?" Trey looked down at the T-shirt and jeans that he was wearing. "What's wrong with what I've got on?"

"Nothing, nothing. I just thought that you might want to get into something a bit more . . . *you know*."

Trey looked at Tom and considered telling him to get lost. His friend was flouncing around the table like some debutante on the eve of her first formal dinner, and he guessed that, for whatever reason, this was a big deal for the Irishman. He blew out his cheeks and turned toward the door. "Fine," he said, pushing it open. "I'll go and get something on that's a bit more . . . *you know*."

"Grand." Tom's smile was open and genuine. "Oh, and, Trey—try not to antagonize Charles tonight. He's not a bad person, and God knows we will want him where we're going. I *need* the two of you to work things out between yourselves."

Trey nodded and left the room, leaving Tom to fuss about the table some more.

Trey walked into the dining room to discover Alexa and Charles waiting for him. Charles was in a suit but had foregone his tie in favor of an open-necked shirt. Alexa was wearing a long black dress and had a necklace around her neck that Trey guessed was extremely expensive. Her hair was scooped up and arranged on top of her head in what he thought was some kind of French twist. They were in mid-conversation as he entered and he tried not to allow the color to rise in his cheeks as Alexa looked over at him and smiled broadly, her eyebrows lifting slightly above her blue eyes as she noticed that he had changed into a jacket and formal trousers. He self-consciously tugged at the hem of his jacket and walked around the side of the table opposite to them.

"Trey, you're just in time. Charles was about to tell me about his theory as to why Caliban might have chosen Iceland as his base." She nodded for him to sit in the chair directly across from her own and reached over to fill his glass with water from the bottle beside it.

"Great," grumbled Trey under his breath as he sat down, "another hour-long lecture, no doubt."

If Charles heard this he didn't say anything, turning in his seat instead to face Alexa. "During the two hours that we've been apart I've—"

"Shouldn't we wait for Tom?" Trey interrupted.

"No need." Tom's loud voice came from behind him and Trey turned around to see the Irishman entering the room wheeling a huge hostess trolley in front of him. "Carry on, please, Charles. I'll dish up the dinner while I'm listening. I've given Mrs. Magilton the rest of the evening off." He shot Trey a look of warning, muttering something about "*making an effort to get on.*"

"As I'm sure everyone else has," Charles said, "I've been wondering if there could be some significance in Caliban choosing Iceland as the site to try out the globe's powers. After we split up downstairs, I went back to the research rooms and searched for links between Nordic countries and zombies, and I was amazed at what I found out. There's a longtime Icelandic belief in the existence of revenants—people that return from the dead. Icelandic legend has it that the Draugr would rise up from their burial barrows and roam the countryside murdering people and killing livestock. They are undead blue-black creatures with superhuman strength who envy the life still possessed by the living. There are countless stories of them breaking into houses and murdering everyone inside, crushing their victims to death with their immense power. Google it," he said, looking over at Trey. "There's simply tons about them on the Web." He shifted his attention back to Alexa and Tom, before adding, "I believe that Caliban may be trying to resurrect these creatures."

The room was utterly quiet. Tom set down the large serving spoons that he'd been holding; the rasping sound they made as their metal surfaces slid against one another reminded Trey of a butcher sharpening a knife against his steel.

"Why?" Tom said in a low voice.

Charles looked over at him and gave a tiny shrug of the shoulders. "The obvious reply is, why not? Caliban might just be exercising his sick desire for chaos and reanimating these creatures for the sheer hell of it. Or maybe, and this theory is something that I do not want to consider, he sees Iceland as the perfect place where he can set up a permanent base in this realm—those long, long nights must have a certain appeal to a vampire. If the Draugr are as vicious and cruel as legend would have it, they could be used to wipe out the human population. That's *if* they can be controlled, which, if our previous experience with zombies is anything to go by, is far from clear."

"Why can't Caliban do that with the demons and vampires at his disposal?" Trey asked.

"Because he wouldn't be capable of creating a portal large enough, or keeping it open long enough, to get sufficient numbers of nether-creatures through. The Draugr are already there. A ready-made army buried in the ground just waiting to be unleashed. All he needs to do is resurrect them. Once he has control of the country he could start to bring his forces through a bit at a time."

"Bloody hell!" said Tom. "Anything else?"

"Not a lot more." Charles reached for his glass and drank a large mouthful. "It's suggested that these Draugr might be capable of increasing their size at will, enabling them to achieve huge proportions while maintaining fantastic speed and strength—although it would seem that they are unable to sustain this for very long. They're described locally as *hel-blar*, meaning blue as death, and they carry the unmistakable stench of death upon them."

"Can they be killed?"

"They're already dead, Tom. But they can be stopped." He glanced at Alexa before continuing. "It's quite ironic when you think why it is that we may have to face these creatures, but they can be dispatched in much the same way as a vampire or a werewolf can—beheading or burning would seem to do the job." This time he shot a look at Trey before going on. "However, there have been no reported sightings

100

of any Draugr for over a hundred years so the background details are a little thin on the ground."

"If they've been buried for that long," said Alexa, "surely they'll be nothing more than bone by now? They'll have been whittled down to next to nothing by the worms and the microbes in the soil."

"Apparently not. Legend has it that they lie untouched in their underground barrows, waiting for an opportunity to rise again and take vengeance on the world for their untimely deaths." Charles shrugged his shoulders apologetically.

"How long have we got?"

"I think that if something as unusual and powerful as one of these Draugr had been resurrected, our people downstairs would have picked it up, so I am assuming that Gwendolin has not been successful—yet."

"Then time is of the essence," Tom said, starting to dish up the food. "We not only need the globe, and quickly, to save Lucien, but we also need to get it away from Caliban to stop him letting loose these . . . Draugr." He ladled generous portions of a creamy chicken concoction onto the plates and passed them around the table before finally sinking into the chair to Trey's right. "I don't know about you lot, but I could do with a drink," he said, and reached for the red wine. "Dig in, everyone. We still have the element of surprise on our side and we'll need all our strength for what lies ahead. We could have done without this added complication, but it doesn't alter our mission—we have to get into Iceland, take the globe from under Caliban's and Gwendolin's noses, and get back here with it for Lucien." He nodded at them, a smile briefly touching his lips. "Piece of cake."

"Can I read through the research that you've managed to dig up so far?" Alexa asked Charles.

"Of course," he replied. "In light of what Tom said earlier about there being a rat in the camp, I've saved everything to disc and deleted any references to either Draugr or Icelandic revenants from the system downstairs. I'll let you have the disc as soon as we've finished here."

Alexa smiled at him, and Trey felt a little sinking feeling in the pit of his stomach as he watched her reach over and squeeze Charles's hand. He looked away, digging into his food and shoveling a huge forkful of the piping hot chicken into his mouth, wincing at the pain it caused to his tongue.

"When do we leave for Iceland, Tom?" Alexa asked.

"All things being well, the day after tomorrow. We have some things that we need to set in place at the other end, and then we'll be on our way. And from what I've just heard, that's not a moment too soon."

"But we still don't know where my mother keeps the globe inside Leroth," Alexa pointed out. "In fact we know next to nothing about the layout of the tower or what to expect once we get inside."

"Trey?" Tom said, raising his eyebrows in the teenager's direction.

Alexa and Charles exchanged a brief look before turning their attention to the boy sitting across from them.

A brief embarrassed smile flashed across Trey's features.

"During the last few months Tom has set me up with sparring partners—various nether-creatures. It was Lucien's idea, to ascertain their strengths and weaknesses. Anyway, one of them—a Murkbeast called Klimbock—mentioned that some years before joining up with Lucien it'd been a guard for Caliban. Caliban crucified Klimbock's brother, so you can imagine that the vampire's no longer on the Murkbeast's Christmas card list."

"What has this got to do with—"

Alexa hushed Charles. "Go on, Trey."

"I asked Klimbock if it had ever been to the Tower of Leroth, and it told me it had, on many occasions. The demon has described its layout to me—some of the guard positions, that kind of thing—and provided us with a map, not a great one, but better than nothing. In addition, it remembers seeing the globe once; Gwendolin keeps it in her private chambers toward the top of the tower."

He looked over at Alexa's frowning face and shrugged his shoulders apologetically. "Tom asked me to keep this to myself until—well, until we were certain who was going and who we could trust."

Then he reached into his pocket and retrieved the hand-drawn map that the Murkbeast had put together for them.

"You're assuming this demon is telling you the truth," Charles said. "How do we know that it's not the traitor? Caliban's insider."

Trey looked back at Charles, his eyes unblinking. "How do we know you're not?"

15

The Necrotroph looked in the passenger-side mirror to ensure that there were no cars entering the street. It glanced down at the printout that it had made from the company's HR files, checking the address once more. Satisfied, it pushed the car door open and stepped out into the cool evening. The smell of freshly cut grass was in the air and the scent evoked a thousand memories inside its head—none of which were its own, and none of which it could truly say that it had really experienced—they were just vague and distant memories from the thousands of bodies that it had possessed during its considerably long existence.

The demon walked along the pavement toward the house and nodded to itself when it saw the black BMW car parked on the driveway in front of the garage. It slowed down its approach, taking deep breaths in through the nose and blowing them back out from a lipstick-painted mouth. These moments before a possession were always the worst, and while it was confident that it would be able to carry out its plans without too many problems, it nevertheless felt something that it guessed was akin to nervousness.

It began the process.

Anyone passing Ruth Glenister at that moment would have considered the look on her face—or rather the complete *lack* of expression on her face—somewhat disconcerting. She resembled a patient who has been placed under a general anesthesia with all vestiges of the life that inhabits the body seemingly absent, as if this middle-aged woman was sleep-walking up the street, oblivious to everything and anything around her.

The Necrotroph turned into the property, neglecting to close the small red gate to the pathway leading to the front door. Pressing the doorbell, it stepped backward slightly and waited on the doorstep for the house's occupant to answer.

The teenage girl who opened the door was perhaps sixteen years of age. She was dressed all in black, with black nail polish and black lipstick finishing off the ensemble. The girl was already frowning as she opened the door, and her scowl deepened as she looked at the strange woman standing on the doorstep.

"Yes?" she said.

"Are you Philippa Tipsbury? Martin Tipsbury's daughter?" asked the visitor.

Philippa Tipsbury stared at the woman standing on her doorstep, noting how she wavered slightly on her feet. Something didn't seem right about this visitor, and the girl wondered for a split second if the woman might be drunk. The way that her expressionless face stared back at her and the swaying motion of her body suggested that this might be the case, but there was something else about the woman that she couldn't quite put her finger on—it was almost as if she might be in shock.

The stranger held up a pass that bore her picture and her name: Ruth Glenister. "I work with your father, Miss Tipsbury, and I'm afraid that I have some rather bad news."

Suddenly it all made sense. The woman wasn't drunk; she *was* in shock. Something terrible had happened to her dad, and for some reason, this poor woman had been sent out by his company to let her know. Philippa's hand flew up to her mouth as if to stifle any sound that might try to escape.

"Can I come in?" asked the woman called Ruth.

"Yes. Yes, of course," Philippa said, standing to one side and ushering the older woman into the hallway. She glanced out onto the gradually darkening street before turning back into the house and closing the door behind her.

16

The possession had gone far better than the demon had any right to have hoped, with the added bonus that the human called Ruth had died during the transmigration process, instead of surviving as some gibbering lunatic who would have to be dispatched before the rest of the plan could be carried out. The demon had looked down at the dead body without the slightest feeling of remorse, despite the considerable time that it had inhabited the human that it had once belonged to. Like all Necrotrophs, it cared nothing for the host that it left behind following a transferral—they were no more than a means to an end.

After dragging the body into the garage, Philippa Tipsbury returned to the house and straightened herself out in front of the full-length mirror that hung in the hall, pushing her hair back into place and examining herself for the first time. She was not unattractive. The clothes that she wore were a statement. Everything was black. She had a small silver ring hanging from the edge of her eyebrow, and when she opened her mouth she could clearly see the large silver stud that pierced her tongue. A mild look of concern crossed her features and she frowned slightly at her own reflection, unable to pinpoint exactly what was wrong, but certain that something was amiss. She had a strange feeling that she had just come in from the garage and the smudge of dirt on her shirt would seem to endorse this belief. But she had no recollection of going into the building or, indeed, what she might have been doing there.

The demon concentrated on dispelling this anxiety, hooking into the area of the host's brain that was controlling these emotions and suppressing them as best it could. This was the most difficult time following a transmigration and it knew that in this instance it had little choice but to let the host retain most of its faculties while carefully closing off the paths to certain thoughts and memories that might cause the human to panic. Later the Necrotroph would assume full control and squash the former inhabitant entirely, but for now it had to walk a treacherous path and bide its time.

Philippa brushed at the mark on her shirt, tut-tutting at herself for being so clumsy. She glanced at her watch and wondered if Liam, her boyfriend, would be home yet from his job. They'd been going out with each other for over a year now and they had planned to go to a party together this weekend with some friends. She glanced at the time again and made her way upstairs to her room. If she called him now, she could make certain of the plans before her dad got home—he thought that Philippa was going to a sleepover at her friend Gemma's house while her parents were away.

She started to cross the room toward the phone on the

bedside table when she stopped, shaking her head in irritation as if to loosen a thought or memory that just eluded her attempts to pinpoint it. Something about her dad. She had some vague recollection of somebody coming to see her about him, and the sensation that he was in some kind of danger.

And then, as quickly as the feeling came, it was gone again. She mentally admonished herself for being so foolish. Picking up the phone, she dialed the number, at the same time moving over to the curtains to look out onto the street below to ensure that her father would not turn up unexpectedly and interrupt her conversation.

The phone was answered on the third ring. "Hello." It was Liam's voice.

"It's me," she said into the handset. "Can you talk?"

"Hey, gorgeous. How you doing? I've just got in from work. I was about to get some dinner. What's up?"

"Nothing's up. I just wanted to talk to you, that's all. How was work?"

"Ah, you know, same stuff, different day. How about you? School still a drag?"

Liam had left school last year. He had done well on his college exams, but instead of going to university he'd decided to take a job in his father's IT company. He was three years older than Philippa, and she knew her dad wouldn't approve of her going out with a boy who was that much older, so she had kept it from him.

"The place is full of losers, Liam. Not a single interesting person in the whole school. They're all just sheep—pathetic, mindless sheep, bleating their way around the corridors between pointless lessons. I hate it, and I hate everyone there."

"Are we still on for the weekend?" he asked. "I've spoken to James, and he said that we can stay the night after the party."

She smiled at the way he stumbled over his words and imagined him blushing on the other end of the line. She was about to answer that she was looking forward to it when the words caught in her throat. She frowned, shook her head and tried again, but all that came out was a thin little croak, and she found it difficult to breathe as her throat constricted again to strangle off the sentence that she had tried to form. A ripple of panic washed through her. Was she having some kind of a fit? Her hand gripped the receiver tightly so that the skin stretched over her knuckles, bleaching them of their usual pink hue, and she stared down at them in horror.

"Hello? Philippa, are you still there?"

"I can't see you anymore," she said. The words tumbled out from her mouth in a torrent.

Her heart leaped inside her and she tried to speak again, tried to correct the absurd utterance that had just poured forth from her, but no words would come. She wanted to scream, and she shook her head in frustration and fear at her sudden inability to control her actions. She tried to pull the phone away from her head but her muscles were locked, the receiver jammed up against her cheek.

"What did you say?" Liam's voice was a mixture of

amusement, concern, and anger. "Is this some kind of joke? Philippa?"

"I . . ."

This time she tried to *stop* the unbidden words from coming, restricting her throat and grimacing, her lips pulled back over her teeth in some grotesque mask. A small mascara-tainted tear slid down her cheek.

"I don't want to see you anymore, Liam. It's over. Please don't call me. I shan't be coming to the party. Goodbye."

She pressed the red button on the handset, disconnecting the call. She stared in disbelief at the telephone in her hand, letting it slip from her trembling fingers and fall to the floor, where it stared back at her mockingly. She shook her head again and slowly stood up from the bed, walking back over to the mirror to study her reflection once more. She wiped the smudges of makeup from beneath her eyes and took a short, sharp breath in through her nose.

Leaving the bedroom, she made her way down to the kitchen. She filled the kettle to make a cup of tea, leaned against the sink, and tried to make sense of what had just happened.

By the time the little ping sounded from the kettle to signal that the water had boiled, she had forgotten that she had ever even made the phone call.

17

Trey rocked back on his right foot, throwing his weight quickly backward into his shoulders and narrowly avoiding the curved claws of the Shadow Demon. He roared, a huge sound that filled the room, echoing off the plastered ceiling and reverberating around and around.

He hooked his own fingers into a fearsome-looking grapnel and raked the air in front of him, where the creature had stood moments before. He sensed it was now behind him and he spun about just in time to avoid the kick aimed at the small of his back. Instead the blow caught him in the hip, pitching him forward slightly and causing a balloon of pain to burst in that area. He regained his balance immediately and veered back around to see that the creature had leaped from its feet and was hurtling toward him, its mouth stretched wide to reveal two jagged fringes of needle-sharp teeth.

Trey dropped his shoulder, and throwing all his considerable weight down toward the floor, he forward-rolled gracefully beneath the flight of the demon, regaining his footing and turning to see the demon land, turn, and ready itself for the next attack all in one movement. The creature was incredibly quick.

The Shadow Demon grinned at him, its red clustered eyes all blinking in unison as it gestured with its hand for him to come at it. Trey pounced, watching to see which way the demon would move to start its next wave of attacks. He saw the telltale flicker as the demon seemed to disappear, moving so fast that his eyes lost it for an instant. But he thought that he had seen enough of its intentions in that fraction of a second. He twisted his body and lashed out with his hind leg to catch the creature full in the face with his foot. The crunch of cartilage suggested that what had passed for the creature's nose was now in a much-altered state, and Trey watched as the demon landed on its back on the canvas. He was on it immediately, pouncing through the air to land with all his weight on the demon's chest and stopping his teeth millimeters from its throat.

"Lucky," the creature said, glaring balefully back at him, before its features cracked into a broad smile. It turned its head to one side and spat a globule of gluey black blood onto the floor.

Trey stood up and morphed back into his human self, smiling back down at the figure of the man in front of him. There was no blood to see with his human eyes now, and despite the fact that the man he was now looking at showed none of the injuries and marks that the demon was still covered with beneath its mantle, he frowned and shook his head in apology.

"Sorry about your nose, Flaug," Trey said.

"Ah, it's nothing," the demon said, tentatively reaching

up and feeling at the nose on his face that from Trey's perspective looked absolutely fine. "You got lucky at the end there though . . . again."

"Yeah, it's funny that, isn't it? The last three times we've sparred, I've got lucky on each occasion. I must be the luckiest bloke to have ever come up against a Shadow Demon." He grinned again and offered his hand, helping the demon up off the canvas.

Flaug had been selected by Tom to act as the latest sparring partner for Trey. He had purposely selected a Shadow Demon because of its phenomenal speed, saying it was the closest thing to experiencing the "misting" that a vampire could perform—the act in which they were able to disappear in one spot and reappear in another instantaneously. Tom had suggested that Trey and Flaug just shadowbox with each other so that Trey could hone his skills and build up his own speed. But the two of them had quickly formed a close friendship and agreed that they could trust each other to try to make the fighting seem a little more real.

Today had got out of hand on a couple of occasions, both of them going at each other with a ferocity that they had hitherto avoided. Trey had enjoyed it at the time—the power and speed that he experienced as a werewolf filled him with something close to elation at times. But now it was over he felt a twinge of remorse and fear at how the fight had gone, and was worried that he had hurt Flaug more than he had intended to.

As if reading his thoughts, his friend came over to him

114

and slapped him on the back. "Don't worry, Trey. You're a werewolf, for goodness' sake. Your natural tendencies are toward destruction and chaos. You should just count yourself lucky that you're able to control those predilections, thanks to the amulet you wear. If not, I'd now be trying to scoop the contents of my throat back together instead of just having a sore nose." Flaug grabbed a towel from a rail on the wall, threw it to Trey, and frowned as he turned to look at his friend again. He walked over to Trey and reached out his hands, placing them on Trey's shoulders and turning the boy slightly to one side.

"Ouch. You might need a stitch or two in that." He nodded toward an area on Trey's back, and as Trey groped behind him he could feel the sticky warmth of blood on his fingers.

Flaug was about to take him off to have his wound attended to when he suddenly looked up toward the closed door on the other side of the gym. "Someone's coming," the demon said.

"It's OK, the door's locked and—"

The handle turned and the door opened.

Trey morphed back into a werewolf and moved toward the door. He was naked—any clothes that he wore when he morphed were instantly destroyed, and the prospect of Alexa walking in on him in the altogether was something that he would rather avoid happening again.

Charles stepped into the room. He nodded in Flaug's direction and then looked up into the orange-yellow eyes of the seven-foot werewolf that was looming over him. "Whoa, now I know how Little Red Riding Hood must have felt," he said in a small voice.

Trey strode over to where his towel had dropped to the floor, and holding it in front of him, morphed back while wrapping it about his waist.

"What do you want, Charles?" he asked. "And how did you get in here?"

"The door was unlocked, so I—"

"That door was locked. I did it myself."

"Maybe you were mistaken. As you just saw, it opened as soon as I tried it."

Trey looked at him through narrowed eyes. He suspected him of using some kind of magic on the door mechanism to allow him entry, but couldn't be bothered to argue right now.

"Well, now you're here perhaps you would be so kind as to tell me what you want?" Trey said, turning to retrieve his clothes.

"You need that looked at," Charles said, indicating the deep puncture wound in Trey's back. "Hold still for a moment and let me see."

Trey paused, looking over at Charles for a moment before shrugging and turning his back to allow his wound to be inspected. Charles gently dabbed at the bloody wound with a handkerchief that he had removed from his jacket. He clicked his tongue in a manner that reminded Trey of his grandmother.

"Hold still," Charles said. He pulled a wallet out of his

116

inside pocket. He opened it and located the item that he had been looking for. Trey looked over to see that he was holding a black needle. There was no thread hanging from it. Charles approached Trey, the needle delicately poised between his thumb and forefinger.

"Charles, what on earth do you—"

"Stay still," Charles warned him again and dug the point of the needle deep into Trey's flesh.

"Ouch! Get off me. There isn't even any thread in that thing!"

"It's a sutura needle, Trey. My father was a sorcerer too and it belonged to him. It uses an invisible thread that will stay in place for about four days before it disappears. *Now keep still.*" He pushed the tip of the needle through the other side of the wound, peering intently at the torn flesh as he worked.

Trey tried to look back over his shoulder to see what he was doing, but the wound was too far around and all he managed to do was get a rather painful crick in his neck.

"What is it used for?" he asked Charles, to try to take his mind off the pain.

"This mostly. They were first used in the Demon Wars for the very purpose that we are employing it for now. This one is practically an antique. I've had it since I was a little kid—great for practical jokes. As a young boy I would use it to sew simple purses together for my mother and fall about in hysterics when all her change dropped out onto the floor at the checkout. All very silly, but enormous fun." He paused for a second, inspecting his work. "There," he said, standing back. "As good as I can do; it'll hold together until you heal up."

"Thanks . . . I owe you one." Trey nodded his appreciation. "You still haven't told me what you're doing here."

"I've come because Alexa has asked me to apologize for what happened yesterday and to try to make peace between us. I wondered if we could go upstairs, have a cup of coffee to clear the air. We're going away tomorrow and I want us to be fine with each other before we set off."

Trey studied Charles's face for any sign of subterfuge but only received an open and honest stare back. Eventually he nodded his head. "OK, let me grab a shower and get changed, and I'll see you upstairs in the apartment."

Charles nodded and turned toward the door. He went to twist the handle, only to find that it would not budge. "Well, what do you know? It was locked after all. There must be a fault with it. I'll have someone come and have a look at it." He turned the small mechanism in the center of the handle, opened the door, and left.

Trey watched him leave. He still couldn't make the guy out—one minute he seemed like the world's biggest asshole; the next, he seemed almost bearable. He decided to give him the benefit of the doubt and wait to hear what he had to say upstairs. He went to grab his clothes and leave when a small cough behind him made him turn around.

"You didn't tell me you were going away," Flaug said, raising an eyebrow.

118

"Yeah." Trey sighed. "Lads' weekend away."

"Oh yeah? Funny, I wouldn't have had you and Charley-Charles down as the best of buddies."

"We're not," Trey said, and left the room with a wave of his hand in the demon's direction.

18

The car carrying Martin Tipsbury pulled up outside his house. He looked out of the passenger's side window, a puzzled look on his face as he noticed that none of the lights were on. He sincerely hoped that his daughter had not gone out to visit one of her friends again. He insisted that she stay at home and do her homework until he arrived back from work in the evenings—not that she seemed to listen to a word he said these days. She had turned into an extremely difficult teenager in the last year or so, and their relationship had suffered to the point where they hardly spoke at all now. His wife didn't help matters, phoning up from Jersey, where she lived with her new man, and poisoning her daughter against him, telling her how useless he was and how she loved her and missed her. If she loved her that much, why had she run away to Jersey with some fancy man and abandoned her? He'd tried to talk to Philippa about the divorce, but she didn't seem to want to listen to him. Only last week he'd suggested that she attend counseling to address her anger issues, but she had laughed in his face and told him how pathetic he was. Before she had gone up to her room she had hissed that she wished he was dead so that she could get on with her life. Things were at an all-time low in the Tipsbury household.

He opened the car door and climbed out, looking behind him as the man who had simply been introduced to him as Mr. Ellington got out of the driver's side and locked the doors. Mr. Ellington was a huge bull of a man with a head that seemed to grow straight out of his shoulders. He moved very slowly and deliberately, and if it was not for the bulging muscles obvious beneath his well-cut suit, Martin would have thought him incapable of any swift or dramatic movement, let alone of being some kind of bodyguard— which is what he secretly guessed he was.

"Is it really necessary for you to come in with me, Mr. Ellington?" Martin asked.

The man slowly turned his head and looked down at him. He wore dark glasses that he hadn't taken off from the moment they had met, despite the fact that it was now quite dark. Martin found this disconcerting, and even now he couldn't be certain if the man was actually looking at him or not.

"Mr. O'Callahan said that I was to stay with you at all times." Even the man's voice sounded like two colossal tectonic plates grinding over each other.

"Yes, but I need to speak to my daughter, explain to her what this is all about. I see no reason why you can't simply wait out here for us."

"Mr. O'Callahan said that I—"

"Yes! I know," Martin said in exasperation. "I know what

Mr. O'Callahan said, *thank you*. I just thought that you might be able to see that this is a difficult situation and . . ." He broke off, looking at the blank and impassive face that stared back at him. He sighed. "Fine. Come on then, Mr. Ellington. Let's get this over and done with."

The Necrotroph watched them approach up the path and hissed in anger when it saw the Maug demon that accompanied the human. It quickly realized that it would be impossible to even attempt to possess the man with such a powerful demon protecting him, and it pulled away from the window and began to pace the room, quickly assessing its options. It resolved to wait, bide its time until it saw an opportunity to strike. It moved to the door as soon as it heard the key enter the lock, turning on the hall light as it went.

"What were you doing in the dark?" Martin asked as he stepped into the house.

"I've not long got in myself," his daughter replied, and leaned forward to plant a small kiss on his cheek. "And no, before you ask, I wasn't around Gemma's. I went to the library to do some cramming."

Martin frowned and regarded his daughter. She never welcomed him home. Never even came out of her room to say hello. And certainly never kissed him.

"Who's your friend, Dad?" she asked as she moved off toward the kitchen to put the kettle on. "You didn't tell me that you were bringing anyone home with you."

Martin walked down the short hallway, followed closely

by the behemoth at his back. "This is Mr. Ellington," he said in a small voice. "He works with me at the firm."

"That's nice. Would you like a cup of tea, Mr. Ellington?"

Martin nearly passed out with shock. He couldn't for the life of him figure out what was going on. Philippa never made tea. It was as much as he could do to get her to make her bed each day. She was behaving extremely odd. He wondered if she had done something very wrong and was trying to cover it up. If that was the case, she was making a terrible job of it.

"Are you all right, Philippa?" he asked.

"Fine. Never better, thank you. Why?"

"No reason." Perhaps this was not going to be as bad as he had thought. He had been dreading telling her that they would have to leave immediately for the airport—as he had been instructed to do by Mr. O'Callahan—and he had not been able to think of a single way that it could be done without her resorting to one of her screaming fits, during which she told him how utterly crap her life was and how he had ruined everything. Whenever they had one of these arguments she would threaten to kill herself, telling him that they would both be happier if she did. Martin was always left exhausted after these rows and never knew what to say, because whatever he *did* say always made things a hell of a lot worse.

He picked up the mug of tea that she had placed in front of him and ignored the pain on his lips and tongue as he took a huge gulp. He looked at her and screwed up his courage.

"We have to leave for the airport. I've been sent on extremely urgent business to the Seychelles and the firm want you to accompany me. The whole trip will be paid for by Mr. Charron, and we have been given an extremely generous expenses budget to spend as we see fit once we get there. We have to leave right away. Now. This evening." The words came out in a long, tumbling stream, and he hunched over the steam coming up off the hot tea, waiting for the inevitable eruption.

The demon inhabiting the body of Philippa Tipsbury was treading a very fine line. It was unable to take complete control of the host in case the Maug sensed something was amiss—the demon bodyguard was watching the whole scene very carefully, and the Necrotroph could not afford to make it suspicious. It had to work subtly now, suppressing the areas of the host's mind that wanted to react violently to this news, while hiding from the Maug's attentions. Its only hope was that the father would react favorably to this new side to his daughter and not become overtly apprehensive in front of the accompanying demon.

"The Seychelles? Just like that? But what about school, Dad? You're always telling me that I need to knuckle down this year and that I can't afford to miss any time from my studies."

"That will all be taken care of by Mr. O'Callahan and Mr. Ellington here. They assure me that my company has strong connections with the headmaster of your school and that they will be able to smooth the whole thing over. They are even going to arrange a tutor to cover anything that you might miss."

A multitude of angry thoughts and vicious retorts sprang up into Philippa Tipsbury's mind, but she was unable to articulate any of her resentment. She had the odd sensation of being on the outside, looking in on this scene as it unfolded. Try as she might she could do nothing to express her anger at the news her father had just delivered.

She opened her mouth, intending to tell him that she wasn't going on his stupid trip. "Oh, well, that's all right then. As long as you're sure that I won't get in any trouble with Mr. Hayter. Sounds great!"

What was she saying? What was happening to her? A wave of panic began to rise up within her, but almost as soon as it had begun to form it seemed to dissipate, replaced by calm and warm thoughts about the great time that she would be able to have with her father. The trip would enable them to get closer again. She looked over at her father and smiled at him. "The Seychelles? Wow, I've always wanted to go there. I'll go and get some things packed, shall I?"

She went out into the hall, and Martin could hear the sound of her footsteps as she lightly padded up the stairs in the direction of her bedroom. He looked over at the silent figure of the man standing next to him and smiled nervously in his direction. He had never been so amazed in all of his life.

125

* * *

Philippa closed the door of the bedroom behind her and leaned against the cold surface of the wall, staring up at the ceiling. The Necrotroph took complete control of the host now, squashing and smothering the swelling thoughts and emotions that had been allowed to build up inside the host while the demon had been forced to hide deep inside, far away from the Maug's watchful stare. It felt happier again now that it could relax a little and thought ahead to what it knew it must do.

The demon had no choice but to leave the country with the feeble little human that was Philippa's father. It regretted that it would not be able to take him over before they were in the Seychelles, but any death at the airport, or on the plane, would cause too much of a commotion and possibly destroy any chance that it might have of finding out what it was this man knew that made it so important to get him out of the country under guard.

No, it would just have to be a little more patient. There would be ample opportunity to take what it needed from the human once they were away from the Maug and in the Seychelles. Then it could report what it knew to its master and still be in a body that presented it with the perfect opportunity to return to the inner workings of the empire of the traitor, Lucien Charron.

Philippa Tipsbury smiled to herself and hummed a tune that she had never heard before. She leaned forward and made her bed, smoothing out the covers and fluffing up the pillow. She hated an unkempt bed.

126

19

"White or black?" Charles asked as Trey walked into the kitchen, dumping his bag on the floor beside the table.

"Not a huge fan of coffee, to be honest. I'll probably just have a fruit juice or something."

"Oh, come on, humor me. I've just made this from scratch, and I've been told that I make the meanest cappuccino in these parts."

Trey looked over to the giant Gaggia coffee machine that was hissing and steaming in the kitchen. He had to admit the smells coming from it were good, and he nodded his head in assent. "Cappuccino it is then. Plenty of chocolate on the top for me, but no sugar."

He sat down and watched Charles busying himself in the kitchen. He moved around it as though he knew where Mrs. Magilton kept everything, opening up the precise cupboards that contained the various items that he needed to prepare the hot drinks. Trey idly wondered how it was that he could know his way about so well.

"Sure you want chocolate and not cinnamon?" Charles said, holding a teaspoon of the brown powder over the frothy foam that jiggled at the top of the bowl-like cup. Trey nodded, and Charles finished the two drinks. He brought them to the table, placing one in front of Trey and sitting in the chair opposite.

"This is all very nice," Trey said, a quizzical look on his face.

"Like I said, I'm here to smoke the peace pipe with you before we get under way tomorrow. Just figured it best to clear the air before the two of us go into the fray, as it were."

The room went silent while the two of them sipped at their drinks and considered what to say next.

"So how—"

"What did you—"

They both spoke at once, and then smiled at each other.

"Go on," said Trey. "You first."

"I was just going to ask how often you sparred like that. From what I could see of the Shadow Demon, and from the look of that cut on your back, it must have been quite a session. I don't imagine that you want to be doing that too often?"

"So you can see them?" Trey asked. "The demons. You can see them in their true form? I thought that you were completely human."

"It's a spell. I can switch it on and off as I need, but to be honest I rarely, if ever, nullify it these days. It helps me to see who is who around this place and that way I know what I'm dealing with. It can be very embarrassing at times otherwise."

"Tell me about it," Trey said with a shake of his head.

"It must be a bit of a bind for you—only being able to see the nether-creatures once you become the werewolf. I'll

128

try to teach you the spell sometime, when we get back . . . if we get back." He looked at Trey, his eyes hard. He took a sip of his coffee and then smiled, adding in a lighter tone, "It's extremely difficult, but if Tom can learn it—even if it did take him over a year—I'm sure that a quick learner like you will pick it up in no time."

"Thanks," Trey said.

"You're very impressive, by the way," Charles said. "The sight of you standing there when I came in through that door quite took my breath away, and I think that anyone who can give a Shadow Demon a run for its money is always going to be handy to have around."

Trey shrugged. "We get together a couple of times a week. It started out all very 'safe,' but we seem to have got a little more intense over the last month or so. We wouldn't hurt each other really."

Charles looked at him for a moment over the top of his coffee cup. "Be careful around Shadow Demons, Trey. You never quite know what they're up to."

"Flaug's a friend."

"All the same, be wary of how much you allow yourself to trust a creature like that. They have a habit of turning *very* nasty very quickly."

Trey matched the look from the man opposite him. His initial willingness to listen to Charles was quickly turning to irritation, and he was about to say something about not feeling that he could trust *him*, when Charles interrupted his thoughts.

129

"You like Alexa, don't you?"

Trey set his cup back down on the saucer and stared across at the young man. "Look, Charles, I don't see what—"

"It's OK. I haven't, and wouldn't, say anything to her. I just wanted to know if my suspicions were correct."

"Well, even if I did, it really is none of your business."

"That's true—it isn't any of my business anymore."

Trey waited.

"But I think that it is best to get everything out in the open now and therefore it's only fair to tell you that Alexa and I had been going out with each other."

Trey's stomach did a funny rolling thing and he felt his throat constrict, making him swallow a large lump that had formed there. He had known there was *something* between Alexa and Charles by the way that she had been with him at the dinner the other evening, touching his arm when she laughed at his stories and fiddling with her earrings whenever he had been speaking (which had been all too often). Trey tried to push these images away, but they kept playing over in his head—a torturous loop of petty jealousies.

"There's nothing going on now, Trey," Charles said, as if reading his thoughts. "We split up a short while before you came on the scene, and she has told me on more than one occasion that there isn't any chance of us getting back together. I just thought that it would be best to lay my cards on the table now, before you found out some other way."

Trey shrugged again. "It's none of my business . . . but thanks." He nodded before returning his attention to the

130

gradually disappearing ring of white foam around the inner circumference of his cup.

They sat like that for a few moments, neither really knowing what to say to change the subject to more neutral ground.

"What do you know about Gwendolin?" Trey asked eventually.

"It's probably better if you tell me what you know and I'll fill in the blanks."

Trey shrugged his shoulders. "Not much at all, apart from the fact that she used to be Lucien's partner and that she's Alexa's mother. I can't seem to find anyone willing to talk about her. Why is that?"

Charles puffed out his cheeks and looked through the window toward the hazy light bouncing in from the river below. "It's the shame of it all, I suppose."

Trey waited for him to continue.

"My father was working here then. He told me that the two of them—Lucien and Gwendolin—met when she was eighteen years old. Lucien was instantly besotted with her. She was stunningly attractive—with long red hair that hung down her back in rolling waves and a face that was not just beautiful, but intelligent and determined at the same time."

Trey's thoughts turned to Alexa and he considered how her face must be an amalgam of her mother's and father's. From this he thought he could picture how Gwendolin might have looked back then.

"They were inseparable. And together they did great work

in thwarting Caliban's plans at a time when his power was at its peak. But as the years went on their relationship started to fracture. It wasn't much of a problem to begin with, but their thoughts and vision for how they saw the way forward began to cause the rifts between them to widen."

"How so?"

"Gwendolin began to explore dark magic more and more. She would seek out the ancient scripts and writings that were believed to have been lost forever—employing a team of people to locate them—and she immersed herself in their teachings. Lucien tried to stop her, but her argument was that they would never truly be able to thwart the evil that Caliban would wreak in this world if they did not understand how it came about." He glanced over at Trey and a quick, nervous smile briefly touched the corners of his mouth before he continued.

"By now she was an incredibly powerful sorceress. She had always been a star pupil—her mother began to teach her from a very early age, and she had a natural gift for magecraft. But now her power was perhaps greater than any sorcerer who had come before her and she jealously guarded her secrets and skills. Dark magic has a way of doing that to people. It's a pernicious force that seeks to consume those who dare to study it. As pupils of magic we all learn aspects of it, but are made painfully aware of the dangers that beset anyone who dares to delve too deeply into its secrets. Maybe it was Gwendolin's foolhardy belief that she was capable of resisting its consuming power, or maybe, having had a taste, she decided that it was this power that she truly wanted, regardless of the cost. Things were looking very bad indeed. And then she became pregnant."

"Alexa?" Trey asked.

"Yes. And with the discovery of her pregnancy, she changed. Or appeared to. She completely turned her back on her arcane studies and immersed herself in the joys of motherhood. It was eight years since the two of them had met, and in the last three years of that time Gwendolin had changed out of all recognition. But the baby . . . the baby transformed all that in a stroke, and almost overnight Lucien and Gwendolin returned to that state of unbridled happiness that they had both known at the start of their union. The baby was like a brilliant light that banished the darkness that had begun to devour her."

"What happened?" Trey asked when the silence that followed had strung itself out for what seemed like an age.

"Nothing at first. Alexa was born, and Lucien and Gwendolin entered that state of ecstasy that all parents do. They doted on their newborn child, and the universe seemed to slot into perfect place for a while. But after a year or so Gwendolin began to renew her interest in magic again—if she ever truly gave it up—although she promised Lucien that she was no longer interested in the dark arts and that she merely wanted to keep up her skills and knowledge. He agreed to allow her to continue her studies as long as she kept to her promise.

"But, as I said, dark magic has a way of getting under

your skin, waiting deep in the marrow of your bones for you to let your guard down before it rises up again and demands its due attention. Gwendolin couldn't resist its allure. She secretly set up her team of researchers again and began to delve once more into murky secrets that were better left hidden and forgotten. She began to lose her grip on reality. She was obsessed by her need to acquire more and more power, and in doing so, more and more of her was lost to those who loved her.

"One day Lucien decided that she was no longer a safe presence to have around. There are places that people can go—in realms other than this one—where poor souls that have lost their way can be sent for help, a sort of rehab for junkies of evil. He walked into her study to find her in the middle of an extremely perilous summoning. She was trying to bring back a demon lord known as Horg, who had been banished from the Netherworld centuries before. The summoning required a sacrifice to be made in order for it to be successful. She had prepared the sacrificial offering and would have gone through with the ceremony, if Lucien had not walked in when he did."

Charles stopped and looked over at Trey, a strange look in his eye.

"Was the sacrifice a human or an animal?" Trey asked, his voice sounding papery thin. The silence in the room was palpable.

Charles nodded very slowly, knowing that Trey had

already come to the conclusion on his own. "It was Alexa," he said. "Gwendolin was going to sacrifice her own daughter."

"Alexa." Trey's mouth felt dry and his mind swam as he fought to take this revelation in. "Does she have any idea—"

"No. She doesn't know. That's why Lucien told Alexa that her mother was dead. What else was he going to tell her?"

"She'll find out."

"Let's hope not, for her sake."

Trey looked at Charles and shook his head. "Why tell me? Don't get me wrong, I'm glad you did, but why tell me?"

"Because you need to know what we are up against, Trey. Gwendolin is pure evil. She and Caliban will stop at nothing to wreck everything that is decent and good and honest in this world. Neither will they stop at anything to destroy the likes of us. And tomorrow we leave to try to steal an ancient and powerful object from right under their noses. This is not going to be like play-fighting with a Shadow Demon—you need to be very, *very* careful out there, Trey."

"Then I hope that you are as good as Alexa says you are, Charles," Trey said, blowing out a long breath and standing up to clear away the things from the table. "Because it sounds like we really are going to need all the help we can get."

Charles nodded in agreement. "She mustn't go in. Alexa can't be allowed to face Gwendolin when we get to Leroth."

Trey turned to face him. "I don't see how you are going to stop her, Charles."

"I agree that it's going to be difficult, but I've been talking to Tom and we've come up with a plan."

20

Their flight to Reykjavik the next morning was delayed. They had begun to taxi toward the runway in Lucien's private jet when they'd slowed and stopped, turning back to their starting point. The pilot had come back into the cabin and explained that there had been an STCA in the skies overhead. "It stands for short-term conflict alert," he said. "Basically it means that two planes up there were too close to each other and they've had to take remedial action. It shouldn't delay us too long. As soon as we get up I'll do my best to make up any lost time, Tom."

"Thank you, Nigel," Tom said, glancing down at his watch and frowning.

In the end, they were delayed for three hours. They left the plane and returned to the private room that was set aside for them inside the airport. They ate and tried to watch some television, but this time they were itching to get away, and the boredom was getting to them all.

Eventually they were airborne, the pilot apologizing for the delay despite there being nothing that he could have done about it.

Trey sat in a comfortable brown leather chair opposite Tom. He looked over at his friend and an uneasy feeling of déjà vu flickered through him. The last time he had been in this plane he had been hurtling toward Amsterdam to rescue Alexa from Caliban, and he briefly considered whether he would ever get the chance to take a *normal* flight, perhaps on a vacation somewhere where there wasn't anybody waiting to kill him at the end of the journey.

Tom looked unusually nervous, his eyes fluttering around the cabin, scanning for dangers that weren't there. He had fished his mobile out of his pocket on at least four occasions, looking down at the screen before returning it with a frown. The full magnitude of what they were attempting to do had only really dawned on Trey as he lay on his bed the night before, staring up at the ceiling and replaying the conversation that he had had with Charles over and over again. He looked over at Alexa and smiled when he saw that she was also looking in his direction. He nodded his head at her before reaching for the newspaper on the table in front of him. None of the four of them seemed capable of speech, so wrapped up were they in their own thoughts and planning. Instead they relied on furtive glances and nods of encouragement like paratroopers moments before their maiden jump into a war zone.

Trey was about to put the paper down again and go to get a drink from the galley when a voice sounded inside his head.

"Are you OK, Trey?" Alexa asked.

He concentrated on the words of the spell that he and Charles had been over countless times on that afternoon in the meeting room, forming them in his mind and going through the mental steps that his tutor had walked him through so carefully. A gentle *nudge* inside his mind told him that the spell had worked and he opened his eyes again.

"Fine, thanks," he projected back. *"Just a bit nervous. Do you want a drink? I was just going off to the galley to get a Coke or something."*

"I'll come with you; I could do with stretching my legs."

The two of them stood up and asked aloud if anyone else wanted anything. Answered by two shaken heads, they walked to the small galley at the back of the jet.

"What's up with Tom?" hissed Alexa as soon as they were out of earshot.

"How do you mean? He just looks a bit nervous."

"Tom is *never* nervous. I've seen him working with my father on lots of things and I have never seen him looking like this. I want to say something to him but I don't know what."

"I'd leave him be, Alexa. He just needs to get his own head right, and you cooing over him isn't going to help him do that. He'll be fine."

"Do you think he's worried about going up against my mother with me in tow? Because if that's the case I think that I need to explain to him that he needn't worry. I'm not at all sure that I—"

"No, Alexa, I don't think that's it," Trey interrupted her. Then, as she looked over at him with a quizzical expression on her face, he had to turn away to hide the embarrassed look on his own.

"What's going on, Trey? What do you know that I don't?"

"Nothing."

"You're a bad liar, Trey. What are you all keeping from me?"

"Please, let's just get a drink." He grabbed a can from the fridge and turned back toward the main cabin of the plane to return to his seat.

He didn't look up at Alexa as she returned to her own seat. Instead he dug in his rucksack to see if he could find something to occupy him for the remainder of the flight. He rejected the handheld gaming console that he had bought a week or so before and chose instead his MP3 player, selecting a Kings of Leon album and settling back with his eyes closed, letting the music wash over him.

21

Martin Tipsbury turned the page of the paperback novel that he had bought at the airport and had started to read in the first-class lounge. He had purchased five books with the intention of reading them by the pool during this unexpected vacation. He never found the time to read these days and this annoyed him because it was only once he sat down with a book that he realized how much he enjoyed the exercise. Now he would have the opportunity to immerse himself for two whole weeks—Mr. O'Callahan had told him that he thought he would be able to come back after a week, but insisted that Martin stay for a fortnight and enjoy himself as much as possible.

Now that he had had time to think about what was happening, he couldn't quite believe his luck—all he had done was carry out the research that he had been asked to and now, as some kind of reward, he had been sent on an all-expenses-paid trip to the Seychelles. He smiled to himself. Maybe his luck was finally changing. He had never been a lucky man, but right now he felt as though he had won the lottery. He took another sip from the champagne flute in his hand, letting the bubbles burst against his nose, and concluded that he really didn't care what was behind it all; he was damned if he was going to let anything, or anyone, spoil this for him.

He glanced over at his daughter and smiled. She had donned an eye mask to try to eliminate the bright sunlight that streamed in through the porthole windows on either side of the plane. Her breathing was shallow and even, and he was surprised at how quickly she had fallen asleep once they had been shown their seats.

He sighed contentedly. Philippa was actually being nice to him. More than that, she was being the nicest to him that she'd been for a very long time. He thought about the row that they had had only a week ago, following advice from his brother that he be a bit firmer with his daughter. He had shouted at her for the first time ever. She had laughed at him at the time, telling him that he was pathetic and how much she was looking forward to moving out of the house and getting away from him. But maybe he had planted a seed in her head and this newfound respect that she was showing him was the result. He determined to take Mr. O'Callahan's advice and treat the whole thing as a vacation that they could use to fix things between them.

He relaxed back into the seat and took in his surroundings again. He had never flown first class before and he was stunned by the amount of room and attention that they were given on board the plane. He'd already had three glasses of champagne and his head was pleasantly fizzing with the effect of the alcohol. He was unused to drinking and he thought that he'd better slow down before he ended up getting sick and spending the remainder of the flight in the toilet. He reclined his seat and stretched out full-length on what was effectively now a bed. A hostess came along and offered him pillows that he accepted, thinking that he would keep the books for the pool and try to get some sleep right now, like his daughter beside him.

He lay back on the bed, a lazy smile of satisfaction playing on his lips.

After a short time, and once the Necrotroph lying next to him was certain that Martin was asleep, it sat up and raised its chair into an upright position. It looked at the gently snoring carcass next to it and struggled not to let the contempt that it felt for this pathetic excuse of a man show too clearly on its human host's face. How dearly it would have loved to perform the possession right now and put an end to this hideous charade. But it would have to wait. It would have to wait for the right time.

Philippa Tipsbury stretched her neck and climbed out of the seat to go to the bathroom. As she did so, the paperback novel that her father had been looking at earlier fell to the floor between their seats.

She looked down at the book, noting how he had abandoned it after only a few pages. A sly smile formed on her face. She bent down to retrieve the book and placed it back on the shelf between the two seats.

She inwardly vowed that he would never finish this story or any other book again.

22

The body of the dead woman lay draped over his legs. The head lolling down toward the floor drip-dripped blood into a neat circular pool that moved inexorably toward the leg of the huge, ornate chair that Caliban was sitting in.

The ancient vampire licked at his fangs with the tip of his tongue, savoring the last of the blood that was there. Gray, paper-thin eyelids closed over yellow irises and black elongated pupils. The feeding had filled him with the power and energy that his kind had craved throughout the centuries and he slowly moved his head from side to side, flexing his neck, feeling his strength growing. He pushed the body to the floor, wiped his chin as he stood up and reveled in the feeling of invulnerability that surged through him.

Caliban heard footsteps approaching the great hall that he occupied toward the top of the tower and wondered who would dare to interrupt him at this time. He ran the palm of his taloned hand over the top of his bald head and drew himself up to his full height, ready to face whoever was on the other side of the door.

He motioned with the finger of his left hand and an inky black tendril emerged from somewhere within the shadows behind his thronelike chair. It snaked along the ground and wrapped itself around the outstretched arm of Caliban's victim, dragging it back into the obsidian darkness. The constant thrumming noise that emanated from the shadows rose to a gabbling din of excitement for a moment before a hiss of annoyance from Caliban restored it back to little more than a background whisper.

The vampire opened the door and looked out at the figure of the Maug demon that stood in the doorway. The creature peered at him from beneath its beetled brow, unwilling to lift its chin to face him fully.

"Why do you disturb me now?" Caliban hissed. "Could it be that you do not understand me when I say that I am not to be interrupted at this hour?"

"She said that it was important, my lord," the creature mumbled.

Caliban waited.

Gwendolin pushed the massive demon aside and stepped into the room. With a slight motion of her hand the heavy door slammed shut in the guard's face.

The hag who stood in front of Caliban bore no resemblance to the sublime and resplendent beauty who had once been Lucien's wife and Alexa's mother. No longer human, the dark powers that Gwendolin had so zealously sought out had consumed her. Gone was the white alabaster skin, the elfin eyes, and the strong but delicate features that had once won his brother's affection and devotion. Instead, these had been replaced with the grim death mask of a nether-creature consumed with bile and hatred for everything that it had once been. She had come to Caliban after his brother had tried to kill her, seeking him out and describing her plans, her schemes, to wreak havoc on the human realm. Over the years she had immersed herself in the dark arts so completely that she now wielded immense power and had become the most important individual in the vampire's empire.

Caliban waited, trying to keep his growing irritation in check, knowing that she would not be rushed. He turned his back on her and returned to his throne.

"Well?" he said, once he was seated again.

She took a few steps in his direction, looked up at him and smiled, revealing blackened teeth that had eroded to such an extent that they were little more than glistening stumps peeking out from the gums.

He smiled back, deliberately revealing the full length of his fangs in the hope that this might prompt her out of her silence.

"We have had some success," she said.

"*Some* success?"

"It would seem that the revenants are even more . . . unstable than we had imagined. As we have only managed to resurrect the one so far, it is difficult to say whether it is just this particular Draugr that is uncontrollable, or whether they will all turn out to be like this. I suspect the latter to be the case."

"We are in the business of chaos, Gwendolin. Surely this creature cannot be as bad as you suggest?"

The smile that had gradually slipped into a grimace finally fell completely from her face and she stared back at the vampire with a look that he found difficult to read. "You need to come and see it," she said. "It's as much as we can do to contain it at the moment."

Caliban inclined his head to one side and considered what she had said. They had worked tirelessly to raise the Draugr from their burial mounds, and each time they had failed. Gwendolin had locked herself away in her room at the top of the tower where her ancient books and manuscripts were kept, until she had emerged this morning with a new invocation that she had found buried in some long-lost script. She had reported this to him, and he had not seen her looking so excited about anything for some time. And now she was standing in front of him with a look on her face that suggested that she wished she had never come across this new information.

"Very well, Gwendolin. Take me to see what we have."

He stepped down, and as he went to leave, the gabble of noise from the shadows behind him rose into a loud cacophony of guttural voices and animal-like sounds that were all layered over and intermingled with one another.

"Hush, my little ones. I will be back shortly, and then you will feed properly."

He closed the door behind him and followed the witch down the corridor.

23

"It's freezing!" Trey said, pulling the zipper on his coat up as far as it would go. "Why's it so cold? It's nearly spring, for goodness' sake!" He was now glad that he had let Alexa talk him into buying the jacket before coming out here. It was a puffer style and was filled with eiderdown. It had cost an absolute fortune, but the man in the shop had said that they were about the best thing available for keeping warm in very cold conditions. Trey hoped that he was right.

"We're in a country called *Iceland*," Alexa said with a smile. "The clue might just be in the name."

They stepped out of the airport and headed toward a car that was waiting for them at the pickup point.

"And it's bloody raining," Trey grumbled. "Why couldn't Caliban have translocated Leroth somewhere tropical? Barbados, maybe. Or Cuba—I've always wanted to go to Cuba."

"It's just a bit of rain, Trey; you're not going to melt," Charles said, shaking his head and putting his holdall in the trunk of the car.

"Ah yes, but it is this particular type of rain that I find so annoying—that fine misty rain that worms its way between the smallest gap in your clothing. It's without doubt the worst type of rain you can get. If there was a top ten list of rain that I most—"

"Will you shut your hole about the weather and get in the car?" Tom said, holding open the back door of the big black van. "In case you have forgotten, we are supposed to be coming into this country with as little fuss as possible, and I really do not want to be standing out here listening to you moan about a bit of rain."

"Sorry, Tom."

As soon as they were all inside, Tom, in the front passenger seat, addressed the man who had sat silently waiting for them all to embark.

"Hjelmar, long time no see," he said, shaking the man's hand. "Sorry about the delay, but we got held up at our end. Some idiot pushing tin almost managed to send two pieces straight into each other's flight path!"

"I received the message, Tom. It is not a problem. No need to concern yourself." The man was about the same size and build as Tom and spoke in a strong Nordic accent.

Tom twisted in his seat so that he could see the others in the back of the vehicle. "Everyone, this is Hjelmar Stefansson. Hjelmar, this is Trey, Charles, and Lucien's daughter, Alexa."

"Nice to meet you all," Hjelmar said. "Alexa, I last saw you when you were just a small child, when your father brought you here. I hope that his condition will improve and that he'll visit us again soon." He pulled the car away

149

from the curb and followed the sweep of the road toward the exit. "I have located a small house a few miles outside the capital in the area that you specified, Tom. I've also left all the equipment that you requested there." He turned his attention away from the road for a moment and eyed the Irishman with a raised eyebrow. "Am I allowed to ask what you are doing here, Tom?"

"No, you're not, Hjelmar. But as soon as the whole thing is over, I'll fill you in on all the juicy details over a bottle of that delicious Icelandic vodka that you're so keen on."

"It's a deal. But I want *all* the juicy details—and you're buying."

Trey smiled at the sight of the two men, now deep in conversation in the front of the car. They were both of a type that seemed to abound within Lucien's organization—tough, rugged men who understood what needed to be done in almost any situation. He turned his attention to the landscape outside the window, taking in the country's backdrop now that they had left Keflavík airport behind them. He was immediately struck by how completely bleak everything looked. It was as if the stark, hard landscape had been painted by an artist who had forgotten to include any colors in his palette except gray and brackish green. Trey had read in a guidebook that NASA had used this environment to simulate the lunar landscape when training the astronauts for the *Apollo 11* mission. Looking out the window, he understood why.

He tried to spy out a tree among the rocky terrain, finally spotting one sheltering from the cold beside a deserted farmhouse. It looked like a lanky, frightened kid hiding in the bike shed from the school bullies, dreading the next beating he was going to receive at their hands.

Charles, who was sitting beside him in the back, must have figured out what he was thinking, because he leaned across in the seat and said in a hushed tone, "Now you know why this place is the suicide capital of Europe."

Trey grinned back at him, adding, "Can you imagine what it's like in the winter when there's no sunlight either? Sheesh!"

"Actually, I think that Norway lays claim to that dubious badge of honor," Hjelmar said in a loud voice from the front of the car. Trey and Charles looked at each other in disbelief, both flushing red in embarrassment. "And the darkness is a good thing—if you happen to like the dark."

Tom turned around and glared at the two of them like a father who has found his kids flipping the bird at the cars behind them. To avoid meeting the Irishman's stare, they buried their heads in the map Charles had on his lap, and held their tongues for the remainder of the journey.

They arrived at the house about twenty minutes later. Tom opened the front door and shooed them all inside as quickly as he could, glancing into the surrounding countryside as he did so. It was nice to step into the warmth from the cold outside, and they unzipped their coats and looked around.

Trey was standing by a heater in the living room when Alexa came in and stood beside him. Nobody was talking much anymore, the nervous anxiety that they all felt upon arriving here had dried up any conversation. Trey puffed out his cheeks and nodded toward the front door, where Hjelmar was fetching in the last of the things from the car.

"You didn't tell me that you'd been to Iceland before," he said.

Alexa shrugged her shoulders. "I hardly remember it. My father helped Hjelmar and his friends to deal with an infestation of vamps. We came as Hjelmar's guests after it was all over. Vampires love places like this—short days and long nights—it's a dream ticket, and they're always trying it on here."

"Iceland has a strong history of magic and sorcery," said Charles, who'd also entered the room now. "It's a key strategic point in Lucien's empire because it is somewhat easier to open portals to the Netherworld here than in other parts of the world. That's why we were able to locate Caliban so quickly once he'd begun to operate here—we keep a close eye on places like this."

"He must have known you'd catch on to his presence here."

Charles shrugged. "Like I said, it's a key strategic point, and with Lucien out of the way at the moment, Caliban must think that we've taken our eye off the ball."

"When you've all finished yapping you might want to help shift these bags out of the way!" Tom's voice barked from the hallway.

Hjelmar came into the house holding the car keys out to Tom. He dropped them into his friend's outstretched hand

and nodded sternly. "Jon is here now. I will go with him. The car is almost fully fueled so use it as you want. If you need to leave in a hurry, dump it wherever you can and give me a call to let me know where to pick it up." He looked into the room where Trey and Alexa were standing and nodded in their direction. "Give my regards to your father when he is up and about again, Alexa. Nice to meet you, Trey. Maybe next time you are here I can take you sightseeing, eh?"

He turned to leave, shouting over his shoulder as he went, "The fridge and food cupboards are all full so feel free to eat and drink anything that you want."

Tom walked into the room. He'd evidently started to unpack some of the items that Hjelmar had left for him because he held an ugly-looking assault rifle in the crook of his arm. "Who wants a nice cup of tea?" he asked.

24

The interior of the room resembled the site of an explosion. Pieces of splintered wood and twisted metal littered the floor and in the center of the room, not far from the strange revenant creature, two dead bodies lay like gruesome islands floating in a crimson sea. One of the dead demons had had its head torn off, although there appeared to be no sign of the missing item. The other body looked as if it had been crushed by some huge weight: organs and other parts that should have been on the inside were on the outside, extruded from it onto the ghastly, slippery mess that had become of the floor.

The remaining two Maug guards were standing against the wall as far away from the Draugr as they could get. In their hands they clutched long, cruel-looking spears, but their eyes reflected nothing but undiluted fear as they eyeballed the creature before them.

"What is the meaning of this?" Caliban's voice cut through the eerily silent room that only a short time ago had been filled with a symphony of agonized screams. He stood in the doorway and eyed the guards with contempt. "Why are the two of you skulking there in the shadows? Clear this mess up."

154

They mumbled their apologies but gave no sign of moving from their position of relative safety.

The vampire regarded the chaos before turning his gaze to the creature standing in the center of the room. He slowly walked in, stepping over the flotsam and jetsam that punctuated the bloody floor. The Draugr regarded him through long-dead eyes, its great barrel chest heaving up and down, watching Caliban approach. Around its wrists were what appeared to be thick silver-gray bands of shimmering light that was fluidlike in the way that it flowed in unison with the creature's movements. The restraints flowed down from the creature's arms to the floor on either side, where they were anchored to some invisible points. The monster was pure power. Great slabs of sinuous muscle lay beneath its bluish black skin, rippling and contracting as it strained against its shackles. There was a putrefying stench of decay and death in the room that was overwhelming, and Caliban had to resist the urge to cover his mouth with a handkerchief. It was impossible to think that this creature had ever been human.

The vampire stepped forward. Judging from the circle of damage, he was now within the creature's range.

"Careful, master," said one of the Maug from behind him.

"Silence, you cretin!" Caliban commanded without looking around at the two terrified demons.

"It's just that it—"

The rest of the sentence was cut off by the deafening roar that emanated from the shackled beast in the middle of

155

the room. Caliban watched as it peeled back black lips to reveal the series of daggers that lined its mouth, its entire face contorting into a mask of fury. A smile flickered across the vampire's features as the creature began to expand in size very rapidly—the thunderous roar increasing in volume to match this sudden accretion. The thing now stood a good twelve feet in height, and Caliban marveled at the strength of the magic that denied it its freedom, watching as the thing raged and tore to be loose from the restraints at its wrists. It lunged toward him—the speed with which it moved a contradiction to its immense size and bulk. The huge open maw hurtled toward the vampire's face, teeth bared and ready to rend flesh from bone.

Caliban waited until the last moment before he misted, re-appearing at a spot no more than three feet back from where he had stood, and watched as the creature's teeth met with a snap around nothing but air. The smile he had worn throughout still adorned his cruel features and he turned to the sorceress by his side.

"Feisty little thing, isn't he? Tell me, Gwendolin, do you think it can be . . . tamed in any way?"

The sorceress regarded the undead monster and slowly shook her head. "I think that my original concerns have proven correct. They have been underground for too long," she said. "The rage that they have built up over the centuries has consumed them. They want revenge against a world that has forgotten them, but they seem happy to destroy anything and everything that they encounter in the mean-time. They appear to have lost all ability to communicate."

"And this is the only one that we have successfully man-aged to restore to life?" the vampire asked.

"Yes. There would appear to be another lying in a burial mound not far from where we recovered this one, but we have put off digging it out. We could do so, and use the globe's powers again to see if we might be successful but I am pessi-mistic. As you know, we have found it much harder than we had thought it would be."

Caliban studied the creature again as it gradually shrank back to its previous size. After a moment he let out a short, humorless laugh.

"Have the other one brought back and see if it too can be resurrected," he said.

"But, master, you've seen . . ."

Caliban raised the prosthetic hand that now adorned his right wrist, cutting her off with the gesture. The curved blades at the ends of the fingers reflected what little light was in the room. He pointed toward the beast, which had not taken its eyes off him since he had entered. "Sadly, they ap-pear to be of no use to me as part of my army. But I believe that any creature with such pure, unadulterated rage is still something that I would like to have restored to the human world." He turned to Gwendolin and narrowed his eyes. "If, and when, you revive the other one, I want you to have them transported down to the capital city of this godforsaken land

157

and then have them set free. If it is revenge that these creatures want, who am I to disappoint them?"

Gwendolin managed a thin smile that she hoped would mask the dismay she felt at hearing this command. She was already exhausted, and now she was being asked to expend even more energy on what was little more than a vicious and diabolical whim. "Very good, master. I shall see to it personally."

Caliban turned to the two guards that were still lurking at the far end of the room. "Be sure to clean this mess up," he said with a careless gesture over his shoulder.

An unkind smile played on his face as he left the room and turned back up the corridor. Perhaps this experiment was not to be a complete waste of time after all.

25

It was the birdsong that woke Martin Tipsbury the next morning, that and the smell of the wild flowers that drifted in through the open windows. He swung himself out of bed and looked out at the view, smiling at the sight. It was like looking at a picture in a glossy travel brochure. Brightly colored birds hopped from branch to branch high up in the tall gardenia trees, whose white blooms produced the strong scent that drifted in to him on the breeze. Beyond the gardens of the villa the white sand of the beach stretched out toward an azure sea that reflected back the late-morning sunshine as white-hot pinpricks of light.

He and Philippa had arrived at the villa a little after three o'clock that morning, after transferring to this island, Praslin, from the main island in a small Bell 206 helicopter. Despite the sleep that they had both managed to get on the plane, the trip had left them groggy and wanting nothing more than to throw their things down and climb into bed. The housekeeper, Mrs. Beauchamp, had been waiting for them when they arrived and had fussed around, arranging for their bags to be placed in their rooms and asking them if they wanted to eat. They had politely declined her offers of food and collapsed on their beds instead. Philippa was in a room just down from his own and he hoped that she too had enjoyed this view when she arose.

Philippa had spent most of the plane journey in silence. When she had not been asleep she had simply stared out of the window at the sea of clouds below. She had eaten little and simply smiled politely and nodded whenever Martin had asked her if she was OK. He sincerely hoped that this did not signal the return of the usual sullen and aggressive attitude that he had come to expect. He still held out some hope that this surprise vacation could be the beginning of a new start for them both. He loved his daughter, but she seemed to be filled with little more than thinly disguised contempt for him, and nothing that he did was good enough anymore. He hoped that there might still be time to put things right before she drifted away from him forever.

He stepped back from the window and stretched, arching his back and letting out a deep sigh of satisfaction. He moved back into the room, humming tunelessly to himself, and noticed the telephone on the bedside table. He walked over to it and studied it for a moment. He wanted to phone Mr. O'Callahan back in the UK. To tell him that he had arrived safely and thank him for this opportunity. Martin could never have afforded a trip like this, and he smiled at his good fortune. He had been told that he was not to call anyone during the trip, but he didn't see what harm calling his boss could do. He picked up the receiver and was about to dial when he heard his daughter's voice on the other end of the line. He frowned, looking down at the device in his

160

hand before returning it to his ear. Philippa was speaking to someone from a telephone somewhere else in the villa.

"That's right," she said, "just the two of us. Tonight . . . Curieuse."

The man repeated the details of the trip back to her, confirming the times that she had obviously given him before Martin had picked up at his end.

"That's fine, thank you. Oh, and there is a very good chance that only one of us will be coming back when you come to collect us, so if you could let the skipper know that in advance—thank you."

She hung up and Martin stared down at the receiver again as if uncertain how it had got there in the first place. A strange feeling came over him. It was something about the way that Philippa had spoken—her voice cold and hard with something else that he couldn't quite put his finger on. *Who the hell had she been talking to? And what did she mean, "Only one of us will be coming back'?* He lifted the phone up to his ear again, but the line was dead. Replacing the handset in its cradle he sat back on the bed and tried to figure out what on earth was going on. He considered how very oddly she had been acting toward him since he had arrived home yesterday. He wasn't used to smiles and kisses and cups of tea. Instead, upon announcing that they had to leave for the airport, he'd expected swearing and violence and vitriolic abuse. Something was wrong. He'd tried to kid himself that it wasn't, but something was badly wrong.

There is a very good chance that only one of us will be coming back.

An uncomfortable idea crowbarred its way into his mind. He shook his head, silently admonishing himself for imagining such a foolish and fanciful notion. But once it had found its way in there was no hope of him ridding himself of the terrible thought he had just had, and the more he tried to ignore it the more convinced he became that it might just be true. Horrifying, yes, but true nevertheless. He was surrounded on a daily basis by demons and djinn and other creatures that he didn't care to think about, deliriously happy that as a human he could not see them for what they really were. But he knew. He'd always known. And Lucien had been honest with him about what his business was and what it tried to do. And Martin had been happy to take the generous salary that he'd been offered, telling himself that it didn't matter and trying not to think about who and what he shared the office with.

But what if something had happened? What if one of those creatures had done something to Philippa, and—

He shook his head, trying to force the thought away.

He leaned forward and tapped out the number of Tom O'Callahan's mobile phone, needing someone—anyone—to speak to.

"Who was that you were calling?" Philippa asked as Martin entered the kitchen area. She was dressed in a red swimsuit with a brightly colored sarong wrapped around her waist.

162

The sight of her in anything that wasn't black halted him for a second. She looked like a different person.

"Calling?"

"I thought that I heard you talking to somebody on the phone when I came in from the garden."

Martin shook his head. "No, not me. I've just this moment woken up and came straight down here. Where is Mrs. Beauchamp?"

"She's popped out for a moment to get some provisions. I told her the type of food that we like to eat. I asked her to get lots of fish for you; I know how much you like fish."

Martin did like fish, but they never ate it at home because Philippa refused to have the smell in the house. She was a vegetarian and the mere smell of fish or meat sent her into fits of histrionics about the exploitation of animals. He mumbled his thanks as he sat down at the table next to her, helping himself to a banana from the large bowl of fruit in the center. He peeled the fruit, considering idly why he was doing so—he had no intention of eating it. He was surprised by how calm he felt (or was it just empty?) and even managed to smile back at his daughter when she asked him how he was feeling today.

"I've been looking through this guidebook that Mrs. Beauchamp gave me," she said. "I think we should take advantage of your company's offer and try to do as much as we can while we are here. I'd like to go on a trip to the neighboring island, Curieuse." She pointed to a picture of a beautiful island rising up from a sapphire sea. She reached over and placed her hand on his arm, giving it a little squeeze.

163

"It's almost deserted," she said. "We could hire a boat and the two of us could go over this evening. Mrs. Beauchamp says that if we are lucky we might even see green turtles coming up onto the beach to lay eggs. She said we should take a picnic and we can watch them from the cover of the trees. So what do you think?"

Martin swallowed hard. He looked into his daughter's eyes and hoped that he was wrong in his suspicions, and that the preposterous theory that he had related to Mr. O'Callahan moments ago was just that. Surely he'd lost his mind if he thought that his daughter could be capable of anything so malevolent. And yet he kept thinking of that voice he'd overheard on the line and how it had terrified him to the core.

"Sounds nice . . . ," he managed to mutter.

"Good. Then I'll nip into town and see about getting us a boat." She gave his arm another little squeeze. "It'll be a night you'll never forget, Dad." She stood up and went to leave.

"You look good in red, Philippa," Martin said in a quiet voice. "Suits you. Makes a change from all that black."

She looked down at the swimsuit and smiled back at him. "I bought it at the airport while you were book shopping. I thought it'd make a nice change. Black's a bit morbid to be wearing in a place like this. I'm thinking of giving up the whole goth thing anyway."

Martin watched her leave the room and walk onto the

164

sun-baked veranda outside. He glanced down at the banana still in his hand and put it back on the plate in front of him.

If he was right, his daughter planned to murder him tonight and he didn't have the slightest clue what he was going to do about it.

26

"Who on earth was that calling you at this time in the morning?" Trey asked Tom as he entered the kitchen.

"Just somebody that needed to update me on something," the Irishman said with a frown, glancing at his watch. "More to the point, what the hell are you doing up at this hour? You don't normally crawl from your pit for at least another five or six hours. Was your bed on fire or something?"

It was five o'clock in the morning. The blackness visible behind the shuttered windows was absolute—there was no street lighting, or indeed any of the light pollution from offices, cars, and houses that Trey was used to, living in the big city—just a complete darkness without any source of light to fix upon.

"Couldn't sleep," Trey said.

"That's understandable. Nerves get the best of everyone, Trey. I myself get the heebie-jeebies before going into something like this."

They both turned around in surprise at the sound of somebody else coming into the kitchen. Alexa was leaning in the doorway, glistening tears tracking down her cheeks. "I've just had a phone call from Dr. Tremaine." She cocked her head to one side and stared at Tom accusingly.

166

"I asked them not to call you," Tom said in a low voice, holding her stare. "I didn't want you to panic if he took a turn for the worse."

"I guessed you might do that so I spoke to Dr. Tremaine before we left and left direct instructions to ignore any orders that you might have given to that effect."

Tom slowly nodded his head.

Alexa looked down at the mobile phone on the table in front of the Irishman. "They called you first," she said.

"Will somebody please tell me what is going on here?" Trey said, looking between the two.

"They called from London," Tom said. "Lucien's condition has deteriorated and they don't think he'll survive for very much longer."

"How long has he got?"

"They're not certain. Two days? A week at best."

A silence hung over them all as they considered what Tom had just said. Trey stared at the table, picturing Lucien lying in the room in London surrounded by machines.

"We need to get to Leroth," he said.

"We will," Tom growled, getting up and retrieving three cups from the cupboard over the sink. "We'll get that globe and get back to London in time to use it to heal Lucien. I won't hear of any other outcome to this mission. We leave tonight as soon as it's dark. I'm waiting on one final delivery—a piece of equipment that I've ordered. Then I think we're ready to go."

"You might as well make me one of those as well," Charles

167

said from the hallway. He walked up to stand behind Alexa. "Looks like we're not going to get any more sleep today so we might as well have a decent cup of tea. I'll rustle us up a good breakfast."

Trey's definition of a *good breakfast* did not consist of anything as seemingly inedible as pickled herrings and a hard bread that he would have labeled as stale and consigned to the bin. Instead, he contented himself with a bowl of muesli and a soft-boiled egg. Showering after breakfast also revealed another delightful feature of this land of rock and ice, the water had a strong and distinct smell of sulphur, leaving him with the feeling that, despite dousing himself with almost a third of a bottle of shower gel, he was going to emerge smelling worse than when he had first got in.

Stepping out of the bathroom, he found Tom in jittery mode again, looking at his watch every ten minutes or so and pacing between the kitchen and the front room to peer out the window that looked over the driveway. After about an hour, a small van pulled up outside the house, and Tom opened the front door to greet the driver on the doorstep.

"Jon, nice to see you," Tom called as the man approached the house. They shook hands, and Trey guessed that this must have been the man who had picked Hjelmar up the day before. "I hope you managed to get hold of the equipment that I requested?"

The tall newcomer inclined his head to one side and pursed his lips. When he spoke it was with a strong Nordic accent. "You know how to set a fellow a task, Tom. This kit was *extremely* difficult to acquire. I had to call in some pretty huge favors."

"Did you get it or not?"

"I got it. I'll need a hand to carry it out of the van."

Trey watched as the two men went down to the van and opened the back doors. They returned with a huge wooden crate that must have been at least four feet in length. They placed it on the floor inside the hall and Jon went to fetch a canvas rucksack that he put next to the crate.

"When you've finished whatever business you have here, Tom, I'd be *very* interested to know how this thing performs," the Icelander said with a nod toward the large wooden box.

"When I've finished here, Jon, I'll let you have it and you can see for yourself. How's that?"

The tall thin man seemed extremely happy with this proposal and gave Tom a small salute as he left the building.

Trey studied the Irishman and grinned. "You look like a kid that's come downstairs early on Christmas morning to see all his presents stacked up beneath the tree. Aren't you going to open it?"

"Go and fetch me a claw hammer from the toolbox inside the back door, Trey. We'll crack this baby open and see what we've got, shall we?"

Trey stood back and looked at the weapon housed on a small stand inside the box. It was about the length of his arm and was khaki in color, with sections made of a dull black metal. At the front was an absurdly large barrel that Trey guessed would quite happily accommodate a chicken egg. Behind this was a short, fat cylinder, whose shape and positioning reminded Trey of the ones that you see on the revolvers used in old Westerns—the kind that the cowboy slowly turns around to check that he has loaded it correctly—except that this one was huge and hung under the weapon like some bizarre udder. Behind all of this were the trigger mechanism and a short shoulder butt.

"What *is* that?" Trey asked, staring at the thing in horror.

Tom stepped forward and picked the weapon up, grasping it by the stubby handle toward the front of the weapon and pulling it up to his shoulder in one swift movement. "This, my friend, is an M32 MGL-140, or a multi-shot 40mm grenade launcher to the likes of you and me. In addition," he said, stooping down and fishing in the canvas bag that Jon had placed next to the crate to pull out a fat, stubby shell that he held up between his thumb and forefinger, "these are thermobaric grenades. What do you think?"

Trey looked at his friend as if he had suddenly gone stark, raving mad. "Thermobaric?" he said in a small voice.

"They disperse a fine, flammable mist into the air, which, being under-oxidized, ignites to create a huge fireball that's impossible to escape. Everything in the proximity of the detonation is burned—inside and out. Nasty," he said with a shake of his head. "And if that doesn't kill you, the pressure wave will." He bent down and replaced the small grenade

170

in the bag before straightening back up and treating Trey to one of his best lopsided grins. "I hope to God that I don't have to resort to it. I've never used one before, but then I've never faced a disappearing tower and a vampire lord's zombie army before. But if I do, anything in range is going to burn. And *everything*—even werewolves and vampires—can be killed with fire."

Trey was still standing looking at his friend in open-mouthed disbelief. He shook his head slowly and looked between the Irishman's solemn features and the killing machine that he was now holding upright. "Remind me never to get on your bad side, Tom," he said, and went to see what Alexa and Charles were up to.

27

Martin and Philippa spent most of the day lying in the hot sunshine that streamed down onto the white sands of the villa's private beach. Martin had come out at his daughter's insistence. He had told her that he didn't feel too well and wanted to lie down in his bedroom, but she wasn't about to let that happen.

"Nonsense," Philippa chided. "Some sunshine is what you need, Dad. Come outside and let the sea air work its magic on you. You'll feel back to your old self in no time."

He had joined her on the beach, trying to appear as normal as possible while listening out for the phone to ring in the villa. As the day wore on he became more and more edgy until it was as much as he could do not to scream out loud. Eventually he'd gone for a long swim in the sea, allowing the action of the waves and the solitude that the ocean provided to soothe some of his anxieties away. He was a good swimmer and despite his slight build could trawl along effortlessly in his local pool, racking up at least a hundred lengths in a session. He found that he was able to think while swimming, the rhythmic sound of his own breathing lulling him into a state that he guessed might be something akin to meditation. After an hour or so he had emerged from the sea and flopped down onto a beach lounge in the shade. Lying there, with his book in his hands, it was not long before the sharp teeth of rising panic were nibbling into him again.

Eventually he became aware that Philippa had sat up and was looking at him, her eyes obscured by the large black sunglasses that she had purchased at the airport before leaving the UK.

"Not very good?" she asked.

"What?" Martin said with a start.

"The book. I assume from the fact that you have been staring at the same page for the entire morning that it isn't exactly a gripping read." She inclined her head to one side. "Are you all right, Dad? You seem extremely twitchy. Is something worrying you?"

"No . . . I'm fine. I'm just enjoying the sunshine. I'm not really reading. Just . . . thinking." This last was true. He had done nothing *but* think since overhearing that conversation this morning, and no matter how many times he turned it over in his mind he always came up with the same conclusion— she was planning to kill him and leave his body on an island as part of a trip that she had arranged for this very evening. If the place was as deserted as she had suggested, they probably wouldn't find his body for months. He imagined his dead body lying in some quiet and secluded part of a beach, the crabs crawling over his cold flesh as they feasted on him and—

He shook his head again. He needed to stop this madness.

173

Because that is what it was—madness. He was being ridiculous. Philippa wasn't *capable* of such a thing. Sure she'd told him countless times in the last few years how much she hated him and wished he was dead—but murder? No. She was just an ill-tempered teenager. He'd got this all wrong. All wrong. Why would Philippa want him dead? Why?

Unless the thing sitting next to him now wasn't Philippa at all.

He remembered the telephone conversation that he'd had with Tom O'Callahan that morning.

His mind racing, he reached down and took a sip of water from a bottle. He considered how she might be planning to do it, running through the options. He didn't think that she would risk any personal injury by trying to throttle him or attack him in some physical way. He briefly toyed with the idea that she might have someone on the island, an accomplice that she had arranged to do the dirty work for her, but he dismissed this almost as quickly as he had imagined it—she simply had not had time to set something like that up—she'd had no idea that they were coming on this trip until the previous day. No, she was going to do for him herself, and he thought that it was possible that she intended to kill him with the food that she had asked Mrs. Beauchamp to prepare for their "midnight feast." That was why she had gone into town this morning on the pretext of booking the boat. To buy rat poison or something like that. Yes, rat poison would do it.

He replayed the telephone conversation: ". . . *there is a very good chance that only one of us will be coming back . . .*"

He had expected Mr. O'Callahan to laugh at him when he had suggested to him that his daughter might be trying to kill him. Instead, the grave Irishman had listened to Martin's recounting of the telephone conversation and after a long silence had asked him if his daughter had been behaving strangely in any way.

A cold shudder had slithered its way down Martin's spine at the way that his employer had posed this question. "Yes," he'd replied. "She's actually being nice to me. That might not sound remarkable, but if you knew how she was before and how she is now, it's as if she's a different person. It's like she's possessed or something."

There had been a pause on the other end of the line.

"Hello?" Martin had said.

"Martin, does your daughter know what you do for a living?" Mr. O'Callahan had asked.

"Good Lord, no. Mr. Charron was extremely explicit about that during my final interview. It was one of the conditions that were made very clear to me—nobody was to know what the data that I analyzed related to, regardless of who they were."

Martin thought about the way that his boss had looked at him when he had stressed this point. Lucien Charron's eyes had bored into him in a way that had made Martin think that he was staring straight into the depths of his soul. Just remembering that moment had sent a shudder through him again.

"Philippa believes that I work for an insurance company," he had told Tom. "Besides, if she ever found out that I work for a company that investigates paranormal activities, she'd never let me hear the last of it. It would simply be yet another weapon in her arsenal of abuse that she could use to humiliate me when we had an argument." He heard the bitterness in his own voice and considered once more why he had let his daughter make his life so utterly miserable for all of these years. "Mr. O'Callahan, does this have anything to do with the work? Is there a chance that my daughter is under the spell of someone or something that is making her behave like this?"

"I don't know, Martin. You did the right thing in calling me. I'm going to get one of our people to go over to your house and have a little look around. In the meantime, don't go on that boat trip this evening. Make out that you are ill or something. I don't care what you have to do, but you just sit tight until you hear from me." He'd paused on the other end of the line and Martin had thought he'd gone when he added, "I don't know what it is, but something's up."

"OK, Mr. O'Callahan."

"And, Martin, for heaven's sake, don't mention to anyone why we sent you over there in the first place. If that should get out, we're all in the smelly stuff up to our armpits."

"I would never do such a thing. You and Mr. Charron can rely upon me, sir."

Martin had hung up then; the adrenaline coursing through him caused his muscles to heat up and the blood to rush around his system at a speed that did not sit well in the hot tropical temperatures of the Seychelles. He closed his eyes and tried to hold back the tears. If he had endangered his daughter because of his work, he would never forgive himself. If that was the case, he'd be better off dead. He had to help her in some way. He had to stop her from doing anything terrible and get back his daughter again. He actually managed to smile at this thought—for years he had hoped that his daughter would change, that she would find a way to break free of the hatred and anger that seemed to fill her for no good reason. And now she had. She seemed happy and carefree and loving. And murderous.

And now here he was, sitting beneath a thatched sunshade in a tropical paradise with the sea lapping at the shore in front of him, wondering what Mr. O'Callahan expected to find in his house and trying to come up with a bulletproof excuse for why he would not be going on the boat trip that she had planned for them that evening.

He glanced at his watch and put his book down. He looked around at the things he had brought out to the beach with him from the house. He checked over and again, lifting towels and crouching down to look under the beach chair, but he failed to find the item that he was searching for.

"Have you seen my mobile phone?" he eventually asked his daughter when it was clear that it was not going to turn up.

"No. You had it on you earlier when you came out." She sat up then, a reproachful look on her face. "Oh, Dad, please don't tell me that you went into the sea with it still in your shorts pocket."

He was certain that he hadn't. But the look on her face suggested that the phone may have ended up in the sea anyhow.

"I don't think so," he said slowly. "Never mind, I'll just use the phone in the house." He stood up and tried not to let her see the anxiety that was beginning to grow within him again.

"They're not working," Philippa said casually, returning her attention to the word-search puzzle that she was doing.

"What do you mean, not working?"

"I was going to call Gemma and let her know how beautiful it is here," she said without looking up. "I couldn't even get a dial tone. The phones are all out."

Martin looked toward the house for a second before returning his attention to his daughter. "Is Mrs. Beauchamp getting them fixed?" he asked.

"She doesn't know," his daughter said. "I gave her the day off today. I thought it would be nice for us to be totally alone so that we can relax properly without her popping out every hour or so to ask if we wanted anything."

"What about our picnic food? I thought that you were going to get her to put that together for us."

"I've decided to do that myself. That way I can be certain that I include all your favorites."

Martin looked out at the sea as it lazily rolled up against the sandy slope of the beach. His breathing quickened until he was panting like a small lapdog. This, and the heat beating down on his head, made the vision at the edge of his eyes *fizz* slightly and he sat down again, realizing that he was in danger of passing out if he did not. He reached out and gripped the glass of pineapple juice that Philippa had fetched him earlier. Ignoring the shaking of his hand, he brought the vessel up to his lips. He was about to take a long gulp when he stopped, looking down at the yellow liquid in the tall glass. He placed it back down on table. *Rat poison.* All he could think of was *rat poison.*

He stood up and slipped his Birkenstock sandals on.

"I'm going to go for a walk," he said. "Get a change of scenery for a little while." The villa was set in the middle of nowhere and he hadn't seen a neighbor for miles when they had arrived in the small hours of the morning. However, he hoped that if he walked far enough he might be able to find a shop with a pay phone that he would be able to use to call the UK. He turned to go, swatting at a fly that at that moment had taken a sudden and keen interest in him, buzzing annoyingly around his face and ignoring his attempts to wave it away.

"That sounds like a lovely idea," his daughter said from behind him, getting up and pushing her own feet into a pair of flip-flops. "I'll come with you. I could do with stretching my legs as well."

179

Martin smiled and nodded his head. He turned away again so that she would not see the disappointment on his face. He had the strange feeling that wherever he chose to go and whatever he chose to do, he would not be allowed to be alone.

28

"Yes, I know that Mr. Ellington was with them the whole time," Tom said into the receiver, "but I still want somebody to go over to the house and have a look round. I have a funny feeling about this whole thing and I'd rather err on the side of caution right now." There was a pause, and Tom looked up to see Trey standing in the doorway, chewing on something. "Yes, it might well be that all of this is in his head, but Martin sounded pretty shaken up when I spoke to him today and I want it looked into."

Tom listened to the person on the other end of the line for a few moments, nodding his head at whatever was being said. "That's grand. Thank you, and keep in touch even if you don't find anything."

"More trouble?" Trey asked between mouthfuls of tuna sandwich.

"Maybe. Maybe not." Tom looked down at the phone. "But our friend Mr. Tipsbury called me this morning from the company villa in the Seychelles and is convinced that his daughter is planning to kill him."

"Blimey. What's up? Doesn't she like the pool, or was their flight delayed?"

"This is no joke, Trey. Something is up. Martin is the only

181

person who knows we're here and what we are here for. If he is worried, there is probably a very good reason. Never underestimate that gut feeling that people get when something's not right. There's something else . . . something that he said that's put the fear of Christ into me."

"What?"

"He said that she was like a different person. As if she had been possessed."

Trey stared at the Irishman—the tuna suddenly didn't taste so good. "What are you going to do?"

"I've got somebody going over to have a look around his house in the UK, and I am trying to arrange for someone else to keep an eye on the villa to see if anything looks fishy. The trouble is, I can't get hold of Martin at the moment. There seems to be a problem with the phones over there."

The two exchanged a look.

Tom was about to get up when his mobile rang again. "Tom here," he said quickly, holding the device up to his ear. He listened for a second, slowly rising to his feet. "When was this?" he asked. A deep frown formed on the Irishman's face. "Then why the hell wasn't I told about it earlier?" he shouted into the phone.

Something about the look on Tom's face as he listened to whatever was being said made Trey step farther into the room, placing his unfinished sandwich on the arm of the chair and wiping his hands on the front of his jeans.

"I want an update in fifteen minutes," Tom said, and pushed the button on the handset to disconnect the call.

Trey looked at the Irishman. He could see the strain in every line of his face. "What now?"

Tom issued a small snort. "There's been another massive jump in the use of the globe detected by our people in London, followed by a signature that they haven't come across before."

"What does that mean?"

"In the same way that a spell sends out a distinct signal when it is cast, each nether-creature also has a telltale signature. You have one when you become a werewolf." Tom stared at the boy. "A little over an hour ago London detected a signature that they'd only encountered once before—yesterday, in fact. Because it was something that they hadn't seen before they put it down to a *glitch*." He shook his head and stared down at the phone

"Do I need to ask where this occurred?"

"About ten miles from here," Tom said, glancing at his watch and then looking out the window. "We've got about an hour and a half until sundown. In no time at all after that it'll be dark. I, for one, have no intention of approaching a place like Leroth without the cover of darkness."

Trey looked at his friend and nodded. "Tom, I wanted to talk to you about this plan of yours. I'm worried about Alexa. If Charles is right, she shouldn't be allowed to see what her mother has become. She—"

"All taken care of, Trey. Alexa and I will set up shop outside and create a diversion, try to draw as many guards out as we can and keep them occupied. That should allow you

183

and Charles to slip inside unnoticed and locate the globe. If what your Murkbeast friend told you is true, you're going to have to get to the top of that place to even have a chance of stealing the globe, and if Gwendolin is using it as much as she seems to be, that is not going to be easy. I'm guessing that as soon as you get your hands on it, all hell will break loose—something like that is bound to have powerful safeguards in place. As soon as you have it, you and Charles get out and Alexa and I will provide us all with the means to make our escape. Who knows, we might all survive to tell the tale."

"I'm guessing that you haven't discussed any of this plan with her. Because it doesn't seem to me like she is going to be overly enamored with the way you see things playing out."

"No, I haven't, not yet. I know that Alexa wants to go in there for a face-off with her mother. She wants to see for herself what kind of woman could abandon her child to go and serve something as fundamentally evil as Caliban. But Gwendolin gave up the last of her humanity when she tried to sacrifice her own daughter to summon some creature from the pit. I don't pretend to know what she has become now, but it is something inhuman and something that wouldn't think twice about finishing off what it started all those years ago with Alexa."

Trey thought about this, eventually nodding his head. "What kind of diversion?" he asked.

"I hadn't really given that too much thought," Tom said,

jabbing at the keypad of his phone with his thick, calloused thumb. "I usually just rely on blowing things up and then see what comes out of the woodwork. Now if you'll excuse me, young man, I need to get a few things sorted out."

Trey wandered back into the kitchen to find Charles and Alexa sitting at the table talking in hushed tones over mugs of steaming tea. He updated them on the phone call that Tom had just received, but didn't mention the discussion that they had had regarding Alexa's planned role on their impending trip.

"It's the Draugr," Charles said over the top of his cup. "They're raising the Draugr from their burrows."

"Couldn't it be anything else?" Alexa asked.

"Possibly," said Charles, but the shrug of his shoulders suggested that he didn't believe so. "But, whatever it is, it's only going to mean bad news for us. The stakes have just gone up again, if that's at all possible. If we thought that our odds were bad before, I fear that they have just got a whole lot worse."

29

Martin walked down the gently sloping hill, his sandals slapping softly against the hot pavement. He'd spied the café from a crossroads at the top of the hill and had immediately turned toward it, ignoring the protests from Philippa about the heat and the distance that they had already covered. She was still following him, but had dropped back a little now, her flip-flops hindering her from keeping up with the pace he was setting.

The building was on the corner of an intersection between two roads, and from the look of it, the owner didn't rely on tourist traffic to stay open. Small tables spilled out onto the narrow pavement, surrounded by an assortment of chairs—none of which appeared to match another.

He reached down and took the front of his shirt between his thumb and forefinger, gently pulling the fabric away from his chest, which was by now slick with sweat. As he approached the front door he noted that the interior was very dark, and his heart sank as he realized that the place was probably closed.

He pushed at the door and thanked his good luck as it gave inward under the pressure.

The heavyset man standing behind the counter momentarily looked up at the sound made by the little bell above the door. Seeing the panting tourist he returned his attention to the glass that he was drying with a dish towel that was itself in need of a good wash. Martin nodded at an old man sitting at the counter nursing a glass of beer, but the gesture was not reciprocated; the old-timer returned his rheumy-eyed stare to the television behind the bar, which appeared to be showing a documentary about deep-sea fishing, although with all of the static and white fuzz that danced across the screen, it was almost impossible to see.

Martin took all this in at a glance, his eyes greedily scanning the dull interior until they rested on the thing that he had been hoping to find. The small pay phone was situated at the back of the room beneath a glowing neon sign advertising the local beer.

He was about to step toward it, momentarily forgetting everything else, when the door banged painfully into the small of his back, the little bell over his head merrily announcing the arrival of his daughter.

"Dad." Philippa scowled. "What the hell do you think you were doing, storming off like that?"

"Sorry, I just got carried away with the thought of a nice cold beer." He eyed the phone with longing, but instead made his way toward the bar.

"You don't drink beer. What has come over you today? Why are you behaving like a bloody maniac all of a sudden?"

"I just fancy a beer now. Anything wrong with that? I am hot and bothered and I think that right now I would like to cool down with a beer. Take a seat and I'll bring you over a drink. What would you like?"

His daughter eyed him suspiciously. He never answered her back, and this sudden show of mettle, along with his tone of voice, took her aback for a moment. She smiled at him, reaching up and removing the oversized sunglasses so that he would be able to see her eyes. "I'll have a lime and soda, please. No ice." She took a table close to the bar.

"Hot out there," Martin said as he approached the owner. "Could I have a glass of that draft beer and a lime and soda, please?"

The barman nodded and prepared the drinks. Martin looked over his shoulder in the direction of his daughter. She was within earshot so he stepped up onto the tarnished brass rail that ran around the base of the bar and leaned his body forward over the high counter to speak to the man as he poured the cold lager into the glass.

"Is your telephone working?" he asked.

The man looked directly at Martin, but when he spoke it was in a strange accent and language that Martin couldn't quite identify. It sounded vaguely French, but the rhythm and cadence were all wrong. Martin guessed that it must be the Creole that was spoken by the majority of the Seychellois. The old man laughed at whatever it was the barman had said, nodding his head and hissing through his gums as though he was sharing in the world's funniest joke.

"Your telephone—does it work?" Martin repeated.

"Yes, the phone is working," the barman said, setting the two drinks on the bar.

Martin nodded. "It's just that we are staying in a villa a little way up the hill and all our phones seem to have stopped working. I wondered if that kind of thing was normal here."

The barman looked at him with thinly disguised contempt. Martin knew how he must appear to this man—another tourist questioning the ability of the locals to get their services and facilities up to the demands of rich Westerners. He couldn't help that now. He just wanted a phone that worked.

"The phone service here is very good. We don't have many problems," the barman said simply, and he turned his back on Martin to join his gummy countryman watching the TV.

Putting Philippa's drink on the table in front of her, he nodded his head toward the pay phone. "I think I might call work," he said. "Let them know that the phones are out and ask them who we should contact."

To his surprise, she nodded and took a sip from her drink. "Good idea," she said.

Martin almost fell flat on his face, tripping over a low stool in his rush to get to the phone. He fished all of the change out of his pocket and hastily fed it into the small slot at the side of the telephone unit. He prayed that it was enough. He jabbed the number of Tom O'Callahan's mobile phone into the telephone keypad. It rang six times before going to the Irishman's message service. "Tom . . . it's me, Martin," he said into the receiver after waiting out the prerecorded message. "Something is going on here and I am very worried about it. My daughter . . ." He sensed a presence behind him and stopped, half turning to see that Philippa had ambled over to stand by him, sipping at her drink and leaning against a pillar no more than three feet behind him. She gave him a little wave of her fingers and smiled at him. He swallowed, turning back toward the phone, ". . . my daughter, Philippa, agreed with me that I should call you and let you know that the phones here are out," he said, thinking quickly to change what he had really wanted to say. "To top it all, I appear to have lost my mobile. . . . If you could get somebody over to look in on us and sort out the phones, I'd be *very* grateful."

He hung up, unable to think of anything else that he could say with Philippa hovering around behind him. He turned to face his daughter, "Voice mail," he said with a shrug.

The cold, calculating stare that she gave him completely unsettled his nerves, and it was as much as he could do to stop himself from screaming out at the top of his lungs.

He looked back at the phone with a little shake of his head. He was on his own. A cold panic gripped him as he realized that whatever it was that his daughter had planned for him he would have to face it without any outside help.

His heart was beating too fast, slamming into his chest. When he looked at Philippa again he thought that he could detect in her eyes the cruel amusement that she must be feeling right now.

She looked at her watch and then back at him. "We'd better drink up and be getting back," she purred. "Our boat will be turning up in a little over two hours, and we need to get ready for our soirée. Come on, Dad." She offered him her arm as if they were going off on a friendly stroll along a seaside pier.

He was suddenly filled with an emotion that he had not felt for a very long time—anger. It boiled up inside him, consuming the fear that he had been carrying around all day. It was a good feeling right now and he allowed it to rage through him. The anger, coupled with a grim determination to help his daughter get through whatever it was that was happening to her, might just be enough to save them both. He hoped so, because he doubted that any other help was going to come.

He remembered what Tom O'Callahan had told him about doing everything and anything he could to not make the journey with her that night. But something had snapped within him. He straightened up and stared back at Philippa with a look that she had never seen before. Taking her arm, he guided her back toward the door.

"Come along then, Philippa. After all, we wouldn't want to miss our midnight feast, would we?"

30

Gwendolin's eyes no longer saw the Draugr as it raged against the invisible barrier that she had constructed around it—the cold gray irises of her eyes had been replaced by the milky whites of the eyeballs themselves, shot through here and there with tiny bloodred lightning forks. It was difficult magic. She was having to maintain a complete sphere of energy around the creature to contain it, while at the same time lifting and maneuvering the entire thing out of the fortress. That in itself was complicated, but not beyond the ability of a mage of her power.

The problem that she was having was the creature's persistent efforts to break free by changing its size, making it very difficult for her to "mold" the spell around it and move it efficiently—she constantly had to recast the spell, resizing the imprisoning sphere and so using up huge amounts of energy just to stop the creature from simply bursting out and wreaking yet more havoc on those unlucky enough to be in its path (of whom she was one).

Her attempt to reanimate the other Draugr, as Caliban had instructed her to do, had failed. They had dug it out of its barrow and brought it back to the citadel. She had performed the magic needed to bring it back to life and for one moment she thought that she had succeeded again, but the thing had simply bellowed in rage before collapsing in a heap. On reflection, she now thought it astonishing that she had been successful at all in her attempts to revive any of these ancient creatures. But having accomplished this feat she now had the dubious task of cleaning up after herself, disposing of the creature—it being too unstable to control and too dangerous to have around—as per Caliban's instructions.

The Draugr really was very powerful, and the energy that she had to expend at this moment to keep it from breaking loose and running amok again was beginning to wear her down, despite the incredible powers that she had built up over the years. A small part of her could only admire the Draugr's raw energy and strength.

They were almost at the opening that she had created at the front of the tower. A huge armored truck was waiting for them. Their plan was to get the monster inside the vehicle, whereupon a small detachment of Maug would take it to the center of the city of Reykjavik and unleash it on the unsuspecting Icelandic citizens while they slept in their beds. She would accompany them as far as the outskirts of the city just in case it should escape before they arrived at their intended destination.

She smiled inwardly at the thought of the behemoth rampaging through the streets of that city, destroying everything and anyone in its path. And after that? She realized that she did not care what became of the creature. This project had proved to be a disaster for her, and more dangerously, it had

193

put doubt in Caliban's mind as to the extent and efficacy of her powers. Let the humans destroy the thing that she had struggled so hard to bring back to life. She cared nothing for it now. The power of the globe when used in conjunction with Skaleb's Staff was beyond doubt now, and she and Caliban would need to consider an alternative use for it. It was too powerful to simply ignore. Caliban had suggested human zombies.

She shook her head ruefully at this. She hated working with zombies—everybody did. They were anarchic and difficult to coordinate, and the longer the body was in the ground the less likely that the reanimated creatures could be controlled. Knowing this, she should have guessed that the Draugr would also prove to be a lost cause. She had convinced herself that they would be different. Legend had said that they would change while underground, drawing on the magic from the land around them and transforming into something alien to the world that they had once been a part of. A monster that would enact its revenge upon the world above it. They did indeed seem hell-bent on destruction, but they were rampageous, chaotic creatures that seemed utterly incapable of being controlled in the way that Caliban had hoped.

She stopped, frowning again as the creature doubled in size and began to assault the field of magic that she was struggling to maintain about it.

Gwendolin would rid herself of this troublesome revenant and then leave this land of ice and rain. She already had a new project in mind, one that involved the creation of a

194

particular type of shape-shifting demon that she would send into the houses of humans to replace newborn babies in their cots at night. The demons would eat everything in sight, their hunger would be insatiable and once they'd discovered the taste for meat . . . the parents wouldn't stand a chance. There was also the matter of Lucien. The thought of his impending death made her smile for the first time in days.

She concentrated, summoning her powers to ensure that there would be no surprises now that they were so close to the exit. From the outside, she had chosen to make Leroth appear to any human looking upon it as some kind of refinery. They had chosen a remote location with no urban developments nearby, but anyone who knew the area and happened to stumble across it would be completely amazed that a giant factory appeared to have sprung up out of nowhere in so little time. It was one of the problems that she had with the translocation of Leroth within this realm. It was very large, but needed to be made to appear to blend in with its surroundings. Quite often she would simply opt to destroy an existing building or group of buildings and fashion Leroth to look exactly as they had. But here, in a country with such a low population per square foot of land, she had simply chosen to *create* a factory from scratch.

To the small number of nether-creatures that lived and worked within its walls, it looked exactly like what it really was—a giant fortress of a tower that rose up into the sky like some fearsome spear, thrusting upward into the heavens. Gwendolin had almost swooned when she had first seen the citadel in the Netherworld many years ago. It was not vast in the amount of ground space that it took up, but it made up for this by its sheer magnificence and height as it towered above anyone who approached it. It was right and fitting that Caliban should dwell within its walls, and that she too should be one of the few beings that he allowed to reside there with him.

They were almost at the portal that she had created in the wall. Leroth had no entrances or exits. Any would-be attacker approaching would be surprised to find that it looked impregnable, there being no obvious point of attack in the sheer obsidian black walls that made up the lower part of the enormous tower. Portals had to be fashioned to allow anyone or anything either in or out, and it was through one of these that she now maneuvered the creature. In the distance she could smell the north Atlantic Ocean, the cold wind blowing in from it cooled her, and she welcomed this momentary distraction from her efforts.

The sheer amount of sorcery that she had to perform now was weakening her by the moment. She was being forced to maintain a number of complicated spells all at the same time and this was taking its toll on her. She wavered for a moment and almost let her control over the Draugr slip. The creature sensed this and renewed its attempts to break free once more. The physical assault that it directed against the invisible walls around it might well have been leveled at Gwendolin herself, and she flinched as the blows thudded into the walls of the magic field encapsulating the Draugr. She breathed in deeply, inhaling the cold air through her nose and blowing it out again slowly from between her lips, silently cursing Caliban for the umpteenth time and wondering why on earth he had not simply agreed to kill this monster when it was clear that it was uncontrollable.

"And where would be the reward for all your hard work if we took that option, eh?" he had said, with a small shake of his head. "No, Gwendolin, I want you to be able to witness the fruits of your labor before we depart this place. Do as I bid and set the creature free on the descendants of those who buried it in the first place. After all, I wouldn't wish to deprive you of your moment of glory."

She knew that she had enraged him with this latest fiasco, managing to successfully resurrect only one of these creatures when she had expressed such confidence to him about the entire project. If she were not as useful to him as she was, he would undoubtedly have killed her there and then. Caliban suffered failure in the same way that he suffered disloyalty, and his retribution was swift and merciless. But for now at least he needed her. He would make sure that she cleaned up her own mess before he let the matter go, and later she would have to find some new scheme to impress him.

"Whatever you say, master," she had said, bowing and shuffling out of the room backward, always keeping him in her line of sight. You could never be too careful with vampires.

"Oh, and, Gwendolin, do it straightaway, please. I do not wish to stay here any longer than we have to. I'm sure that there are other . . . more serious matters that have arisen while we have been here on this little diversion."

He held her eyes and she stared back into those fearsome dark pools. She had never got used to the deep emotions that his look always created within her—a mixture of terror and excitement, and she tried not to let the shudder that ran through her show too obviously.

It had always been like this between them. He had initially allowed her to join him simply to spite his brother, but as the years had passed and her powers had grown she had become more important to him. The Tower of Leroth was the perfect example of this. Before she had joined Caliban, the tower's formidable powers had been allowed to fall away, forgotten, and were eventually abandoned. The citadel had stopped being used as a portal between the human realm and Netherworld, becoming merely a focal point of legend within the demon world. *She* had unlocked the powers of the bastion that had lain dormant for so long and revived the fortress back to the power base that it had been during the great wars at the start of the Netherworld's history.

The Tower of Leroth was perhaps the most revered monument in the Netherworld, with stories abounding about how it had played a crucial role in deciding the outcome of the Demon Wars that were waged between the two ruling demon lords, Skaleb and Azsnog. The Netherworld had been ruled by the brothers together for thousands of years before Azsnog had decided that he was unhappy with a shared realm. He attempted to unite the Netherworld under one banner—his own—and the Demon Wars, which were to last millennia, began. It was argued that the Tower of Leroth was the single most important factor in Skaleb's eventual defeat of his brother. Skaleb had not wanted the fight. He had no wish to rule the Netherworld alone, and in the final battle, in which his beloved brother was killed, Skaleb had disappeared from the demon realm and the fortress's secrets had been forgotten. That was, until Gwendolin had rediscovered them thousands of years later through her diligent research. And once her powers had grown to a degree where she was confident of unlocking the citadel's powers again, she had done so and made herself indispensable to Caliban.

The cold night air revived her from her mental wanderings and she shook her head in irritation at her momentary loss of concentration. She forced the Draugr out through the opening. The Maug that were to transport the revenant from here stepped back in fear at the sight of the creature. They had already heard of the devastation that it had caused for the few seconds that it had broken free earlier, and they were right to be fearful of it.

Gwendolin steered the creature toward the open doors of the truck and paused for a second, summoning up the strength that she would need to lift it up into the air and deposit it in the back of the armored vehicle.

Once the creature was inside, the Maug slammed the doors shut, locking them from the outside. Gwendolin allowed herself to relax for the first time since she had begun the task of removing the creature from the fortress. Inside

199

the truck, the Draugr was in a demented frenzy, smashing into the confines of the heavily reinforced steel box. She looked up at the vehicle as it rocked and swayed on its suspension.

"We need to get moving as quickly as possible," she said. "That thing will not hold it for very long."

The demons nodded. Two of them climbed into the front cab of the truck, looking fearfully behind them at the sounds emanating from within the vehicle. Gwendolin joined the remaining two guards in the car ahead. She would see that the creature was released as per Caliban's instructions and then return to Leroth, where she would make preparations for their immediate departure.

31

"Will you be OK to drive, Charles?" Tom asked as they left the house. "I'd like the chance to make a few last-minute phone calls."

Charles nodded and caught the keys that Tom threw to him. Alexa jumped into the front of the car next to Charles, and Trey squeezed into the backseat with Tom, eyeing the military hardware and paraphernalia that surrounded the Irishman.

"Did you get hold of Martin?" Trey asked as they pulled out of the driveway.

Tom shook his head and looked down at the grenade launcher on his lap, running his fingers across the ugly weapon's metallic surface. "No," he said in a low voice, "and what's worse is that I couldn't manage to get hold of anyone over there to have a look in on the place. The housekeeper, Mrs. Beauchamp, appears to have disappeared and the phones are all out. I've left messages at the Beauchamp house for her son, Tiny, to go over and check the place over for me, but I have no idea whether he's gone yet or not. I hope to God that Martin is OK," he said. "If he is not, and we have been compromised, the next hour or so is going to be a lot more interesting than we hoped."

After this revelation the interior of the car went silent and stayed that way as they drove out into the Icelandic countryside. The rain had started up again, the wipers making a soft, low moaning sound as they swept the water from the windshield. Trey pulled his coat around him to ward off the cold that the car's heater had still not managed to chase away and looked out into the darkness beyond his window. His thoughts inevitably led to Lucien lying in the darkened room in London. His nerves were starting to get the better of him again and he wished that his guardian was with them now instead of on his own, back in the apartment. Of course they wouldn't *be* here if Lucien was not dying in that bed right now. They had to get the globe and save him.

Trey thought of the life that he had now, trying not to dwell on the things that he guessed might be yet to come in the future. He knew that he would not be able to get through it without Lucien around to help and guide him. But it was more than that. It was more than just some selfish need that made him so determined to save his guardian. He allowed himself to imagine that Lucien was dead—hating himself for doing so—and he experienced an all-too-familiar sinking feeling. He had lost everything and everybody that had ever mattered to him in his life. All the things that other people seemed to take for granted had been peeled away from him until there had been next to nothing left. If they failed tonight, he would lose yet another person who had come to mean so much to him. Despite the very short period of time that Lucien had been directly involved in his life, over the last few months Trey had become acutely aware of just how much he wanted him—needed him—around. He couldn't face this world of nightmares unless he had Lucien to steer him through it.

He looked at the back of Alexa's head as they plunged ahead into the night. He wouldn't allow Caliban to do to her what he had done to Trey. Caliban had already taken her mother from her; he mustn't be allowed to take her father as well.

Trey watched the nightscape flash past and determined that they would rescue the globe from Caliban. Not only that, but they would all escape Leroth safely.

Unfortunately, he was correct in only one of these assertions.

They pulled up at the bottom of the gently rising hill and climbed out of the four-by-four vehicle. Trey looked over at Charles and was surprised to see how nervous he looked—the mask of arrogant self-assurance was gone for now, replaced with an anxious scowl that started at the eyes and spread out to every facet of his countenance. The apprehension that he was displaying made Charles appear his true age, and Trey was suddenly reminded that he was really only a few years older than he was. He sidled over to him and gave him a friendly slap between the shoulder blades.

"How are you feeling, Merlin?" he said in a voice that belied his own feelings.

Charles turned to him and forced a smile. "I guess I'll be

happier once I know exactly what we're up against. What about you, dog-boy?" he asked.

"Crapping myself," Trey admitted, nodding his head and staring off into the distance.

Charles laughed loudly. It was a strange sound under the circumstances and Alexa turned around to look at them, a nervous smile playing on her lips.

"Shall we go then, Tom?" she asked.

The Irishman hefted the big gun in his hands. He pursed his lips and nodded slowly, lifting his face to the sky so that a thin, slick coating of rain washed over it. "Might as well," he said. "As my old ma used to say, 'You'll never plow a field by turning it over in your mind.'" He turned to Trey, nodding at him. "You'd best be doing your thing—we don't know what's up ahead."

Trey removed his clothes, stripping down to his underwear, and morphed. The violent and sickening rush of pain was over almost as soon as it began and he opened his eyes to see his three friends looking up at him—a look of horror and fear on their faces. It saddened him, knowing that no matter how many times they had seen him like this before, the reaction they were showing now would always be the first thing he saw when he opened his eyes as a werewolf.

The world was suddenly very loud and the usual sense of dizziness swept through him for a few seconds before he could better adjust to the assault on his senses. He closed his eyes again. Bright yellow and green washed across his vision as the smell of the sea blew in on the wind, these

204

colors flecked with a mixture of browns, greens, and curiously deep purples from the smells of the earth and rocks around them. His wolf senses gave him a curious synesthesia—allowing him to experience smells as colors. Another scent carried on the wind, which set his nerves on edge and brought a lake of saliva into his mouth—it was a reddish brown smell and he knew in an instant what it was: rabbits. There must have been hundreds of them around, buried away in their underground houses beneath his feet, and the smell of them sent his head reeling. He took a deep breath through his mouth, fighting the animalistic urge to start digging at the ground to try to unearth the creatures.

The new sensations, and the emotions they stirred up, rolled over him like a great wave, and while the amulet that he wore around his neck enabled him to maintain control, aspects of the wolf inside him battled against his efforts to suppress them. He loved the feeling of being outdoors in his werewolf form. It was as if when he was outside, like this, the true realization of his powers was almost within his grasp. He wanted to throw back his head and howl, and this desire was coupled with an even stronger one—to run off into the night, letting the wind and rain rush past him as he sprinted through this vast open landscape. To run . . . and to hunt.

Stop it, Trey, he told himself. *Get a grip, and remember what you are here for.* He reached up with his huge clawed hand and fingered the Amulet of Theiss that hung around his neck, knowing that without it he would have no control over the base urges that nagged at him.

205

He looked around him, taking in the details of the land and noting the topography, his wolf eyes observing the nuances of the rocky ground up ahead and instantly assessing the best routes to provide the maximum amount of cover as they ascended the hill. He felt good. The power that coursed through him was as invigorating as ever, and this, coupled with the adrenaline in his system, made him feel something akin to invincible.

He nodded down at his group of friends again. Even through the rain and the wind he could smell the fear and anxiety that came off each of them, his own scent mingling and merging with theirs. He tried to ignore the smell, choosing to look ahead up the hill rather than take in the thick, sluggish brown color that clung to his companions.

"Let's go," said Tom, and they started their approach to Leroth.

32

Trey effortlessly jumped the twelve feet between two craggy rocks on either side of a grassy depression. His friends would have to climb down into the hollow, and he would wait here in order to help them up onto this side.

The terrain was easy enough for him, his long powerful legs making light work of the undulating ground that seemed to be hard and unyielding at one moment, soft and malleable the next. He had taken it upon himself to scout ahead, trying not to go too far as the others struggled along behind him.

He crouched down on the large rock he was standing on and looked back through the darkness. He could see that the effort was taking its toll on his friends, the rain making the going that much harder, especially for Tom, who was not just older than the other two but also carrying a significant amount of extra weight in the form of the equipment he had brought. (He had already refused Trey's offer to carry it for him.)

The wind blew the rain against him, but he did not feel the cold. He used his nose and ears to scan the land ahead for any sign of the citadel that they sought. He stopped, keeping perfectly still for a second and cocking his ears to take in the tiniest sounds up ahead. He heard it again, the sound of a vehicle somewhere over the ridge that lay about fifty meters away.

He turned back at the sound of footsteps to see Charles approaching the other side of the depression. "Anything yet, Trey?" he asked. Alexa had caught up with him now, and much to Trey's relief, he could see Tom bringing up the rear.

"Not yet, but I thought I caught the sound of an engine starting up somewhere close by, so hopefully we are not too far away now." Trey formed the words in his mind and pushed them out to all three of his friends, glad now that he had allowed Alexa to bully him into learning the spell.

"If that's the case, no more talking for a while," Tom said, taking hold of Trey's proffered hand and allowing the werewolf to haul him easily up over a line of rocks that formed the steep wall in front of him. "Any noise will carry for a long way out here, even with this rain. And I think that we should avoid any magic for a while too. There's no telling how much security there is around this place or what they'll be looking out for."

The rest of them nodded and they moved forward toward the tall bank of rock and earth that rose up ahead of them, slipping as they tried to climb up its steep incline. Trey, pausing near the top, clearly caught the harsh scrape of two metallic surfaces rubbing against each other, but when he looked back down the slope at his friends it was obvious that he was the only one who had heard the sound.

Holding out his huge clawed hands, he signaled them to stop. He pointed up to his ear and then again forward. Tom nodded and slowly climbed up to join him, staying in a low crouch that was copied by the others as they neared the crest of the ridge to look over at the scene below.

The fortress was huge. A giant black tower that thrust its way skyward as if some monstrous dagger had been set into the earth, handle down. It appeared to have been carved from a single piece of rock, and Trey couldn't imagine how such a thing could have been created. The edifice seemed to resonate with a dark energy. To Trey's ears it seemed almost to hum, like overhead power cables do in a downpour, except that the energy that was coming off the vast black structure filled him with a raw and undiluted fear that bit down deep into his bones. There was no sign of any entrance into the tower. It rose out of a base of gigantic roughhewn rocks that Trey's eyes scanned again and again for any hint of an opening.

He was about to point this out to the others when a large section of the rock seemed to *pulse*, shimmering in a way that suggested it had changed at some molecular level. Just as suddenly, a huge creature appeared in the opening, trapped inside what appeared to be some globe of energy, its outline visible as the rain bounced off its surface. A car that had been waiting on the ground below switched on its lights to illuminate the scene.

"What is that thing?" Alexa asked, sidling up next to Trey to look down at the huge blue-black creature below them.

"Draugr," Charles said in a low voice. "And from the look of things, it doesn't appear to be particularly pleased to have been resurrected."

The creature bellowed up into the night sky, hammering at the invisible envelope that imprisoned it. Even from up here Trey could smell the unmistakable stench of rotting putrescence that emanated from it—the smell mirroring perfectly the color of the creature itself.

"Where are they taking it?" Alexa asked.

"Away," Charles said, shifting his weight a little and causing a trickle of stones to cascade down the slope behind them. "My guess is that they underestimated the volatility of these creatures and have now decided that they will be better off cutting their losses and getting rid of it while they can."

"They can't just set that thing loose!"

"I think you'll find they can, and quite happily will."

Suddenly, shuffling out from the entrance, a new creature was picked out in the car's lights. It shambled forward, arms stretched out in front of it, hands held palm out, like some ancient evangelical preacher. It appeared to Trey that this new creature was somehow responsible for keeping the giant monster from breaking loose and destroying everything in its path.

"Gwendolin," Charles said in a small voice.

Trey glanced around at the sharp intake of breath at his side and saw Alexa looking with undisguised horror at the person who had given birth to her. "It can't be," she said. "That . . . *thing* can't be my mother."

Charles turned to look at her. "You're right, that thing is not your mother any longer. The being that once inhabited that body and that loved you and your father has long since gone. The thing that we call Gwendolin is now little more than a husk to house the creature of darkness that she has become. I'm sorry, Alexa."

"How do you know that's her?" Alexa hissed. "You can't be sure."

Charles looked across at her before turning his attention back to the scene below. "Whoever that is down there is simultaneously performing three separate, and very difficult, spells. They are containing the Draugr, moving it at the same time, and have created that entrance to the tower. Perhaps my father could have accomplished such a feat when he was younger and at the peak of his powers, but there is only one mage that I can think of that is capable of it now."

The Draugr was now almost fully inside the truck, and had begun to roar again, the noise making the hackles on Trey's back bristle and his lips involuntarily draw back from his teeth in a snarl.

The demons that were standing by rushed forward to slam shut the heavy doors of the armored vehicle.

The sorceress appeared to visibly sag, her shoulders dropping at least an inch or two and her head lolling forward.

Eventually she turned to one of the Maug demons that

were hovering behind her, barked an order, and moved off toward the car that was waiting.

She had opened the door and was about to climb inside when she stopped. She turned slowly and looked up at the ridge that they were hiding behind, scanning it for the something that she could sense was concealed up there. Trey and the others held their breath and watched as the sorceress stood staring up in their direction, a puzzled look on her features.

There was an enormous bang from the inside of the armored truck and a large convex dent appeared in its roof like some great metallic ulcer had suddenly erupted on its surface. Gwendolin's attention was swiftly drawn back to the task at hand and she shouted something to the driver of her car and climbed inside, slamming the door. The truck, with Gwendolin's car in front and a second bringing up the rear, started its engine and began to pull out.

"Bloody hell!" said Tom. "I thought for a moment we were done for."

"We can't let them take the Draugr away from here, Tom. If they free that thing, thousands will die."

"We need to get into Leroth, Alexa. With Gwendolin and that many guards leaving together, this is our best chance. We can see about sorting this other mess out once we've got what we came here for. It's not good, I know, but we need to get inside that place before they up and disappear again."

Alexa had turned her attention back to the vehicles. "We may not get the opportunity," she said. "Look."

The banging and bellowing emanating from the truck had intensified, and the entire vehicle started to rock violently on its suspension, shifting forcefully from side to side in time with a series of deep, hollow bangs. The demon sitting in the driver's seat was looking about wildly. The sound in the truck's cab must have been deafening. As the driver attempted to turn the vehicle to follow the leading car there was a surge against the opposite side of the truck. For just a split second the wheels on the side nearest to them lifted clear off the ground, the tires spinning in the air and throwing an arc of mud and stones out behind the vehicle. The tires, back down on the ground again, struggled to find purchase in the muddy ground, and the vehicle now swayed violently from side to side as a result of the Draugr's savage attacks on the walls of its prison. There was an enormous crash and the entire vehicle pitched to one side again. A metallic groaning sound suggested that the vehicle was not built to endure such treatment. Trey waited for the truck to crash back down to earth when from the corner of his eye he saw Charles throw an arm out, the palm of his hand extended like a traffic cop commanding an onrushing car to halt. Trey watched in fascination as the truck started to topple, the wheels now at least twice the height from the ground that they had been.

That low groan of metal buckling under pressure was louder and unrelenting now, punctuated by a staccato hammering, like the beating of an anvil with a blacksmith's mallet, as steel approached its breaking point.

The truck tipped farther until gravity had its inevitable way. An enormous crash filled the air, hurting Trey's ears, and he stared down at the truck on its side with its wheels spinning against nothingness.

Charles was still in a trancelike state, his face a mask of concentration and effort. A small grunt escaped his mouth and his right hand suddenly jerked upward. The back door of the truck flew open.

The Draugr charged out of the opening and lifted its head to the heavens, roaring in anger and frustration.

Trey watched the creature leap up onto the side of the overturned cab, smashing at the thick bulletproof glass of the side window with its fist. The laminated glass shattered under the blow but held in place even after three more heavy blows were rained down on it. From their vantage point Trey could see the two demons inside cowering backward in fear, believing that the monster would break through at any second. The Draugr stopped its assault and hunched forward to peer in at the creatures trapped in the steel shell, tilting its head to one side as if studying animals in an enclosure at the zoo. Suddenly it leaped high up into the air. At the same time its size increased so that at the zenith of its ascent it was the size of some colossal bear. It plummeted down with tremendous force, landing with both feet directly on top of the cab and crushing it inward as if it were little more than a tin can. The door buckled, the metal screeching in protest.

The Draugr jumped again, crushing the already-mangled metal repeatedly until it was completely flattened. The screams of the demons inside had stopped.

The car containing Gwendolin came skidding to a halt, the brake lights creating little islands of red in the black rain that still poured from the sky. The sound made the giant creature stop and turn. It jumped down from the cab and started to run toward the car, sensing that it would have a much easier time of smashing it, and its contents, to pieces than it had enjoyed with the larger vehicle.

The Maug were out of the vehicle and running to meet the Draugr as Gwendolin got out. She shrieked angrily at them to destroy it, raising her hands to her head and clawing at her own wet and matted hair in fury. Three more demons of a type that Trey had never seen before ran from the opening in the wall. They were carrying long, vicious-looking spears and they fanned out to approach the Draugr from behind in a semicircle.

Tom turned to Trey, who was looking down at the scene with a mixture of horror and fascination. "You'd better be going, lads," he said. "I don't think that we're going to get a distraction any better than this one right here." He nodded to Charles and Trey before turning to face Alexa. "You and I are going to stay here and see that these two have every chance of getting out once they've rescued the globe from Caliban."

"Are you kidding, Tom?" Alexa shouted above the rain and the noise of the mayhem that was unraveling below them. "This is not what we discussed. If you think I'm waiting back here with you while these two—"

"This is the plan, Alexa," Tom said, his voice harsh and firm. "Trey and Charles are the two best equipped on this team to get into Leroth and get out again with the globe. I'm sorry that we didn't discuss it with you, but we knew how you'd react." He turned to look at Charles again. "Have you got the map?" he asked.

Charles nodded and patted his back pocket.

Alexa stared at the three of them as what Tom had just told her sank in. "How could you?" she said, looking hard at Trey. "How dare you make plans behind my back?"

Another roar exploded from below, followed by the wailing screech of a demon in its death throes.

"Do you think that I might lose it in there if we were confronted by my mother?" Alexa continued over the din. "You've seen that thing down there. Do you think that I harbor any feelings except utter contempt for that? You complete and utter—"

"It wasn't like that, Alexa." Trey used magic to communicate with her, momentarily forgetting that they had agreed not to.

"Forget it, Trey. You knew about this before we came out here, didn't you? Some friend you turned out to be! And you, Charles—what's up with you? Nothing to say?"

Charles flushed a bright pink and turned his attention to a muddy clump of grass growing just in front of him.

"We don't have time to argue this out now, Alexa," Tom

216

said sternly. "The boys will need our help when they get out and I will not be able to do that on my own. I might be able to blow things up with this," he said, nodding toward the grenade launcher, "but if it comes down to sorcery, I'll need help." The Irishman fixed her with a cold look. "Your father would understand what's needed in this situation. I hoped that once we got here and had to face this moment, you would too."

Alexa looked at him. He'd hit a nerve with his last comment and he knew it. She took a deep breath and very slowly nodded her head. "OK, Tom. I'll stick here with you. But the three of you should have had the balls to discuss this with me. I thought that you might have held me in enough regard to do that."

"OK," Tom said, and addressed Trey and Charles. "Go on now," he said. "In and out again as quickly and quietly as you can. And don't either of you go taking any stupid risks. Remember what it is that we came here to do, and stick to the brief. Look out for each other in there."

Trey and Charles nodded at Tom, but Alexa refused to meet their eyes. They set off, clambering down the slope to their right, Trey ahead, with Charles just behind him. They were almost at the bottom of the hill when a high, keening scream cut through the night. It was a painful noise. Trey looked behind him to see Gwendolin and the demons facing the Draugr, the scene lit by the lights of the truck that was lying on its side. The deafening wail was coming from Gwendolin and as Trey watched she began to transform in front of him. She had already changed dramatically—she had taken on a dark gray hue from head to foot so that her skin looked like charcoal—and then the very air around her began to dance and shimmer like the surface of a road on a hot summer day. Trey turned to ask Charles what was going on when suddenly thousands of tiny stones and pieces of grit began to fly through the air at tremendous speed. The two boys dropped to the floor to avoid being hit, but even so fine particles bit into their flesh and they could feel the ground beneath them being drawn as if by some irresistible force. The stones came from every direction, flying straight toward Gwendolin and sticking to the howling sorceress like iron particles attracted to some super-magnet. Layer after layer coated every part of her until she was completely covered. The stones continued to fly through the air, larger and larger ones until eventually she was attracting stones and broken fragments of rock the size of a small fist that created a sharp, cracking sound as they met. The sorceress appeared to have doubled in size.

"She's invoked an Elemental," Charles said, shouting above the deafening noise. "That's difficult to do." He shook his head in dismay. "I've no idea how she could still have the strength to do that after raising the Draugr. That's not a good sign." He was watching the scene, his eyes wide in wonder.

A low growl brought him out of his reverie. He looked back at the werewolf, whose attention was on the opening in the wall of the fortress little more than twenty feet away. "You're right, Trey, we need to get inside."

Trey sprang to his feet and half dragged his companion toward the breach in the wall, the two of them passing through it without so much as a backward glance. They would miss the battle between the Draugr and Gwendolin that had just begun.

33

Tom and Alexa watched as Trey and Charles slipped unnoticed through the opening in the wall and disappeared from sight as soon as they stepped into the darkness. They checked the scene unraveling before them, making sure that no one else had seen the two boys enter. Gwendolin and the demons had enough to occupy them. The demons that had emerged from the tower advanced on the Draugr, their spears held out ahead of them. The revenant, like everyone else, had stopped and watched the transformation that Gwendolin had undergone moments before. It had been impossible not to.

"What in the name of Mike is *that*?" Tom asked, looking down at the huge stone-and-rock *thing* now standing in front of the Draugr.

"She's summoned an Elemental," Alexa said, staring down at the giant stone-monster that had been her mother. "She wants to take on the Draugr by force."

Tom looked over at the sound of Alexa's voice and saw the unmistakable look of admiration on the teenager's face.

"Let's not forget who we're rooting for here," he said under his breath.

Alexa fixed him with a cold, hard stare. "I'm rooting for

one person and one person only, Tom. And if you think that I've forgotten that the failure of this mission could mean the death of my father, you're not the man I always thought you were. Yes, I'm impressed that that . . . *creature* is capable of pulling off one of the most difficult summonings ever known, but that's only because I know that I will never be able to do it."

She turned her face slightly away from the Irishman, to keep her attention on the scene below. "I don't have any feelings for her, Tom. I know what she is and I know what she has done." She stopped, and when Tom glanced over at her he could see that she was struggling to hold back tears. "And, yes, I even know that she was going to use me as a human sacrifice all those years ago."

"How long have you known about that?" Tom said after a brief pause.

"People like to gossip, Tom. And a story as juicy as that?" She blew out her cheeks. "That's a doozy. There's *no way* that people can help but talk about something like that. I picked up snippets here and there and eventually I worked the whole thing out. I still thought that she was dead though. I thought my father had killed her."

"He would have. But she disappeared." Tom's voice sounded hollow to his own ears.

"I wish he had. I wish he'd wiped her off the face of the earth right there and then."

"I'm so sorry, Alexa. You shouldn't have had to find out something like that about your past."

221

She nodded her thanks. "By the way, you were right not to let me go down there. I'm sorry I said those things to you all, especially to the boys. I hope that Trey and Charles are OK in there."

"I'm sure they're doing grand."

Alexa was about to reply when a huge roar ripped through the night air.

Below them, the Draugr had transformed in size again so that it must have stood a good fifteen feet in height. The creature roared its fury into the night sky and threw its body forward toward the vast stone-and-rock-clad Elemental, trying to topple it. The Elemental swung its arm, and the heavy stone fist crashed down onto the Draugr's back, smashing the creature to the floor. A deep, ugly sound came from the mouth of the Draugr as the force of the blow shook it to its core. It looked up just in time to see the Elemental lift its foot in an attempt to stamp on its head. But the stone-monster was slow—incredibly powerful, yes—but slow, and in the time it had taken to raise its bulky leg to deliver the fatal blow, the Draugr had rolled to one side and regained its feet in a single movement. The revenant jumped impossibly high into the night air, thrusting its feet at the head and shoulders of the Elemental, pushing out with its muscular legs to maximize the impact. Great chunks of stone and rock fell away from the Elemental, rattling and tumbling onto the floor at its feet. It groaned under the assault and staggered to one side, only just maintaining its balance by putting an arm out and pushing back up against the ground. To Tom and Alexa, it wasn't clear how it would have got back up again had it gone over; it was obviously extremely heavy, and if the Draugr did succeed in toppling it, the Elemental would be at the complete mercy of the rampaging revenant.

The Draugr closed in again but had forgotten or was oblivious to the Nargwan demons advancing toward it from behind with their long spears. Suddenly one of them broke forward, stabbing the Draugr, thrusting the weapon viciously into the creature's flank and twisting the blade inside the flesh. It was the last thing the demon ever did. The Draugr turned on its assailant, grabbed at the shaft of the spear and snapped it. Shooting an arm out, it snatched up the retreating demon by the neck and lifted it into the air. Dashing the demon to the ground, it turned back to the Elemental just in time to meet the rock fist that slammed into its face.

There was a sickening crunch as tooth and bone shattered under the force of the blow and the Draugr staggered backward, shaking its head like a heavyweight boxer caught with a flailing right hook in the first round. One side of its face was a ruined mess and it spat a great globule of black blood and broken teeth on the ground, staring down at the gory mess. It was as if the sight of its own spilled blood made something inside the giant creature switch. The creature's great inky blue head lifted, eyes as black as coal regarding the stone monstrosity before it. It took a huge breath, filled its barrel chest to its fullest, issued a deafening bellow, and charged at the Elemental again.

The revenant had hit the thing of stone and rock three or four times before the Elemental knew what was happening. As great chunks of masonry fizzed off into the night air the Draugr launched salvo after salvo of heavy blows at the rock-thing, smashing its fists into the creature, which was now backing away under the severity of the attack. One blow sent what had been the lower jaw of the Elemental spinning off into the darkness in a shower of rocks and pebbles. The Draugr was impossibly fast and agile for a creature of its size. Leaping high into the air, it clasped its hands together over its head and brought them down like a hammer onto the head of the Elemental, which staggered under the force of the blow. The Draugr would certainly have finished it off, but for the second spear that buried itself deep into its back. This spear was quickly joined by another that ripped through the flesh of the Draugr's thigh, the metal-tipped head emerging on the other side in a fountain of blood and gore.

The giant revenant roared, bellowing its fury at the injustice of being denied its victory. It stumbled to one side, still reaching out to inflict one last blow before it collapsed. The stone-monster rocked back on its own heels, barely able to keep upright and reeling like a drunk on board a ship in high winds.

Slowly the demons closed in on the Draugr like hunting dogs encircling their prey. One of the Maug produced an axe, hefting the weapon in its hand, readying itself to make the final blow to decapitate the Draugr and end the creature's long and pitiful existence.

"We need to do something, Tom," Alexa hissed. "If this ends now, Charles and Trey will be trapped inside Leroth."

The Draugr was down on one knee, its ruined leg held out stiffly to one side with a torrent of black flowing freely from the wound onto the rocks and stones that now littered the ground. It looked about in anger at the demons that were gathered around it in a tight circle, but its strength was ebbing away—carried from its body in the dark ribbons that snaked their way down into the ground. It was incapable of doing more than watching as the demons prepared to dispatch it.

The Maug eyed a spot on the Draugr's neck and swung the long-handled axe through the air in a vicious arc that was intended to hack through bone and muscle and tendon. But the Draugr had one last ace up its sleeve. It waited until the very moment that the axe was due to bite into its flesh before instantly shrinking back to its original size. The axe sailed effortlessly over its head, its momentum carrying onward through its deadly arc until it buried itself deep into the chest of another demon standing to the left of the revenant. The Nargwan looked down in stunned disbelief at the sight of the protruding axe head before sinking to its knees, dead.

The low, rasping laugh that came from the Draugr rang about the open space and it looked around at its executioners with contempt, but its strength and fight were gone. It was now too weak to even face its opponents. Instead, it hung its head, waiting for the final blow to come.

The Draugr heard the grunt of the Maug as it swung the axe for the final time, but it never felt the cold steel of the blade cutting through its neck.

Instead, the world around it erupted in a rolling wave of flame that consumed everything in its path.

34

Trey and Charles hurried through the opening into what appeared to be a low corridor hewn through the glassy black rock. Trey tensed and scanned the passageway that disappeared off in both directions from where they stood, to ensure that they were not in danger of encountering a fresh batch of reinforcements making their way to join the melee outside.

It was eerily quiet and this sudden and complete lack of sound struck Trey as soon as they had entered—the noise of the battle outside would not be joining them in here. It had disappeared entirely the second that they had stepped through to this side of the wall—like some invisible shutter had slammed down, trapping the clamor behind it. Charles noted Trey's confusion and reached out, tapping on the great fur-covered forearm nearest to him. "You're not in the same plane anymore," he explained. "As soon as we came through that aperture we stepped out of our world and into the Netherworld. Those sounds don't belong here and won't carry through to us."

Trey looked toward the opening and noted how his view of the outside appeared to continue for only about twenty meters or so beyond the walls of the fortress, whereupon it simply fizzled out. The world beyond this that was Iceland was simply replaced by a swirling gray haze. Trey thought that he could see *things* moving around within the murky curtain, small dark things that darted around incredibly quickly as soon as his eyes fixed upon them. He wondered what was happening outside, and if Tom and Alexa were still OK.

"They'll be fine," Charles said, looking up at him. "Tom won't allow anything to happen to her."

Trey's golden lycanthrope eyes seemed almost incandescent in the darkness. Very deliberately, Trey looked first left and then right before returning his attention to Charles.

"You can communicate like this, now." Charles's voice came to Trey as though he was murmuring straight into his ear, even though his lips had not moved. "This place only exists because of magic," Charles said, talking normally again, "and the only person who could detect us easily is outside at the moment with her hands full. We're in the Netherworld now, at least a part of it that has been transported to the human realm. I'm in much greater danger of being discovered here than you are, Trey. I'm human. I don't belong here—you do." The sorcerer looked up at the lycanthrope, a worried-looking smile on his face. "I will not use sorcery until I have to, as I'll need to save my energy. I suggest that you do the same and only *talk* to me when you need to."

Charles watched the werewolf stare down at the floor

again, concentrating on the spell. His lips moved around the huge teeth set in his jaw and a series of rumbling growls issued from the great wolf head. *"OK,"* Trey said eventually. *"Which way do we go?"*

Charles nodded in Trey's direction. "You've really got the hang of that; you must have had a damn good teacher."

The low growl came from deep within the werewolf's chest. Trey peeled back his lips to reveal to Charles the full array of massive teeth set into his jaws. Charles guessed that it was the werewolf equivalent of a smile, but nonetheless an involuntary shudder skittered its way down his backbone.

"I just had a terrible thought," Trey said. *"What if Gwendolin has Mynor's Globe on her? Out there."* He nodded toward the opening.

"She wouldn't take an object as precious as that out of the tower. No, we have to believe that your information is correct and that it's kept in her personal chambers."

Charles turned to his left and right, peering at the twin walls of darkness that the corridor disappeared into. He pulled the map from his back pocket, but the light was low and he could hardly make it out. "This passageway must encircle the inner courtyard and the tower itself. There must be an entrance somewhere along it. If I could see this map properly, I'd—"

He looked up and saw the huge figure of the werewolf heading off down the corridor to their right without so much as a backward glance.

"OK. Fine. Right it is then," said Charles, and set off after him.

The passageway was completely unlit, and as they left what little light had spilled in through the opening behind, they plunged ever deeper into a blackness that was now almost complete. Trey's eyes were perfectly adapted to this environment; the structure of his werewolf eyes, with their much higher ratio of rods to cones, allowed him to see in the dark almost as well as he could in daylight. But he was aware of how acutely Charles was struggling behind him, losing his footing and stumbling every time the pitch of the floor changed beneath their feet, so Trey was forced to go much slower than he would have wanted to, sticking close to the other man and allowing his own presence and bulk to be a guide to the way ahead.

Eventually it became apparent that they were approaching a new opening set into the inner wall on their left. A peculiar purple light spilled into the darkness up ahead. Trey swiftly approached it, keeping close to the wall and moving silently to assess any new danger that might be waiting for them. Now that he could see again, Charles quickly caught up with him.

A light breeze blew in from the doorway, and as Trey approached the opening, the stench that it carried assaulted the most acute of his senses, making him reel backward as if he had been physically struck.

"Are you OK, Trey?"

The stink was incredible, like nothing that Trey had ever encountered before—as a human or a werewolf. The acrid reek of rot and decay was overlaid by harsh and metallic and sulphurous smells that crowded over each other, competing to dominate. Trey gagged and fought to keep himself under control—his synesthesia transformed the smells into multitudinous colors, a conflagration of yellows, greens, reds, and browns that crushed in on one another in front of his eyes and made his head spin.

"The smell, Charles! What the hell is it?"

Charles took a sniff and screwed up his own face. He swallowed audibly, fighting to control his stomach. "Whoa! Yes, it's pretty rank, I'll grant you. Must be a hell of a lot worse for you. Are you OK?"

Trey shook his head but took a step toward the door. He shuddered as his stomach heaved in protest. He opened his mouth to breathe through that instead, but only succeeded in tasting the foul odor as well as smelling it. He fought to ignore it as best he could and approached the opening again to look up at the tower that rose into the sky overhead.

"Impressive, isn't it?" Charles said behind him.

Trey looked up at the sky, and the sight sent an icy trickle of fear coursing through him. The black sun still burned high overhead in the deep purple firmament.

"This is a small inner bailey," Charles said, able to see the map now. "It separates this outer wall from the inner tower.

Strange, because it wasn't at all obvious from the outside. It looked just like one huge tower rising out of rock from out there, eh?"

Trey scanned the colossal citadel that rose up in front of them. There appeared to be a series of cages hung from chains suspended from outcrops in the walls high above their heads, although there seemed no way that these could be accessed as there were no apertures in the walls of the giant fortress until about two-thirds of the way up, and these appeared to be little more than tall, vertical arrow slits of the sort that Trey had seen in pictures of castles in the human realm.

Charles followed the line of Trey's sight. "Gibbets," he said. "For displaying the tortured and mutilated bodies of Caliban's and Gwendolin's enemies. By the look of them, quite a few appear to be occupied. It clearly doesn't pay to get on the wrong side of the master of this place."

The smell was still bothering Trey, making it difficult for him to focus fully. Suddenly there was a flash of movement overhead, quickly followed by another and another. Small black shapes appeared to detach themselves from the beams supporting the dangling metal cages and swooped down in their direction. Trey watched as maybe twenty or so of these shapes approached from different directions, growing in size and detail as they flew down from their perches. They began to circle in the air above them, hissing noisily.

They were the first winged demons that Trey had ever

seen, and while they were small—about the size of a domestic cat—he considered how these creatures perfectly fit the image that he would have conjured up in his imagination if anyone had asked him, back when his life had been *normal*, to think of a demon. They had black humanoid bodies with leathery wings that grew out from between their shoulder blades. Muscular legs hung down from the torso, and the feet ended with disproportionately large and curled birdlike claws protruding from the toes; the same needle-like talons were also visible at the ends of the creatures' fingers. Mean, sharp faces stared out at the intruders through baleful black pinprick pupils set into red eyes that never blinked. The wings flapped in a scooping motion to keep the demons in the air. But it was the tail that caught Trey's eye. Long and ringed like a rat's tail, it ended in a small triangular barb that Trey could remember drawing on pictures of devils and demons that he had made as a young boy.

Trey and Charles stood and watched the acrobatics of the tiny demons as they wheeled in the air above their heads. Then, without warning, one of the small creatures swooped down toward them, folding its wings in behind it and dive-bombing the pair. It shot past Charles's face—a flashing blur of black—raking at his flesh with its small, daggered hands, before rejoining the flock overhead.

The wound didn't bleed immediately. It was as if the nerves and blood vessels were momentarily paralyzed—in a state of shock—from the damage that had been inflicted upon them. Then, as quickly as the small demon had swooped

233

down out of the sky, Charles's face began to spout a crimson waterfall of blood that spilled vigorously down his cheek and neck, instantly soaking into the material of his shirt. His hand instinctively flew up to the wound and he pressed the torn ribbons of flesh hard against his face with a splayed palm.

Another demon dive-bombed Charles, quickly followed by another that had peeled away from the gathering flock and followed its companion in a racing dive through the air. Trey threw out a clawed hand and tore the first of them from the sky above Charles's head, sending the demon crashing to the floor no more than a meter from where they stood. Raising his foot, Trey stamped down on the creature's prone body. At the sight of the other demon's death, the second attacker quickly veered away from Charles and headed directly for Trey's face, its lips curled back to reveal rows of tiny teeth that reminded Trey of a piranha's. Trey waited until it was nearly upon him. He could clearly see the vehement look on the creature's ugly little face, its hooked claws extended toward his own as it sought to avenge its companion's death. At the very last second Trey rocked to one side, twisting his head and snapping his huge jaws together to sever the creature's head from its body. He watched the decapitated torso crash to the ground, wings still flapping, unaware that the signals being sent to them were the last they would ever receive.

Charles was twisting and ducking to avoid the increased attacks that were being made upon him too. A demon had landed on his back and was clinging to him, its talons buried deep into his flesh. Trey ran over, crushed the creature in his hand, and threw it to the ground.

"Trey," Charles shouted, "can you keep them off me for a second?"

Without a word, the lycanthrope leaped up into the swarm of winged demons, clawing and biting at any foolish enough to come near him. Their attention concentrated on him and the swarm regrouped to launch a concerted attack on the werewolf.

Behind him, Charles stood stiff-backed, hands held out before him with the palms upturned. He closed his eyes, oblivious to the river of blood that still poured from his face.

Trey rocked back again, narrowly avoiding an attack, catching the wingtip of one of the creatures between his incisors and throwing the demon to the ground with a twist of his head. He glanced behind him toward the young sorcerer and saw Charles's body stiffen, then jerk violently, his fingers suddenly closing to form two tight fists. Trey dodged as another of the demons dropped toward him, but didn't take his eyes off Charles. The sorceror's body jerked again, his eyes flew open and he thrust both hands into the air over his head as if throwing invisible dust at the heavens.

There was a moment of pure and complete silence, a millisecond of utter *nothingness*. Then the fifteen or so demons still wheeling around their heads burst into flames and fell from the sky, hitting the ground with low thumping sounds as their still-burning bodies crashed into the dirt.

Trey looked back at Charles, who was reapplying pressure to his wound, trying to staunch the flow of blood. He looked pale, and Trey worried that he might be in danger of going into shock. Charles returned Trey's look, nodding that he was in fact OK.

"What was that?" Trey said.

"Never mind. Did any of them escape?" Charles said. His speech was slurred and he spat a large globule of blood onto the ground in front of him.

Trey looked around him at the little islands of fire and then up into the sky. *"No, I think you wiped them all out with whatever the hell it was that you just did."*

"Good. We need to get out of the open quickly. Then I need you to patch me up."

They ran toward the base of the tower, relieved to discover an enormous door no more than forty feet or so from where they had been standing. Trey was not surprised that they had not seen it immediately upon entering the bailey. It was black and appeared to be made from a solid piece of some strange metal that was icy cold to the touch. Set into the inky walls it was almost invisible. There was no handle and no lock, and even when Trey put his considerable weight against it, the thing wouldn't budge.

"Sew me up, and I'll get us inside," Charles said. Fishing in his pocket for his wallet, he retrieved the sutura needle that he had used on Trey's injury after his bout with the Shadow Demon back in London.

Trey reached out and grabbed for the needle, but his great wolf hands simply weren't dextrous enough to grip the small and delicate instrument. He took a deep breath, and glancing quickly around to check that they were not in danger of any imminent attack, transmogrified back into his human form, taking the needle from his friend.

"I'll hide us as best I can, Trey, but you need to hurry up—like me, you are extremely vulnerable here in your human form."

Standing stark naked in the shadow of the giant tower, Trey didn't need Charles to tell him how vulnerable he was. He took the needle between his forefinger and thumb and reached forward to pull Charles's hand away from the deep gashes in his face.

"Oh man!" he said with a shake of his head. "I don't know what I'm doing here. I don't even know where to start."

"Just sew it up as best you can to stop the bleeding, Trey. I'm not expecting a perfect blanket stitch or anything."

"Fine. But if I do this too badly, you're going to end up with one side of your face looking like a chewed-up piece of gum." He squeezed together the two sides of the deepest wound, trying not to get too much dirt from his fingers into the bloody mess. Jabbing the needle into the flesh beneath the tear, he pushed it up through the other side, repeating the process again and again and cursing in frustration each time that his hands slipped in the sticky blood. After a while he'd succeeded in getting the bleeding to stop. He stepped back

237

to look at his work, shaking his head at the pinched and puckered mess that was now one side of Charles's face.

"How's it look?" Charles said. It was the first sound he had issued since the work on his face had begun, and Trey marveled at how stoically he had borne the ministrations. He opened the swollen eye on the mangled side of his face and looked over at Trey.

Frowning, Trey pushed his bottom lip out and considered the best way to respond. "Let's put it this way," he said finally. "You're not going to need to buy a mask to wear next Halloween."

"Great," Charles said, reaching up and tentatively touching the newly repaired flesh. "You need to change back as quickly as possi—"

The werewolf was standing over him, looking down at him with its lips drawn back over its teeth in that snarling smile again. The black-and-gray pelt that covered Trey's body blended in perfectly with the stone behind him and he turned to look at the door again.

"Come on," Charles said, moving toward the entrance. "Let's get inside as quickly as we can."

Trey watched as Charles placed the palm of his hand on the icy surface of the door, ignoring the pain that it must have been causing to his bare flesh. Satisfied with whatever he had discovered, Charles closed his eyes, moving his lips as he began to utter some silent incantation.

Trey didn't hear anything to suggest that Charles had

succeeded in opening the door, but suddenly it swung inward effortlessly.

"We're in," Charles said.

They pushed the door fully open, and entered the Tower of Leroth.

35

The sound of the engine had cut and their captain, a young man wearing a brightly colored Hawaiian-style shirt and a baseball cap, jumped deftly from the front of the boat, a long coil of rope clutched in his hand. He splashed into the low breakers and pulled the boat farther up the beach.

Martin watched from the terrace outside the kitchen as the young man hauled on the rope, the muscles in his arms rippling with the effort. He became aware of his daughter standing behind him, and his body involuntarily tensed. A cool breeze blew in off the sea, carrying the metallic briny smell of the ocean with it. He breathed in a great lungful of the stuff, savoring the smells, as if for the last time.

"Ready?" she asked.

"I think so," he replied, and turned to look at her.

Philippa had put her hair up into a bun, piling it up on her head and securing it with long, glossy black chopsticks that stuck out from her head at acute angles. She had reverted to the familiar black lipstick and she wore a black dress with black leggings underneath. She looked up at him with an expression that Martin was unable to put his finger on.

"You look very nice," he said eventually.

"Thank you," she said. She held his eyes for a moment, but Martin could detect no hint of warmth in her cold and calculating look. The daughter that he loved was not at home behind those twin globes. He wasn't certain what was.

"Come on then, Dad. We don't want to keep the man waiting any longer than we need to, do we?" She started to walk out of the house in the direction of the beach.

"Aren't you forgetting something?" Martin said from behind her.

She turned and looked at him, a small frown creasing her forehead.

"Our hamper," he said, leaning over to pick it up from where she had placed it beside the fridge. "We don't want to forget the food for our late-night turtle watch, do we?"

"How silly of me. Can you bring it, Dad? I'll be down by the boat." She walked off, hoisting the thin shawl that she was wearing back up over her shoulders.

Martin watched her go, picked up the hamper, and pulled the terrace door closed behind him. He had no way of knowing it, but at that very moment Mr. Ellington's team had just opened up the large chest-freezer in his garage back in England to discover the frozen corpse of Ruth Glenister staring back up at them with dead eyes. Neither could he have known that if he had delayed for no more than another ten minutes before climbing aboard the small boat with his daughter his life would have been saved by the arrival of Tiny Beauchamp—son of the missing

Mrs. Beauchamp—whom the team in England had finally been able to contact, asking him to get over to the villa as quickly as he could. But Martin Tipsbury had never been a lucky man. And in approximately ten minutes' time he would find out just how truly unlucky he really was.

36

It was cold inside the tower. Even Trey, covered with a thick pelt of fur, could feel the intense drop in temperature as they entered, and he looked over in concern at Charles to see how much he was suffering. To his surprise, Charles seemed completely unaware of the cold, and Trey was once again impressed by the sorcerer at his side and his ability to put up with things that Trey knew he himself would not be able to bear if he was in his human form.

They stood just inside the door that they had closed silently behind them, and Trey peered into the gloom, scanning the darkness that surrounded them for danger. There was very little light down here, but what there was allowed him to see that they were standing in a vast, circular space—perhaps fifty feet in diameter—that disappeared up into a murky blackness overhead. The smell that bombarded them inside the tower was almost as bad as that outside: rot and decay and neglect. In the center of the space was a low stone building that appeared, from the darkness beyond the windows, to be unoccupied. Behind the building, set a little way back, was what at first appeared to be some kind of flagpole.

There was something about that pole that bothered Trey,

and he strained his eyes and peered up at it disappearing into the darkness. He thought he could just make out the outline of something . . . something vaguely human-shaped that appeared to be hanging from a wooden beam protruding from the tall pole. He stared at the object, but it was too high overhead in the shadows to make out any more detail. A small shiver suddenly snaked through him.

"Trey." Charles nudged him. "We need to get moving."

The werewolf stole one last glance at the shape overhead before turning to follow his friend. A low moaning sound startled him. He tensed, anticipating some kind of attack. Charles cautiously moved toward the sound, Trey catching up with him until they both stood at the foot of a huge staircase where they stopped, looking about to locate the source of the noise.

Trey's eyes were adapting to the almost-complete darkness now and he peered around him at their surroundings once more. The huge circular staircase wound around the entire base of the tower, following the contours of the walls, but set in from them by about six feet. There didn't appear to be anything supporting the flight of stairs from above or below, and Trey marveled at how the huge stone steps seemed to have nothing but each other to cling to as they rose up into the gloom. Radiating out from the staircase at intervals were small ramplike bridges, connected to the outer walls by ropes, and these linked the staircase with what appeared to be a series of small black caves set into the outer wall.

Another moan drifted down to them and it became clear that whatever creatures were making the pitiful sounds were housed in these small fissures.

"Onward and upward," Charles said in a low whisper. He nodded at the stairs, and Trey signaled that the sorcerer should take the lead. "Fine with me," Charles said, stepping up ahead of the werewolf. "Just make sure that nothing comes out of these caves to follow us up. I don't like it in here one little bit."

They began to climb, desperately trying to keep their ascent as silent as possible. Trey was happier that he could see quite well now, and he glanced again at the thing suspended up near the rafters, although it was still too indistinct to make out. He had a nagging feeling about it. Like an itch you can't scratch, it bothered him, increasing the nerves and anxiety that he was already battling to keep under control.

They carried on like this until they were almost halfway up the staircase—about fifty feet above the ground—when another of those miserable low moaning sounds came from their right, stopping them in their tracks. The groan was very close to them, and Trey leaned out from the step that they were standing on, peering across the gap to see if he could make out what had produced the sound from the small, black hole. Whatever it was sounded as if it was in terrible pain.

"What are you doing, Trey?" Charles hissed. "Let's just keep moving. We have to get to the top of this place, and even then we have no idea where Gwendolin might be keeping the globe."

"Wait there," Trey replied. *"I just want to check something out."*

The lycanthrope placed his foot onto the bridge that linked the staircase with the outer wall, pushing down hard against it to test its strength. It creaked and swayed slightly against the ropes that were holding it in place, but he thought it would hold.

"Trey, for crying out loud, we don't have time for you to start exploring. Let's go."

Trey ignored him and stepped out onto the wooden bridge. He moved across the short distance, stooping down as low as he could to peer into the cell. Because by now it was clear to him that that was what it was. Heavy bars made of some black metal were set into the floor and roof of the small opening. There was no obvious means of entry, and Trey had the horrible suspicion that anything that might be unfortunate enough to be confined within the tiny, dark space behind those bars must have been placed there first, with the bars put in place afterward, sealing them in forever.

He looked into the gloom. The stench coming from the cell was brutal and Trey retched as the contents of his stomach made another bid for freedom. And then something moved in the darkness. The thing shifted itself around within the tiny confines and crawled toward him, pulling itself along on its belly to approach the tiny opening.

Trey was not sure what the creature had once been. It

was impossible to tell if it had been human, demon, or animal when it had been placed in its cell, but he was sure of one thing: It appeared to be close to death.

"Did the angel send you?" it said in a voice that even Trey's ears struggled to make out. "Did she send you?"

Trey knelt down and pulled at the metal bars, hoping to wrench them free so that he could help this poor pathetic creature.

"It's no good," the thing said. "Only she can free us. Only she can save us." The wretch looked up over Trey's shoulder, high up into the shadows at the top of the cavernous room.

How long has this poor creature been confined in there? Trey wondered. And what could he do to try to free it from its appalling prison?

As if reading his thoughts, the creature shuffled an inch or two closer and fixed Trey with its rheumy eyes. "Only the angel can save us now," it repeated, and cut its eyes up toward the ceiling again.

Trey immediately knew what the thing behind the bars was looking at. He turned his head and followed the gaze of the creature trapped behind the bars. He should have listened to his gut a bit more. He had somehow known the importance of that man-shaped thing suspended up there in the gloom—that nagging itch that had started inside him as he peered at it should have told him that he couldn't simply ignore it. And now he thought he knew how to scratch the itch.

247

Trey looked through the bars at the imploring face of the wretched creature. He nodded his head in its direction in a gesture he hoped it would understand.

"I'm going to get you help."

He stepped back across the small bridge and looked up at Charles, who had continued to climb the staircase ahead of him.

The young mage was staring back at him, shaking his head in annoyance. "What is it?" he asked.

"Wait here," Trey said. *"There's something I have to do."*

"Trey, stop!"

"Wait there."

Trey had gone. Charles watched as the werewolf leaped effortlessly and silently down the steps that they had ascended together, disappearing into the darkness.

Trey crept up to the building that they had seen upon first entering this place. He moved without noise, his powerful limbs propelling him swiftly and silently through the darkness. He tuned in to everything around him, his wolf senses taking in every scent and sight and sound. He felt invigorated again in the same way that he had when he first transformed into his werewolf self out in the Icelandic countryside. Then he had wanted to hunt rabbits; now he was preparing for something that he sensed was much more dangerous. He hugged the shadows of the building's walls, invisible among them.

He moved toward one of the windows, listening. As he

248

suspected, there were creatures inside. They were moving around, and from the sound of things, preparing to leave their post, perhaps to reinforce those nether-creatures already outside with Gwendolin. Trey knew that he did not have much time. He looked about him, catching sight of a huge metal structure against the far wall that looked for all the world like a shark cage that he'd once seen on television. He loped over to it and tested its weight. It was extremely heavy, and even with his supernatural strength it was an effort to move the thing without making any noise. He heaved it off the ground and staggered back over to the guard house, placing it as best he could in front of the door to the structure.

He crept around the back of the building and approached the base of what he had thought was a flagpole but now knew to be a gallows, letting out a small sigh of relief as he saw the chain secured to a cleat that was set into the wood. The remainder of the chain was piled into a heap at the base of the pole. He had had a vague idea that there might be no mechanism to lower the thing to the floor, which would have left him completely impotent—wolves are good at many things, but climbing isn't one of them.

He carefully unhitched the coils of chain, bracing himself for the sudden increase in weight as he unsecured the last few turns. As soon as he had the full weight of the thing in his hands he paused, listening carefully for any sign that he had been discovered. Looking up at the series of pulleys that secured the chain he very slowly began to feed a small length of chain upward, wincing at the sounds that the metal links made as they passed through the pulley wheels. He stopped again, listening. He continued like this for the next few minutes and then emboldened by his progress began letting out longer and longer lengths of chain, feeding them slowly through his hands until eventually the thing at the other end began to swing into view.

The gibbet was grotesque. Unlike those that Trey and Charles had seen hanging from the walls in the courtyard, which were little more than circular cages, this one appeared to be custom-made. It was constructed entirely out of lengths of black metal that had been bent and shaped to form a giant, human-shaped enclosure, complete with arms and legs that were angled slightly away from the body so that the whole thing reminded Trey of the stick figures that he had drawn and suspended beneath the rope during games of Hangman as a small child. As big as the cage was—he thought that it must be at least as tall as he was in his werewolf form—the thing inside was simply too large for it. It was pressed tight up against the cage; the rough metal bars that made up the contraption were deliberately cut with spiteful, jagged edges that were bent backward toward the prisoner to bite deeply into the flesh.

The gibbet swung slowly around and turned to face him. Now that it was nearer, Trey could see the face of the thing trapped behind those tortuous metal straps. It was female. A huge Amazonian creature that was easily the same size and build as he was himself. She was gagged—great strips of leather had been bound around her head to cover her mouth, but her eyes looked down on him now, and despite the excruciating pain that she must have been experiencing, the ice blue globes that sought out his face appeared to be smiling.

She was no more than twenty feet off the ground when he ran out of chain. He looked down at the little that was left. There was enough to tie it off onto the cleat, but the gibbet was still too high up off the ground for him to reach it. He looked up at the imprisoned creature again, not knowing what to do.

"You'll have to let her drop," Charles said from behind him.

Trey jumped at the unexpected sound, swinging around to see Charles standing no more than five feet away from him, staring up the gibbet.

The sorcerer looked back at the werewolf, a strange expression on his face. "We have to get her out," he said, "and we can't do that if she's dangling above us like some Mexican piñata. Let her drop, Trey."

"Look at all that metal that is already embedded into her, Charles. If I let her drop, it could kill her."

Charles stared up at the thing suspended overhead, and when he turned back to Trey the werewolf realized what the expression on his face was—it was fear.

"If that is what I think it is, Trey, you won't kill her. Let her drop. Just let me get a bit nearer so that we can get that thing open as quickly as possible because I'm guessing that it is going to make one hell of a noise, and when it does all hell is going to break loose here."

Trey watched Charles walk out and stand just to one side of where he expected the hanging cage to land. He looked down at the final length of chain in his hands, took a deep breath, and let go.

37

The boat cut through the calm waters, churning a V-shaped wake behind it that spread out slowly before disappearing back down again into the vast body of the Indian Ocean.

Martin sat alone at the front of the boat, looking forward into the late-setting sun that was clutching at the horizon, determined to shed a few more rays into the world before the night took it over completely. The drone of the engine was strangely hypnotic, and this, coupled with the rocking motion of the boat, somehow managed to assuage the rising panic that he had allowed to build up inside him throughout the day. He was still convinced that Philippa was going to try to kill him, but an inner calm had somehow developed within him in the last hour or so and he was determined to use this trip to try to understand the rage that had somehow spored and grown inside his daughter.

Or maybe it wasn't her at all. Maybe his hunch—that something to do with his work was responsible for all this, a spell or some other magic—was correct. He almost hoped this to be the case, because if not it meant that he had failed as a father. It meant that she was so angry at the world, and him in particular, that she thought that violence was the only way she could resolve it. He thought of the recent cases he had read about in the US where teenagers, unhappy with the world, had gone on terrible killing sprees. He recalled how all these tragedies had ended in the perpetrators taking their own lives, and he winced—he would not lose his daughter. He would tell her that he knew she planned to kill him and he would find a way to stop her and keep both of them safe.

It still came as a terrible surprise when he heard his daughter ask the pilot of the boat to stop the engine. They were only about ten minutes into the boat journey and he could see the island of Curieuse—their supposed destination—up ahead in the distance, looming darkly out of the water. Another boat, much larger than the one they were in, was anchored in the ocean about four hundred meters away, and when Martin turned to look at his daughter it was this that she was eyeing suspiciously.

Becoming aware of his scrutiny, she turned her face to his and looked at him with an expression that was impossible to read.

"Why have we stopped?" Martin asked.

Philippa ignored him, looked over at the larger boat again, and studied it for a moment or two. There was nobody on board and all the lights were out, suggesting that the crew had anchored for the night and taken a smaller boat over to the island in the distance.

"I said, why have we stopped?" Martin asked again, his voice cracking a little.

Philippa glanced at him before switching her attention

to a large fishing gaff that was lying on the deck near her feet. She picked up the tool, which was about a foot long, and studied the great curved hook at the end of the aluminum pole, bringing it close to her face and turning it around slowly before her. She hefted the device in her hand, feeling its weight.

Martin's heart hammered away inside him and he rose slowly to his feet, holding out his hands in front of him. "Philippa, put that down. Do you hear me? Put that thing down at once!"

Philippa smiled at him. Then she swiveled swiftly on her heel, swinging the pole through the air in a wide arc that ended at the head of their Seychellois captain. The pole caught him a painful blow and he cried out in surprise at the unexpected attack, looking up at the girl in front of him in wide-eyed terror. Philippa pulled hard on the handle of the pole, dragging the huge hook at the end of the implement into the skipper. She watched, her head cocked slightly to one side, as the man stood up in the back of the gently rocking boat, his hands flying up to grasp at the metal hook, his fingers attempting to gain some purchase on the now-slippery metal. His mouth dropped open and he emitted a long, rasping hiss as a stream of blood poured down his chin.

Martin could only watch in mute horror as his daughter leaned her weight to one side, and putting all her strength into the gaff, heaved the man over the side of the craft and into the dark waters below.

"Oh my God!" said Martin in a voice that he hardly recognized as his own. "You've killed him. You killed that poor man."

Philippa turned to face him, frowning slightly as if surprised to see him there. She looked back over her shoulder as if to check that the man had not somehow survived the horrific attack and come bobbing to the surface, but he had sunk down into the dark waters without a trace. Very slowly, she turned back to Martin with a look that sent a zigzag of icy fear coursing down his spine.

She stepped toward him, a malevolent smile creeping over her lips as she watched him back away from her with his hands still held in front of him in a supplicating gesture.

"Please . . . ," he said. "Please, Philippa, we need to talk. We need to help you. You know that, don't you? You know that you need help?"

The laugh that came from his daughter was like no human sound that he had ever heard in his life, like a saw being dragged over knotted wood. And the voice that accompanied it was cold and dark and other. It was a voice that should never have come from his daughter's mouth.

"Kill you?" the creature that inhabited Philippa's body said. "And why would I want to do that, Martin? I need you alive. Oh, yes, very much alive."

Martin stepped back again until the backs of his legs banged up against the heavy picnic hamper that he had placed in the front of the boat with him. He considered leaping over the side of the boat, but images of her running him down in the craft, the propellers ripping through his flesh as she drove the vehicle over his half-submerged body, formed in his mind's eye.

She approached him again. She no longer had the fishing gaff, but he doubted whether she needed it. She looked capable of killing him with her bare hands. She stopped no more than three feet away from him. Martin stiffened, expecting an attack. Instead, his daughter's body slumped as if all of the muscles had suddenly lost their strength, and she swayed on the spot before him like some drunken cobra that has been forced from a snake charmer's basket. Her face was slack, the eyes staring through him, blank pools of nothingness. She opened her mouth and uttered a strangled gasp that petered out into a long, ragged breath. A death rattle.

Her body jerked suddenly, the lifeless arms that had been hanging at her sides jerking involuntarily, making Martin jump with fright at the anticipated attack he was still sure was coming.

Still staring blankly at him, she opened her mouth wider still, stretching and elongating the oval farther and farther, and he was suddenly reminded of the silent screaming figure in the Edvard Munch painting, staring out into the world with the same cold, dead eyes. She coughed and gagged.

And then the Necrotroph's face appeared at the back of her mouth.

It squirmed and writhed out of her throat, its contorted features twisted into a mask of effort as it struggled to free itself. Martin watched in horror as the thing struggled and

257

rolled violently, forcing its way out until suddenly a long length of it sprang forth—a twisted face at the end of a glistening, wormlike body that snaked out of his daughter's mouth and writhed in the air in front of him. Tiny hands with no arms waggled in the air from the sides of the torso, and below these a ring of smooth, slender tentacles that ended in what appeared to be hooks swayed and danced in the air.

Martin's head shook from side to side, his body denying the terrible scene before him as he stared at the thing emerging from his child. The black eyes were fixed upon him now and he had the sensation that the *thing* was grinning at him. He opened his own mouth to scream, and in doing so Martin Tipsbury sealed his doom.

The creature suddenly shot forward across the small distance that separated them, its head burrowing into his mouth. He could feel the small hands grasp on to the edges of his lips, pinching and grabbing at them as the demon struggled to force its way deeper inside the open cavity. The last of the demon's body slithered free of his daughter's mouth and she crumpled to the floor, the unblinking eyes still staring up at him.

My God, Martin thought as he looked down at her. *Is she dead? Please don't say that she is dead!*

He took an automatic step backward and tripped over the hamper, falling onto the deck. He tried to grab hold of the *thing* and yank it free. Clamping his hands around one of the body segments, he gripped the tubular body as tightly

258

as he could and pulled. He had to get this thing out of him so that he could help Philippa.

One of the tentacles waggled in the air for a second before reaching out and delicately touching the back of his hand. Martin felt a huge bolt of pain, like an electric shock, and he would have screamed if the demon's head had not been firmly wedged in his esophagus. His hands flew open and he felt the demon burrow inside his throat another inch or two. The edges of his vision were beginning to gray out and he had the familiar buzzy-headed feeling that he got as a child when he held his breath for too long at the deep end of the swimming pool. The tiny hands had got a good purchase on his rear molars now, and Martin clamped his eyes shut as he felt the demon, with a huge effort, pull itself deep inside him, slipping down his gullet and descending into his alimentary canal.

He took a huge staccato breath that came back out in a gush and he lay on his back, trembling all over, staring up at the stars. He tried to get to his feet, but doubled up in pain as something twisted deep inside him. A low groan escaped him as a series of small electric shocks fired off inside his body, followed by a hideous cutting sensation that caused him to scream into the night air, tears springing to his eyes and cascading down his cheeks.

He thought that the pain would kill him; his legs thrashed wildly and he writhed in agony on the deck of the boat. Then as suddenly as it had begun, the pain vanished, replaced with a strange feeling of calm that rolled over him like a warm blanket, somehow letting him know that everything was going to be all right.

He staggered to his feet, staring about him wildly until his eyes settled on the body of his daughter. He frowned down at the carcass and a great wave of sadness welled up inside him. The demon inside him tried to quash these thoughts but the depths of emotion were too great, and Martin knelt down to take his daughter's body in his arms.

Something inside him was telling him to pick Philippa's dead body up and throw it overboard. A lance of pain stabbed through him again, making him gasp, and he stood up, straining to get to his feet while holding her in his arms. He looked down into her face, tears welling up in his eyes.

And then she took a breath.

Martin gasped and sank to his knees, fighting the commands that the demon was sending him and ignoring the electric bolts of pain that coursed through him. He laid her down on the deck, hovering over her. She opened her eyes a little and looked up at him. "I love you, Dad," she said.

He was about to reply when the pain took him over completely. His smile faded, replaced by a grimace. He fell backward onto the deck and let the pain take over.

When he climbed to his feet again he had forgotten that Philippa was there. He stared about him and took in his surroundings, shaking his head and trying to remember something that he was sure was of great importance to him. A small uncomfortable pain shot through his spine, like an electric shock, and he quickly forgot everything once more.

He knew that he had to get back to the villa as quickly as possible. He needed to contact his master and tell him what the humans were planning and . . .

Who the hell was his master?

Another bolt of lightning went off inside him and he shivered, shaking out these strange thoughts. He crossed to the rear of the boat and bent forward to grab the pull cord that started the motor. Resting one hand on the engine housing, he pulled sharply on the handle, smiling as the machinery coughed into life. A feeling of elation ran through every part of him, and he sat down, taking hold of the tiller arm. He was about to twist the accelerator handle when his eyes fell on his daughter's body again, her chest rising and falling rhythmically now. Then he looked over at the picnic hamper still lying on the deck at the front of the boat. He let go of the tiller, stood up, and walked toward it, grimacing in pain at the series of shocks that went off up and down his spine and inside his head. He bent forward and picked the case up, staring down at the black leather straps and buckles that held it closed.

She wasn't going to kill me, he thought. *She might not have loved me as I wanted her to, but she would never have killed me. It was that thing. That thing that was inside her!* And now it was inside him, she would never be safe.

Agony exploded inside him. He gasped and staggered forward, almost losing his grip on the hamper.

The tiny part of him that was still Martin Tipsbury forced his body to straighten up. With a greater effort of will than he had ever shown before in his life, he forced his legs to work and walked toward the edge of the boat. Artillery shells of pain exploded within his body, and his brain was screaming at him to stop, but he somehow ignored the thing inside him, and clinging to the last vestiges of his humanity, he forced his body to obey his will. Placing his foot up onto the gunwale of the boat, he expelled a huge breath from his lungs, clutched the heavy hamper to his chest, and leaped over the side of the boat into the black waters below.

The Necrotroph had underestimated him. It had thought of him as weak and malleable and because of that it had not taken the time to get everything right before it had started to control him. It had rushed, trying to get back to the house to contact its master. And it had underestimated the bond between the man and his child. Now it was trapped inside this human body, plummeting toward the sea floor with no other being around that it could transfer to.

The demon raged inside Martin. It tried to take control and force the stupid creature to let go of the box and kick back up toward the surface, but the more it tried to impose its own will the more the human battled it, determined to end both of their lives. It felt the crushing pressure of the water pressing in on it from all sides and then suddenly the seabed rushed up to meet the human's feet.

The Necrotroph knew that they were a long way down beneath the surface. Panicking now, it shrank back, hiding deep inside the human, hoping that the host too would suddenly become flooded with fear at the situation it was in and try to save itself. The Necrotroph was fairly certain that it could assist its human host in getting back to the surface but it knew that it was counterproductive for it to force the situation right now. For the first time in its very long existence it felt a shiver of fear and contemplated its death at the hands of this foolish, insignificant, and inferior being. It hid away and tuned in to the thoughts of the human, hoping against hope that it would choose life over this end.

Martin felt the release inside him as the demon retreated back away from his consciousness. He opened his eyes and looked at the blackness around him. He thought about his life and the good things that he had enjoyed in it and all of the things that he still wanted to do and see. He thought of Philippa and of the happier times that they had spent together. He thought of her as a baby and how his world had been complete somehow when she had been born. In his head he told her that he loved her. Then he opened his mouth and took in a huge lungful of salt water, flooding his lungs and consigning himself to death.

The demon screamed out from inside the human as it felt its host begin to slip away. It took control of every part of the human and this time there was no resistance. But it was too late—the host was too far gone. The creature screamed again as it realized that it would be trapped inside this body-coffin for its last few moments in this realm, until it too died.

For Martin Tipsbury, it was the only brave thing that he

had ever done in his life, and as the black hands of death began to pull him into their final embrace he could feel the demon inside him squirming in its own death throes.

Martin Tipsbury died with a look of grim satisfaction on his face.

38

Tom fired two of the grenades in quick succession into the tight knot of demons below them. He had spoken to an acquaintance about the thermobaric explosives before leaving for Iceland, trying to ascertain if they would be the right tool for the job. His friend had described the incredible explosive power of this relatively new weapon and assured Tom that if he needed to kill large numbers of enemies within a relatively small area, there really was nothing better.

The grenade launcher spat the small bombs down into the knot of nether-creatures with an almost-apologetic coughing sound that did nothing to prepare Tom and Alexa for the scale of the destruction that was to ensue.

The grenades detonated upon impact and the resulting cloud of fire spread out in a vast, ground-hugging mushroom of flame that obliterated everything within its deadly reach. The demons and the Draugr were first engulfed in a superhot cloud of fire before the pressure wave slammed into their bodies, tearing them apart and sending the pieces into the air like strips of sodden rag. It was all over in an instant.

As the smoke cleared, Tom and Alexa looked down at the carnage below.

"Well, that went better than I expected," Tom said in a small voice.

"Come on," Alexa said, getting to her feet and moving down the hill toward the scene of destruction.

"Where do you think you're going?" Tom shouted after her.

"I want to check something," she said, and set off down the slope.

Tom climbed to his feet and started after her. The hill was steeper on this side and he almost slipped twice, nearly pitching headfirst down the grassy bank that Alexa was tackling with the grace and sure-footedness of a mountain goat.

"Alexa, stop," he called after her. "This is not what we're supposed to be doing. We are meant to stay in position to provide covering fire for the lads when they come out." He glanced toward the opening off to his right, hoping that Trey and Charles did not choose this particular moment to come running out, hotly pursued by Caliban and his demon guards.

Alexa had come to a stop at one side of the great area of burned land that marked the killing circle of the grenades. She looked down at the ground, frowning. She stood like this, unmoving, until Tom finally caught up with her.

"Come on, Alexa," he said, taking hold of her arm and trying to steer her back in the direction of the hill.

"Look," she said.

Tom looked down at the area that she was staring at. "What?" he asked.

266

"She's not here."

Tom looked again at the area in front of him. A huge swathe of rocks and stones had been scattered across a large area that radiated outward from the epicenter of the explosion. Most were blackened and had been broken up into much smaller pieces by the force of the blast.

"But she turned into that *thing*, Alexa. She was turned into stone. And from what I see here, that stone has been blown to bejabers like everything else down here."

"No. I saw her leave, Tom."

"Alexa, you can't possibly tell me—"

"I know what I saw, Tom. My eyes never left her the whole time, and just as you fired, the Elemental looked up in our direction. It knew. And just as those bombs of yours were released I saw these rocks simply collapse in on themselves. She'd already gone before the explosions went off, Tom."

Tom looked over again at the opening in the black tower behind them. As he watched, he could see what appeared to be movement in the darkness behind it. At first he thought that it might be nothing but a trick of the light, but as he watched, it happened again—the blackness of the opening seemed to shift and expand as if it was stretching outward. He took hold of Alexa's arm and she turned to see what it was that he was staring at. Suddenly a vast living cloud of bats burst free into the night sky. Thousands of the creatures poured out of the gap, a torrent of darkness that wheeled in an arc just outside the opening, gained height, and turned to swoop straight down toward them.

Tom stared up at the vast black colony. "What the hell are—"

"Run!" Alexa shouted, and propelled Tom ahead of her, checking back over her shoulder to see how close the creatures were. "The car, Tom! Get into the car or we're dead!"

They ran over to the car that Gwendolin and the Maug had abandoned earlier. It had been much farther up the road than the truck, and while it hadn't entirely escaped the shrapnel of rocks and stones that the explosion had thrown up, it was still in one piece. They jumped in through the open doors at the rear of the vehicle and slammed them shut just in time to avoid the first wave of the creatures. As they looked out, the entire colony of bats swooped and veered around outside the car. The bats attacked the glass windows, throwing themselves full tilt at the transparent panes. Their bodies made a satisfying *thonking* sound as they crashed into the toughened glass before sliding to the ground. Some would catch the car body at a slight angle and veer off helter-skelter, crashing to the ground. But they were relentless in their attack. The sheer number of the creatures throwing themselves at the vehicle created a huge din inside, a hailstorm of tiny bodies hell-bent on destroying the human occupants. Some shuffled their way up the hood, using their wings like leathery oars to propel themselves forward, and now their ugly, vicious faces were pressed up against the front windshield, tiny rows of white teeth revealed in hungry mouths that were set in front of black pinprick eyes.

"What are those bloody things?" Tom said, unable to take his eyes from the windows.

"Skaleb's Brood," Alexa replied. "The demon lord kept them as pets and would release them in the first wave of attack during a battle."

"Vampire bats?"

"No, Tom, if only they were. I suppose the closest comparison I can think of in the human plane would be something like piranha fish or army ants. These things can strip a body of flesh in minutes. They hunt in vast colonies, hundreds of thousands of them swarming together to wreak devastation on anything that is unlucky enough to come into their path."

"What are they doing here?"

"Well, the Tower of Leroth belonged to Skaleb; I guess that the original colony stayed on after their master disappeared. Caliban probably allows them to stay in the tower as another means of defense. Either that or he can't get rid of them. Who knows?"

"Great," said Tom, looking out of the rear window toward the tower. "And how are we going to get Trey and Charles safely away from here with this little lot wheeling around out here? If they come out now, the boys'll be dead before we can do a thing."

Alexa climbed over into the driver's seat. There were no keys. Tom watched as she closed her eyes and placed the palm of her hand over the ignition, her lips mouthing words he was unable to hear. Seconds later, the engine burst into life. She turned to him and gave him a little nod. Switching her attention back to the front windshield, she flicked the wipers on for a moment, throwing leathery-winged creatures off on either side of the car.

"Hold on to your hat, Tom," she told him as she put the car in gear. "We're going to lead them away from here. We have to get them far enough from the entrance so that they're not a danger to Trey and Charles when they come out."

"And then what?"

"I don't know. I haven't thought that far ahead yet." She pressed the accelerator down hard, making the car leap out into the darkness of the Icelandic night.

39

The cage hit the ground with an enormous crash, toppling over onto its front so that the creature inside was facedown in the thick dust on the floor. Charles immediately dropped to his knees beside it and placed his hands over the two locks that held the thing secured on one side.

Trey could hear the occupants of the guardhouse now. The surprised shouts had quickly turned to shrieks of anger as they found their exit blocked by some immovable object barring the door. Orders were shouted out and he could hear them begin to attack the wood with their weapons. He turned to look at Charles again.

"Quickly, Charles. We're in deep trouble here."

The sorcerer answered with a sharp nod of the head. Beads of perspiration were running freely down his face, which was a mask of concentration. A second later there was a metallic crack and Charles opened his eyes, glancing up at Trey with a look of jubilation. "It's open," he said.

Trey scrambled over and helped Charles lift his side of the gibbet, heaving it open against the hinges on one side of the grotesque exoskeleton and letting it crash back down to the ground. There was little point in trying to be quiet any longer—the guards were already smashing at the wooden door with their weapons and soon they would break free of the obstruction that Trey had placed over the entrance. The creature inside slowly began to raise itself onto its knees, and Trey noticed for the first time that its entire back seemed to consist of feathers. Huge black feathers were plastered against its back and a number of them fluttered to the ground as the creature began to straighten its considerable frame. Trey looked at Charles, who simply shrugged his shoulders and continued to stare up at the thing in front of them.

The creature had risen to its full height now. Its back was still to them and it slowly twisted its head from side to side as if trying to remove some uncomfortable knots from the muscles of its neck. It reached up and unwrapped the lengths of leather from its head. When it turned around to look at Trey, he gasped (although what came out sounded more like a short bark). She was beautiful. And terrifying. She stood about seven feet tall and was dressed in black leather armor that appeared to be scored and marked from numerous battles. Her eyes were a cold gray-blue—the color of the sea just before a storm—and when Trey looked into them he felt the shadow of death fall over him for an instant. It was impossible to maintain contact with her stare. She smiled at Trey, revealing teeth that were sharp and pointed, as if they had been filed to make them so. A huge scar corkscrewed its way from the center of her forehead across the bridge of her nose and down through both lips before finishing at her chin. Yet despite the teeth and the ruinous scar Trey thought that she was the most beautiful creature that he had ever laid eyes on.

272

She nodded her head toward them both in turn. "Thank you, Trey Laporte. Thank you, Charles Henstall," she said in voice that was both wonderful and appalling at the same time. It should have been a beautiful voice, but it seemed to Trey that it promised nothing but death and destruction to anyone who heard it.

"How do you know our—"

There was a sound of splintering wood and Trey looked around to see the metal cage that he had used to block the door falling away. It crashed to the floor with an almighty din and the guards burst free.

There were four of them, all demons. Three looked similar to the Shadow Demons that Trey had encountered before, two carrying short swords, the third an axe that Trey guessed had been used to break through the door. But the fourth demon was a creature that Trey had never seen. It had to stoop down low to get through the wrecked doorway and it lumbered after its companions. It was a huge, foul-looking thing with white skin hanging from its body in sagging folds. A great boarlike head sat atop hunched shoulders, and the greedy eyes that crested the vast snout were constantly on the move. Great tusks curved down from its upper jaw, giving it a saber-toothed look, and it carried a huge, heavy-looking crossbow in its arms. The guards had rushed out, but as soon as they caught sight of their erstwhile prisoner standing next to the werewolf and the human, they slowed to an almost-complete stop, approaching no more than inches at a time.

A sound began to come from all around the cavernous room. It started as just a whisper, the same word being chanted over and over. It seemed to be coming from the cells set into the outer walls.

"Moriel . . . Moriel . . . Moriel . . . Moriel . . ."

Trey looked around at the guards as they fanned out and began to creep forward. He reached his hand over to Charles, trying to push his friend behind him where he might be safer for a moment or so at least, but the sorcerer gently waved his friend's hand away, choosing to stay by the were-wolf's side.

"Moriel . . . Moriel . . . Moriel . . ." It had grown louder now, like a chant in a school playground when two children square up for a fight.

The angel looked at the guards with thinly disguised hatred before turning to Trey and Charles. "You two must leave now," she said. "You have important work to do here."

"I don't think *they* are going to simply let us walk past somehow," Charles said, nodding at the demons. "Besides, we can hardly leave you to face them alone."

The angel looked at the demons creeping slowly toward them, her scarred lips curling up in a look of pure contempt. "Why do you think that they advance so slowly? They know that they are already dead," she said.

Trey looked between the magnificent warrior angel, Moriel, and the demons and instinctively knew that she was right. The four nether-creatures looked petrified and he guessed that it was only a greater fear of their master, Caliban,

274

that kept them from turning around and running from the place.

Moriel took a slight step away from Trey and Charles and snapped her giant wings open behind her. Trey gasped again. She was magnificent. Her wings were huge and shimmered in what little illumination there was in that place—the lustrous black feathers seemed to suck up the light and reflect it back off the millions of tiny spines that they were made of. The sight of the angel unfurling her wings had stopped the demons in their tracks. She stepped forward again, leaned down, grabbed Trey and Charles around the waist, and leaped up into the air, beating those great wings like a colossal eagle taking off for its mountain aerie. She flew straight up into the darkness, higher and higher until Trey could make out the wooden ceiling above them. She banked slightly and, using her wings to slow down, alighted with them on a small landing at the top of the stone staircase.

There was a ladder leading up to a heavy wooden hatch set into the ceiling and she nodded her head toward this. "Through there you will find the remainder of the tower. Be careful as you ascend. Luckily a number of the guards are out with the sorceress now, but you must still take care. Avoid the vampire, whatever you do. You cannot hope to defeat him here in Leroth—no one can." She turned to look at Trey again, her eyes seeming to pierce through into his very soul. "Caliban has something of your father's that he took from him shortly before killing him. Once I have finished with the business in hand"—her eyes shifted for a second toward the dark void

275

below them—"I will try to retrieve it for you. It is yours, and the vampire has no right to have it."

Moriel, I—

There was a shout from below, followed by a smashing sound over their heads and all three of them were showered with tiny droplets of liquid. A crossbow bolt skittered over the landing, doing a neat little pirouette at their feet, before falling off the edge into the darkness. Instead of an arrowhead, it appeared that the bolt had been equipped with a glass vial of some toxic substance. Trey could feel the areas of his pelt where the liquid had touched him already beginning to burn.

The angel looked back down below her into the darkness. Her wings were smoking in a number of places. "Scum," she hissed. "Go now. Quickly, before they fire again. You will need to wash that acid off you as soon as you can. Go." She nodded her head at them, turned and leaped out into the fetid air, snapping her wings open and swooping down into the darkness in the direction of the demons.

Trey looked over at Charles, who was staring back at him with wide-eyed incredulity. There were little curls of the same smoke rising up from the young sorcerer, and he had large holes in his clothing where the acid had already burned through.

"Come on, Charles. We need to find something to wash this stuff off before it burns any deeper." He put his shoulder against the hatch above their heads and pushed upward, relieved when he felt it give under the pressure. The large

wooden door fell back with a crash and Trey pushed Charles through the opening ahead of him. He pulled himself through and slammed the hatch shut behind him, having taken one last look down for a final glimpse of Moriel.

The pain was exquisite and excruciating. Although they had both mercifully avoided most of it, the skin where the acid *had* burned through was already little black puddles of bubbling flesh. And the stuff was still burning, releasing a foul stink of charred skin and hair as it did so. It wasn't clear to either of them when, *or even if*, the acid would stop burning through the tissue, and they looked at each other with alarm.

Charles had attempted to wipe the acid away from a spot on his shoulder with his hand, and now his fingers were also coated and erupting in a series of angry-looking blisters. "We need some water!" he shouted, looking around the room in desperation.

They were in what appeared to be a large storage area. Shelves encircled the walls, and these were piled with all manner of objects and paraphernalia.

They both ran to and fro, batting at their burns with open palms, desperate to find something with which to douse their wounds.

A menagerie of stuffed animals was heaped up in one part of the room, their taxidermed faces staring out at Charles and Trey with lifeless glass eyes. Wooden boxes and crates were piled up in small islands here and there, and to Trey's left was a mass of wooden chairs and other furniture that he guessed were stored here in between banquets that Caliban might hold for his evil cohorts.

Charles ran over to the far side of the room. In front of a vast array of wine bottles laid down in racking against the wall lay two huge wooden barrels marked ALE.

Trey looked questioningly at Charles.

"It's all there is," Charles said with a shrug.

Trey's back was becoming excruciatingly painful as the acid burned through fur and skin to the flesh below. He grabbed one of the large barrels out of the rack and set it on its end, driving his fist down through the top. Bending forward, he lifted the barrel high over his and Charles's heads and rained the brown liquid down on the two of them, soaking their bodies in the strong-smelling liquid.

They sank to the floor, rolling in the last of the ale until the pain had almost disappeared. Charles turned to look at the sorry figure of Trey. His normally magnificent coat was plastered to his skin with the sticky beer. He looked like a bedraggled dog after a downpour. A laugh escaped from Charles. It was an alien sound in this environment, and Trey turned to look at his companion, a puzzled expression on his features.

"I have to say," said Charles, once he had managed to gain control of himself again, "I personally am not having the best of days so far." He looked down at his blackened fingers and grimaced at the pain that still nagged at the flesh.

Trey looked over at him. *"What was that thing? Was it really an angel?"*

278

Charles nodded. "She's a battle angel—an Arel. There are very few of them left. They were hunted down and destroyed after the Demon Wars. She was pretty impressive, huh? Would have been a bit of a looker too if somebody hadn't carved her up like that."

"She was amazing. Just about the most amazing thing that I've ever seen. How did she know our names, Charles? Nobody's supposed to know that we are here."

Charles shrugged. "I don't know. Just like I don't know why we both felt utterly compelled to get that thing down from the ceiling without knowing what it was or why we were doing it. I don't have all the answers, mate. And when it comes to Arel battle angels I don't even know the questions."

"An angel," Trey said with a shake of his head. *"When you think of angels you imagine them playing golden harps on white fluffy clouds. But she was . . . fearsome. Do you think she'll be OK? There were four of those demons down there, and she wasn't armed."*

"From what little I've read about the Arel, I think that she'd be fine if there were a *hundred* and four demons armed to the back teeth down there."

Trey nodded. Somehow he knew Charles was right. He stood up and shook himself, his thick fur sending a fine shower of beer flying off in all directions.

"Thanks for that," Charles said, wiping his eye. "Are you sure you don't want to cock your leg and pee on me while you're at it?"

The werewolf shrugged his massive shoulders. His own neck and back still felt painful and tender, but he had had the benefit of his fur to shield him from the worst of it and guessed that it must be much worse for the young mage. He held a hand down to Charles and lifted him back up onto his feet, noticing the wince of pain on his face. He reached out and lifted the barrel up off the floor again, holding it up with one arm and letting the dregs of the fluid dribble out. He moved Charles under the stream again, turning him around and patting at the areas of flesh that were most badly scorched.

When he was finished Charles looked up at him, nodding his thanks.

Trey moved off, looking for a way up into the next level of the tower. Spotting a staircase in one corner he started to move toward it, signaling for the young sorcerer to follow.

Charles ran after him, almost bumping into the werewolf, who had stopped suddenly, peering intently at something in a crate close to the stairway.

"What is it?" Charles said, moving over to stand beside Trey.

Inside the large wooden crate were hunting trophies; the heads of the creatures had been mounted onto black wooden plinths, their faces frozen forever in bloodthirsty snarls by the taxidermist. The heads were all from the same type of animal—giant wolf faces with lips drawn back to reveal ivory fangs and baleful eyes that glared back at the world.

Charles could feel the anger radiating from the werewolf standing beside him and he gingerly reached up to place a hand on Trey's shoulder. "Remember what we're here for, Trey. We need to get going." He waited a second and then moved to the foot of the stone staircase. "Come on," he said.

The werewolf took one last look at the contents of the crate before turning to join his friend.

The stairs wound around the walls of the tower's interior and they climbed them slowly, heedful of the angel's warnings, expecting an attack at any time from around the next bend. It seemed to be getting colder as they ascended, and this struck Trey as odd. Their breath hung in the air before them as they pushed on up into the heart of the tower.

The only light came in from tall, thin arrow-slits set into the walls at regular intervals and from these came a low moaning sound as the wind outside blew across them, setting the two interlopers on edge every time they approached one. The higher they climbed the more nervous the two of them became. Suddenly Charles stopped, holding his hand up and cocking his head. They stayed like that for what seemed like ages, listening out for a repeat of whatever it was that he thought he'd heard. Eventually the young sorcerer shook his head. "Must have been the wind," he said, and they carried on, creeping upward with all their senses dialed to maximum.

When they reached the top a great wooden door barred their way. Trey reached out to twist the heavy metal hoop that served as a doorknob, but Charles put a hand on his arm. "This has all been too easy. What if this is a trap? What if Caliban's waiting on the other side of that door?"

Trey looked at Charles's ruined face and the burn marks on his clothes and skin. *"If you think this has been easy, I'd hate to see what you think is a tough day at the office. We've got no choice,"* he said. *"We came here to get the globe, and the only way to do that is to go through this door."*

Charles sighed, his breath hanging in the air before slowly dissipating. "You're right," he said. "Onward and upward, eh?"

They pushed the door open and stepped through.

40

Alexa's driving was terrible. She'd only had six lessons, and in her haste to draw the bat colony away from the tower's entrance she was crashing through the gears in a way that made Tom think that, of the three of them, it was probably the car that was in more danger of being imminently killed than either himself or Alexa.

The bats had followed them though. They still attacked the windows and bodywork of the car as it drove along, and Tom was astonished that they had not given up their ineffectual attempts to break through.

After about a mile they stopped. They had come off the road and pulled into a small field, the vehicle's four-by-four capabilities making light work of the off-roading.

The bats still swarmed around the car, but the full-frontal assault seemed to have abated a little. They were circling the car now—a giant black moving hoop of creatures intent on killing.

"What next?" Tom asked.

Alexa stared out at the creatures and then glanced at her watch, calculating how long the boys had been inside Leroth. She turned to look at Tom, who was still sitting in the back of the car.

"What is it?" the Irishman said. "Come on, out with it. You've got an idea, I can see that, so let's hear it."

"I *have* got an idea, Tom, but it's a pretty rubbish one, I think."

"Well, Alexa, even a rubbish idea is a damned sight better than no idea at all, which is precisely what I have got right now. So come on, what is it?"

Alexa glanced outside again before continuing. "I think I have a spell that would wipe out all these creatures in one go. It can be cast over a wide area and anything that is moving within that area will be killed."

"Marvelous! Let's do it."

"There's a problem, Tom. Well, actually there are two problems."

"And they are?"

"Firstly I've never cast this spell properly before. I think I can do it, but it is going to take just about everything I have to make it work."

"Would you be putting yourself in any danger?" Tom asked, staring at her intently.

"No, Tom. As long as you and I keep *totally* still when it's being cast there isn't any immediate danger. It's just that this is a *big* spell. For someone like Charles it probably wouldn't be any great shakes, but I'm not Charles." She held up her hand to stop Tom from interrupting her. "But I do believe I can do it."

The Irishman nodded slowly. "Right. That's the first problem. What's the second?"

"We need to get out of the car for it to work."

Tom swore under his breath.

"It gets worse. I can start the incantation inside the car. I can get to a point where it will merely require me to climb out and utter the last few lines for it to work. But I will not be able to do that if I am under attack. I'm going to need you to get out before me and draw them away from the car. Then you'll have to stay completely still with those things attacking you until I can kill them all."

Tom looked out of the window. At that precise moment one of the tiny creatures threw itself at the glass, its evil little features pressed for a fraction of a second up against the surface before it fell back to the ground. Tom turned back to Alexa and puffed out his cheeks. "I'll take a borrow of that padded coat that you're wearing to put over my head. There's little I can do about my hands and legs." He nodded his head and tried to put on a brave face. "Let's do it."

Alexa rested the back of her skull against the front seat's headrest. She closed her eyes and began to chant the words of the spell. Tom had zipped his own jacket up around his neck and placed Alexa's over his shoulders so that he could pull it up over his head quickly. He took a deep breath and looked over at Alexa. They had agreed that when she raised her left hand he would open the door and make a run for it. His idea was to get about thirty feet away from the vehicle before dropping to his knees and balling up on the ground to protect as much of himself as he could.

The sounds of the spell were in a tongue that Tom thought

must have died out a long time ago because there was no single word that even vaguely resembled anything from his world. The interior of the car was getting incredibly hot. The heat seemed to be generated by Alexa as she intoned the words in a flat, harsh voice, and he would dearly have loved to undo the zip of his coat.

Alexa stopped. She took a huge breath and held it in her lungs. Her eyes were still closed and she sat perfectly still for a second before raising her left hand and flexing the tips of her fingers slightly.

Tom took a big breath of his own and yanked on the handle of the door. He jumped out of the car as quickly as he could, pulling his hands inside the sleeves of the coat as he did so. Tucking his chin down onto his chest, he sprinted as quickly as he could away from the car.

They were on him before he had even taken a couple of steps. The entire colony seemed to converge on the Irishman as he leaped from the car and tried to run through them. There were three of the creatures on his face already, one on his cheek, one with its teeth sunk into the bridge of his nose and another one that seemed, judging from the blood pouring into his right eye, to have already taken a bite from his eyebrow and now seemed to be working on its second helping.

After fifteen or so strides, Tom dropped to his knees. He ripped the three creatures off his face and covered as much of his head as he could with Alexa's jacket. His backside was horribly exposed, as were his legs and back, and it felt as if the entire colony of bats was now feasting on these areas.

The pain was incredible. He hurt in a thousand different places and he could do nothing at all to defend himself. He wanted to thrash out and remove the things from him but he knew he had to stay still—utterly still.

What was only nine or ten seconds seemed to last for an eternity.

Alexa stepped from the car no more than a second or so after Tom had leaped out. The colony ignored her—it was too intent on feasting on the running prey that had so foolishly offered itself up to them.

She turned to face the swarm, her eyes still closed and that same breath still held in her lungs, despite her thrashing heart's demands for fresh oxygen to feed her adrenaline-charged muscles.

"*Iglaron ashnaffen zogren Atall. Ishnok skim'zath orok MEHAN!*"

She opened her eyes, keeping utterly still, not even daring to breathe. For one horrible second she thought that the spell was not going to work as the bats swooped in on Tom's body, each tiny creature battling for a spot to feast on.

Then they were dust.

The bats simply burst into clouds of fine black dust that drifted slowly to the ground. Thousands of them had been wiped out in one go.

Alexa went to take a step to see how badly Tom was hurt,

but the world went black, and she collapsed into a heap beside the car.

After a moment or so Tom lifted his head. There was no sign of the bats. In fact, there was no sign of anything at all except for an irritating powder in the air that got into his nostrils and made him want to sneeze.

He slowly climbed to his feet, closing his eyes against the pain and discomfort that he was feeling. He was bleeding from a multitude of wounds.

A small shiver swept through him and he thanked his lucky stars that he was still alive.

He turned back to congratulate Alexa, when he saw her lying on the ground by the driver's door. He moved over to her, ignoring his own wounds. Kneeling at her side, he checked that she was still breathing and was relieved to find a weak but steady pulse at her neck. There were no lesions or bite marks on the young sorceress, and Tom guessed that she must have collapsed as a result of her exertions. He picked her up in his arms and gently maneuvered her into the back of the car, laying her out across the backseat.

Grimacing, he managed to get himself in the driver's seat and behind the wheel. He clenched his teeth, trying not to think about the sodden wet mess at his back as he pressed himself against the leather upholstery.

After a final glance at Alexa, Tom wiped the blood from his eye, put the car into gear, and turned the wheel to take them back in the direction of Leroth.

41

The first demon looked down incredulously as its innards spilled out of the huge gash that Trey had opened up in its abdomen. They snaked downward, a grisly pendulum of steaming blood and guts that pooled on the floor, where they were quickly joined by the rest of the body that had once housed them. Trey spun around to deal with the second demon, only to watch as it crumpled to the floor, collapsing like an empty sack, all life extinguished from it.

Trey looked at Charles and was met by a nonchalant shrug. "Weak heart?" he said. "Let's go, Trey."

They ran up the corridor, keeping close to each other now. Passing an open door to their left, they slowed down to look inside. The room had been the scene of death. There was blood, still wet and sticky, covering the stone floor, and all the furniture that had once inhabited the space had been smashed and wrecked, with pieces of it strewn about the place.

"I'm guessing this is where they reawakened the Draugr," Charles said, stepping into the room. The smell of death filled the space, and Trey looked around him, expecting one of the creatures to leap out at any moment.

The room was austere. What little furnishings had been

present had been pushed out to the edges of the room. The walls were covered with long, ancient-looking tapestries that made way at intervals for elaborate wall lights. Charles moved into the center of the room, the soles of his shoes becoming covered with the bloody mess there. He closed his eyes and stood perfectly still for a few seconds, swaying slightly. Eventually he turned to Trey with a small shake of his head. "It's not here. The globe *has* been here, but it is not in this room any longer."

They left the carnage behind and continued on up the passageway. Aware that they were nearing their prize, they moved at speed, forgoing the stealth and secrecy that they had adopted up until now.

Two doors were set into the wall, separated by no more than twenty feet or so. As they approached these, Charles put out an arm to slow Trey down, and the lycanthrope turned to look at him.

"What is it?"

"Caliban. He's near. I can feel him."

Trey looked up ahead into the gloomy corridor. A chill ran through him as he thought of the vampire, surrounded by his minions, lurking somewhere up ahead, waiting for them. He thought back to the apparent ease with which they had reached this point and how they had only encountered those two guards during their ascent up through the tower. His mind raced and he told himself that this was all part of Caliban's plan—to lure them in, lulling them into a false

290

sense of security before springing his trap and crushing them. But then he thought of Moriel, and he knew that there was no way the vampire would have allowed them to free the battle angel had he known that they were here. He forced himself to believe that somehow they had not been discovered, that their presence in this place was not known and that it was fear and paranoia that was now paralyzing them both, stopping them from doing the thing that they had come here for. He took a step forward.

"Which door, Charles?" he asked, looking over at his companion and then ahead into the murk.

Charles looked up at Trey and then nodded. He took a deep breath, his eyes rolling back, and when he looked at Trey again his face was awash with hesitation.

"Which one, Charles? Come on."

"The first one," the mage said with a nod.

"You're sure?"

"The first one," Charles repeated with greater certainty.

Trey moved forward, his huge frame hugging the wall, blending in with the shadows. Arriving at the door, he reached forward and grasped the heavy metal handle, pausing for a second to look around at Charles and offering him an encouraging nod. He opened the door and stepped inside.

Trey didn't know what he had expected, but the room that he had stepped into was not it. It was too *normal.* It was a large room dominated by a huge desk strewn with manuscripts and books. The walls were filled with books of every size, and those that could not find a place on the shelves were stacked up in great piles on the floor like huge leather-and-paper termite mounds. A glass jar, like those that he had handled in school biology classes, sat on the desk, and as he and Charles entered the room he could have sworn that the shriveled fetuslike thing suspended in the clear liquid had turned to look at them. It hung there now, in suspension, staring at them with blank, dead eyes.

They closed the door behind them. "It's in here," Charles said. "The globe is somewhere in this room."

They began to search. It was difficult because of the chaos and disorder all around, and not helped by the haphazard way in which they tackled the task, shoving papers and manuscripts to the floor and emptying drawers out on to any clear surface to sift through the contents.

Trey stopped, standing up straight and looking over at Charles who, sensing that his friend was trying to get his attention, turned to look back.

"How big is this thing?" Trey said. *"I'm looking for Mynor's Globe, and I have no idea what it is or what the hell it looks like."*

Charles smiled and continued to rummage through the desk drawers. "It's about the size of a tennis ball," he said. "It doesn't look like much—just a plain dark glass ball really."

Trey looked back at the desk that was now strewn with

the contents of the drawers that he had emptied onto it. He carefully lifted up a sheet of paper and pointed to what he had assumed was a paperweight.

"A bit like that, you mean?" Trey took a step back, half expecting the globe to emit some kind of magical alarm now that it had been discovered.

Charles straightened up and looked over to where Trey was pointing. The glass ball sat on a small black stand that itself rested on a round tarnished metal plate. A smile lighted up the mage's face. He moved around to stand next to Trey before reaching forward and picking up the prize that they had come for.

"You're a bloody marvel, Trey Laporte," he said, moving toward the door and steering the werewolf ahead of him. He put out a hand for the handle.

The air shimmered and coalesced in the room behind them.

There was a low sighing sound like poisonous air escaping from an ancient sealed sarcophagus, and Trey felt a sickening *pulling* feeling in his body. He turned to look behind him to locate the source of the sensation and flinched as the air suddenly became searingly hot, making him squint and turn his face away.

From nowhere, the hunched figure of the sorceress appeared. Her back was to them and her entire body was racked with convulsions that made her twitch and shake violently. Slowly, she managed to lift up her head and move toward the desk, looking for the one thing that could alleviate the agony that she was in.

Charles pushed the globe into Trey's hand, looking up into the huge wolf's eyes. *"Go,"* he said. *"Don't wait for me, and don't try to help. Just go. Now!"*

As if she had heard the silent words, the sorceress turned to face them.

Trey looked down into the inky black innards of the ball in his hand. Something swirled and moved in there, something that seemed almost alive, and he began to lift the thing closer to his face to—

"GO!" Charles shouted, bringing Trey back to his senses. The sorcerer pulled the door open and shoved as hard as he could against the great bulk of the werewolf, forcing him from the room before slamming the door shut.

Gwendolin let out a huge scream of rage as she sent the first fireball in his direction.

Charles was ready for the onslaught. He had waited all of his young life for a moment like this—a chance to face down an opponent as skilled as himself. The years he had spent studying his craft and honing his powers with his father had culminated in this moment. He was, he believed, ready for her. But as he fended off her first attack he could feel the raw power that radiated from her. He'd expected her to be exhausted, her energy spent after her labors that day. But he had underestimated just how powerful she had become during her time in the Netherworld, and the sheer force of dark, malignant magic that seemed to burn off her made him, if just for a second, wonder if he really was skilled enough to defeat her.

Gwendolin had straightened up as soon as she became aware of the two of them at the door—all thoughts of the agony that had engulfed her seconds before suddenly forgotten. She watched as the young mage (she could sense the magic in him and the strength of his powers now) pushed the globe into the werewolf's hand, and she suddenly knew who they were and what they were here for. She also knew that unless she could recover the globe she was done for, so she summoned up every drop of strength within her and attacked. But she had been too slow. The lycanthrope had been bundled out of the room by his companion before she could stop him. She would have to dispatch the human sorcerer as quickly as possible and then deal with the werewolf before he could get away.

Her face twisted into a foul-looking mask of fury and she sent a huge ball of fire at the young human standing barring the door. He didn't blink. He countered the spell, the room exploding in light so bright that it made them both turn their heads away for a second as the burning sphere detonated in the space between them. When she looked at him again he stared back at her with a show of insolence that she had not been subjected to in a very long time. He was skilled for one so young, and she smiled at the prospect of breaking him.

They stood that way—sizing each other up across the

room—before they both raised their hands at almost the same moment and the air between them became a thick soup of energy that danced and shimmered and boiled.

Even though she was impossibly tired, Gwendolin grinned across at her opponent. In the crackling and swirling magic that now filled the room, she knew everything that she needed to about him. His entire life was there woven in among it, all mapped out for her (as her life and powers were to him), so that she knew his strengths as well as his weaknesses. She felt him inwardly blanch at the knowledge that she had forsaken her humanity to become what she was now and she reveled in his dawning realization that, for all his training and dedication, he was not capable of defeating her. She would have looked forward to killing him in a slow and delicious way if it was not for the fact that she needed to stop the werewolf before he could get free of the fortress.

He was strong—perhaps the strongest mage that she had faced in a very long time—but his weakness was his own fear of the dark arts; he had been afraid that they would consume him if he delved too far into their secrets, and so he had left himself vulnerable—especially here in the Netherworld where the dark forces were at their strongest.

He was beginning to weaken, his belief in himself and his abilities ebbing away now, and she could sense his desperation at the realization that he was merely forestalling the inevitable. She closed her eyes and smiled to herself. Then she summoned up all her powers and felt his own strength buckle under as a result. Raising her arms, she lifted him high up into the air above her head. He struggled against the magic, but he was a beaten thing now. She slammed him down into the desk and laughed aloud as the wooden furniture exploded under the force of the impact—great shards of splintered wood flying in every direction. He tried to break the link between them; he was thinking quickly and she knew that he was trying to summon a fire strike of his own, but she was always ahead of him, reading his thoughts and countering everything he tried.

Her eyes rolled back into her head and she silently mouthed ancient words in a long-dead tongue. A pool of fire appeared in the center of the room—its black flames gobbling up the oxygen and making the skin on their bodies fizzle and char from its immense heat. She easily lifted him again, this time hanging him up over the burning hole and watching him squirm and struggle to break free from her.

He would die far too quickly for her liking.

She paused then—a delicious and evil thought filling her twisted mind. Once she had recovered Mynor's Globe from the werewolf, she would use it in conjunction with Skaleb's Staff to bring this miserable human being back to life. Then she could kill him again, *properly*, over and over again, until she eventually became bored with him. Only then would she behead him and have her trophy mounted on the metal stake that was set into the wall of the room for this very purpose. She watched with grim satisfaction as the young sorcerer became aware of her plan and his eyes flickered toward the spike protruding from the wall.

She knew that Caliban would demand the lycanthrope be handed over to him, but she would be willing to make this trade—she had no interest in the werewolf boy.

Pleased with her hideous plan, she began to lower Charles's body down into the fire.

42

The door flew open and Gwendolin barely caught sight of the blurred figure of the werewolf flying through the air toward her, clawed hands outstretched and the vast, open jaws hurtling straight for her throat.

She had never imagined for one second that he would return of his own volition. Nor could she have predicted the ferocity of the attack that the were-creature launched against her, or the speed with which it moved.

She felt the claws rip through the skin of her face and her hands flew up to the wounds. She momentarily forgot everything except for the pure and exquisite pain that exploded through her. The black flaming pit instantly disappeared as her control over the magic needed to sustain it slipped and vanished. Charles fell painfully to the floor, burned and bleeding badly.

The wolf's mouth was upon her now and would have destroyed her had she not somehow managed to get one of her arms down in time to avoid the creature tearing her throat out. Instead the beast bit through the flesh of her forearm, sinking its teeth through muscle and sinew and tendon, deep into the bone below. She screamed at the pain of it, crying out for her master, Caliban, to save her. Knowing that she would die if she did not do something, she delved deep inside herself, summoning up every last drop of strength and energy that she could muster. Her eyes rolled back in her head again, and she *pushed* the giant lycanthrope away from her, the werewolf lifting up off its feet and slamming into the book-lined wall opposite.

Trey looked up in time to see the ruined desk rise up off the ground as if lifted by some huge invisible being. It flew across the room at him. Pieces of the broken furniture smashed into him. He raised his arms, attempting to fend off as much as possible, but a broken splinter of wood, the size of a chair leg, speared his side, causing him to howl in pain. He felt the blood spew from the wound.

But the desk had merely been a diversion, a means of distracting his attention.

Trey looked up to see that the sorceress had transformed into a hideous beast. The demon was almost the same height and build as he was and appeared to be hewn out of pure muscle. Sharp horns of bone grew through the thick red hide that covered its body, to go with the larger curved and twisted horns that grew from the sides of its head. The demon leered at Trey, its pupils tiny pinpricks of black inside the yellow orbs. It moved toward him, peeling its lips back to reveal a black tongue that flickered across teeth designed to rip and tear.

They met in the middle of the room. Trey lunged at the demon's throat, but his opponent rocked back, driving its knee into Trey's thigh, where a huge horn growing from the

300

kneecap ripped a gaping hole. The demon smashed a fist into Trey's face, spiked knuckles inflicting terrible damage and sending a shower of crimson into the air. Another fist followed the first, but Trey turned his head and sank his teeth into the creature's wrist. A loud hiss came from the demon and its eyes rolled in pain. They broke apart for a second, slowly circling each other and looking for an opportunity to attack.

Suddenly the demon charged. It flew across the space separating them, its head lowered, hoping to impale the lycanthrope on those cruel horns. But Trey was quicker. Hours of training with Flaug and the other demons had honed his reflexes and he saw his opportunity. He grabbed one of the nether-creature's horns, forcing the head lower and putting the demon off balance, twisting his own body at the same time to avoid the impaling weapon. With his other hand he reached toward the demon's spine, where more of the curved spikes grew. Grabbing one, Trey hauled the creature up into the air, using all of his strength until he had it suspended high over his head. The demon screamed, flailing its arms and legs in an attempt to make contact with the werewolf below.

Trey took a deep breath, ignoring the agony in his leg and side, concentrating on keeping his balance.

The demon screamed out, still thrashing around wildly and trying everything it could to break free.

"I know what you tried to do to Alexa, Gwendolin." Trey transmitted the words into the sorceress-demon's mind before throwing it at the wall.

It sailed backward through the air before coming to an abrupt halt with the great metal spike protruding from its torso. The demon changed as Trey looked on, morphing back into the figure of the sorceress, whose eyes gawked down at the rusted metal skewer that she was impaled upon, her fingers fluttering along it as if she could not believe what her eyes were telling her. Gwendolin lifted her head to take one last look at the werewolf. It stared back at her mercilessly . . .

And watched the sorceress die.

Trey rushed across the room and knelt down by his friend's side. Charles was still alive, but only barely. He carefully lifted his unconscious friend and draped the limp body over his shoulder as gently as possible so that he might carry him in a fireman's lift and still have both his hands free. He felt his own side with his hand, looking at the blood there. His wounds were hurting more than ever now and he took a deep breath, trying to push the pain away, ignore it. Cocking an ear to check that Charles was still breathing, the werewolf turned and left, grabbing the small glass globe that he had left on the threshold of the room as he went.

Trey didn't look back. He ran as quickly as he could down the stairs and through the doors that they had used earlier, ignoring any thoughts of making his escape through guile and stealth. His breath sounded ragged in his own head, and at every turn he expected to run headlong into a troop of guards dispatched to find and kill them. He could hear

302

from the shallowness of his breathing that Charles was in a very bad way, and he was adamant that they would escape as quickly as possible, and that his friend would not be allowed to die in this place.

It wasn't until he got to the hatch in the floor that led down to the dungeons that he paused. He didn't want to go down into the darkness again. He didn't want to have to see what might have become of Moriel at the hands of the demons. He stood there, his cargo draped across him, and listened to the sound of his own heart as it thumped against his chest, staring down at the trapdoor and willing himself to move forward again.

At that moment a scream of rage seemed to emanate from the very walls of the fortress itself—Caliban had found the dead body of his sorceress.

The sound was enough to galvanize Trey into action again. He pulled the hatch in the floor open, letting it crash down against the floor on the other side. Forgoing the ladder, he jumped down onto the landing below, bending as he landed to soften the impact for Charles as much as possible. He took the stairs three at a time, leaping down into the darkness. As he descended he glanced about. The cells were all empty; the bars that had sealed in the prisoners had been torn free of the walls and it was clear to Trey, even at the speed he was going, that the tiny tombs no longer contained the poor souls that had been so cruelly imprisoned within them.

When he came to the bottom of the stairs he slowed to take in the devastation all around him. There were body parts scattered everywhere. The floor was strewn with dismembered limbs that looked as if they had been torn, not cut, from the demon bodies that they had once adorned.

He needn't have worried about Moriel.

He turned his back on the scene and jogged over to the door that led out into the bailey. Relieved to find that there was a huge handle on his side, he reached out to grab it, but stopped himself from actually opening the door. He and Charles were not far from freedom now and he wanted nothing more than to throw it open and sprint across the open space on the other side. He knew that he could cross it before any flying demons were able to get at them and then it was simply a matter of getting through the tunnel and escaping to the portal in the outer wall. He didn't want to think what would happen if it was not still there, if Gwendolin had closed it before returning to her room in the tower.

Come on, Trey, he told himself.

But something still halted his hand. A small icy shiver ran down him and he looked behind him into the dungeon, expecting whatever it was that had set his senses on edge to come at him from out of the gloom.

He shook his head, telling himself that he was being foolish, that he was risking his and Charles's safety by stalling here. He threw the door wide-open, emerging into the bailey—and straight into the onrushing attack of Caliban.

43

Trey stood, looking in disbelief at the sight of the vampire, unable to imagine how he had got down to this level so quickly. He had either misted to get here, or there was some other, faster way down the tower—perhaps the route that they had used to transport the Draugr. The vampire flew at the werewolf in an apoplectic rage, a whirling flash of fangs and talons and rampant hatred. Caliban's eyes burned a deep red against the gray-white of his flesh, his mouth an open maw of fury and destruction, intent on tearing out the throat of the werewolf. Trey saw all this in a fraction of a second, powerless to defend himself against the unexpected attack. He shifted his weight, dropping his shoulder in an attempt to let Charles fall to safety, but instead the young sorcerer wrapped one arm around the lycanthrope's neck and thrust the other in the direction of the vampire. Caliban was hurled backward through the air, legs and arms thrown out ahead of him, his body propelled viciously by some invisible force. But the vampire was on his feet almost before he had landed and glared back at the two teenagers, a loud hiss coming from his lips. He misted, disappearing to appear immediately before them again, the metal blades of the prosthetic hand flashing in the air to tear the throat from the werewolf. The vampire had won.

And then he was gone.

Trey reared his head back, knowing that he could not escape death at the hands of the vampire lord, when a black shadow blurred past his vision, removing the vampire just as it was about to deliver the blow that would end the teenager's life. The shadow moved so quickly that the boy had no chance of making out what it was. But he knew. He shot his head around, trying to track Moriel as she flashed up into the sky high overhead. Caliban was slashing at her face and throat as he struggled to wrestle himself out of her grip, but the battle angel ignored his attempts at freedom.

"Go, Trey Laporte. Now!" Her voice filled the sky. "Run!"

Something slipped from the battle angel's grasp, falling through the air and landing with a thump on the ground ahead of where Trey still stood in the doorway.

"It is yours now," Moriel cried over the furious screams and shrieks of the vampire lord. "Now go!"

Trey sprinted for the exit carved into the rock on the opposite side of the bailey, dipping slightly to scoop up whatever it was that Moriel had dropped for him on the way. He tore through the opening and plunged down the tunnel, his huge thighs powering him through the blackness toward the portal up ahead. Charles lay across his shoulders, a lifeless rag doll.

As he neared the opening he thought that he could smell

exhaust fumes in the tunnel. He shook his head at the tricks that his mind was playing on him in the state of panic that he was now in, and pushed ahead around what he hoped was the last bend. He saw the incredible sight of Tom sitting inside the car that he had backed all the way into the opening, waiting for them with the engine ticking over. Trey gratefully breathed in a huge lungful of the hard, metallic reek, thinking how the pollutant had never smelled so good. He wrenched the rear door open, then stopped, laying Charles down on the ground next to the car.

"Trey?" Tom's voice called out to him from inside the car.

Trey looked down at the young sorcerer and then crouched over him, placing his head against his chest. The lack of any sound told Trey what he already secretly knew, that his friend was dead, that he had died in that last desperate act to save them from the vampire's attack.

The werewolf lifted his head and howled. The long, ululating cry bounced back and forth across the rock walls, filling the tunnel with its desperate sound.

"Trey?" Tom's voice seemed to come out of a fog. "Trey, we must go. Now."

Trey looked up at the Irishman, tears coursing down the short hairs on his face. *"He's dead, Tom. Charles is dead."*

"Oh, lad." Tom shook his head, turning to look out of the windshield, for once lost for words. When he looked back at Trey his eyes had hardened again, his mouth set determinedly. "We won't leave him here," he said. "Put him

307

in the back next to Alexa, but we have to get out of here or his death will have been for nothing."

Trey did as he was told, gently placing Charles in the back of the car before folding his great frame into the front seat next to Tom, who crunched the car into gear and shot forward through the gap into the nightscape of Iceland.

44

They drove straight to the airport. Tom had broken the silence of their journey only once, calling Hjelmar to make arrangements for their departure.

Trey sat staring out of the side window, glad for the quiet in which he was able to try to get his head around everything that had happened. He had transformed back into his human form and now sat in the front seat, wrapped in a blanket that Tom had retrieved from the trunk.

"It's OK, Trey," the Irishman said in a low voice. "We're free of that place now."

Trey nodded and cut his eyes toward his friend for a moment. "You're bleeding an awful lot, Tom."

"You're not doing so badly yourself on that front, lad."

After about twenty minutes, Alexa came around. She gingerly sat up in the back of the car, cradling her head in her hands and looking about her as if in a daze.

"Did we get the globe?" she asked, her voice little more than a whisper.

"Yes," Trey answered, his eyes never leaving the landscape flying by outside the car. "We got the globe."

Alexa sat up, a small groan escaping her lips. She frowned in Trey's direction and was about to say something when she caught sight of Tom's eyes in the rearview mirror. Something had gone horribly wrong. She looked down at the prostrate figure of Charles next to her, and instantly knew.

"Oh, no, Charles!" she cried.

She pulled his body toward her, placing his head on her lap so that she could stroke his hair. Her sobs filled the confines of the car and they drove like that for some time, the only sounds those of the road and Alexa's crying.

Eventually Alexa looked up, her breath coming in harsh, ragged little gasps. "What happened?" she asked.

Trey told them about his and Charles's experiences inside Leroth, recalling the dangers that they had faced on their way up through the tower. He told them how Charles had forced the globe into his hands and bundled him out of the room to face Gwendolin alone, but he stopped short of describing the terrible scenes that followed inside the sorceress's chambers. Alexa had gone very quiet, and it was left up to Tom to fill in the other side of the story from their perspective. Finally Trey told them how the young mage had given his life to save him from Caliban. He stopped then, too choked to continue.

"I think he knew," he said eventually. "I think he used up everything he had to cast that last spell to save us from Caliban. I felt him collapse into me afterward, as if all his life force had suddenly *gone* from him. I think he knew, but he still went ahead and . . ."

Trey stared down at the glass sphere nestling on the seat

between his legs. The price to attain it had been so very high that he prayed their efforts would not have been in vain. It was terrible that a life had been sacrificed to retrieve something with which they hoped to save another life. He picked the object up, holding it in front of his face, looking into its depths again. He drew in a sharp, sudden breath, turning in his seat to face Alexa, who was looking back at him, already shaking her head.

"Its powers are only effective on nether-creatures," she said. "And Charles is dead, not ill. Even if we had also taken Skaleb's Staff and used them together to bring him back, he would not be alive in the sense that you and I are; he'd be . . . something else." She looked down again at the head still on her lap.

"Let's get him home," Tom said.

Charles's coffin was carried aboard the plane by Hjelmar and his people. Tom had made all of the arrangements, bypassing the authorities, who would no doubt have insisted on having reams of paperwork filled out before they would release the body. Trey, Alexa, and Tom stood on the tarmac and watched their friend being taken aboard, Alexa huddling into the two men's arms as they all grieved. An hour later they were all aboard, and the plane leaped up from the runway into the heavy skies over Iceland.

Trey had changed into the clothes that Hjelmar had thoughtfully provided for him. He'd settled down in his seat and slept for most of the journey home, only waking toward the end of the flight when he sensed that someone was looking at him. He opened his eyes and looked across at Alexa. She was staring at him, a sad smile on her face.

"Are you OK?" she asked.

"No. You?"

She shook her head, her eyes never leaving his.

Alexa asked the question that Trey had been dreading, even though he knew that it was inevitable.

"What happened to Gwendolin?" she asked.

Trey thought back to the horrific end that the sorceress had met and how her dying eyes had stared back at him in her last moments.

"She was killed." Trey glanced toward the back of the cabin, where Charles's coffin lay. "She was going to kill Charles," he said by way of an explanation. "I'm sorry, Alexa."

Trey waited, his body tensed against whatever was coming. Alexa leaned forward and very gently put her hand on his knee. "That thing wasn't my mother, Trey. My mother died long ago. She left my father and me to join Caliban because she loved the power more than she ever loved us. It sounds cold, but I feel nothing to learn that what little was left of her has now been destroyed. I'd say that I hope she rots in hell, but I think that she has been doing that for an awfully long time."

They sat in silence, the sound of the aircraft's engines filling their ears.

"Tell me about the angel," she said. "What was she like?"

Trey frowned, a short humorless snort escaping him. "Not like anything you've ever seen on top of a Christmas tree. She was . . . magnificent. And she was beautiful, and . . . scary. Scary as hell—terrifying, in fact. Terrifying and beautiful." The words came rushing out of his mouth too quickly and he looked back at her, feeling himself blush. "She saved us."

"What do you think happened to Caliban and her?" Alexa asked.

"I don't know. She was taking a lot of punishment from him. She told me to run. So I did." He paused, frowning as the scene replayed itself to him. "There was something else though," he said. "Something about Caliban's expression as he realized what it was that had grabbed him and carried him up into the sky."

"What?"

"Terror. It was all over his face. Even as he was hacking at her with that metal hand, you could see that he was petrified of her."

"Let's hope his fear was justified and that she polished him off once and for all," Tom said in a low voice, looking up from the table that he'd been working at. His rucksack was on the chair beside him. Trey had given him the globe just before they'd taken off, and Tom had treated the thing as if it were one of the explosives he was so fond of, placing it carefully in the bag.

"Yeah," Trey said, glancing up at his friend. "Let's hope so."

But something inside him didn't believe it. Something told him that the vampire had not perished at the hands of the Arel. And while this *intuition* depressed him, there was something else that occurred to him that lifted his spirits for the first time since escaping Leroth. It was another one of those gut feelings, another one of those instincts that he had recently begun to trust more and more, and it told him that Moriel was also still alive. The Arel battle angel had survived Caliban's attacks and escaped him once more.

Trey thought back to her face as she stood in front of him and Charles after they had released her. He thought of her icy cold eyes and the scar that wound its way across her features and how she had addressed them by their full names in a way that had seemed so formal at the time. They had only met for a matter of moments, and yet he felt a connection between them. Something that he couldn't put his finger on, but felt nevertheless. He searched himself now, trying to tap into that *connection*, and the more he did the more convinced he became.

Yes, he was certain of it—she was still alive.

"We'll be landing soon," Tom said. "Better get yourselves strapped in." He nodded at the small leather-bound book that Moriel had thrown down to Trey from the sky. "Do you want me to put that in my bag?"

Trey looked down at it and shook his head. "No, I'll hang on to it for now. Thanks."

45

The man called Christian surfaced out of the ocean about twenty feet away from the boat. The moonlight jumped off the small waves that were playing on the ocean surface, the light a harsh and unwelcome contrast to the velvety blackness from which he had just emerged. He pulled up his mask and swam over to the rear of the dive boat, climbing up the ladder and onto the deck, where he started to remove his tank and the rest of his diving gear.

"Where the bloody hell have you been?" Max shouted as he strode across the deck toward him. "We said that we would return to the boat immediately if we were separated. What the hell do you think you're playing at? And what happened to your surface marker buoy? We had no idea what had happened to you, or where you were."

Christian looked at him and frowned as if he couldn't understand why this man was standing in front of him and screaming into his face. He shook his head a little and dropped the weight belt that he was holding onto the deck among his other kit.

A painful jolt—like a small electric shock—fired into his back, making him wince. He smiled back at his friend. "Sorry. I got a bit disorientated down there for a while. It took me a while to get my head together and then I came back up. I'm fine."

He could not remember how he had got separated from his dive buddy. They had been swimming near an old wreck when something in the distance had caught his eye. He had swum toward it, thinking that it might be a part of the wreck that they had missed when they had explored it during the day.

As he approached the shape he realized to his horror that it was—

He hissed through his teeth as another balloon of pain burst inside him.

"I need to go and lie down," he said to Max. "I'm feeling a bit strange right now and I really could do with just lying down in the quiet for a while."

He walked past his friend, who was now staring at him worriedly, and descended through the hatch into the galley below.

There was a strange sensation in his stomach and he fought off the need to rush to the head and be sick. Instead he slumped down onto one of the seats, lying out along its length, and closed his eyes.

The Necrotroph shut down all of the host's body mechanisms that were not essential to keeping the human alive and plunged him into a deep unconsciousness that allowed the demon to do what was now necessary.

Against all the odds, it had survived. It would need to contact its master, Caliban, to explain what had happened.

He would be enraged that the demon had allowed itself to be discovered in the way that it had. Also, in its panic to survive, it had neglected to discover the secret that Martin Tipsbury had been harboring. But it was confident that Caliban would give it another chance to get back into Lucien Charron's organization again.

It set about preparing the new host. It would not make the same mistakes that it had made with the last one. It would be thorough now and bide its time until it could wreak its revenge on those that it had been sent to infiltrate.

It would find a way back into the vampire Lucien Charron's world and help its master to destroy it from the inside.

EPILOGUE

Alexa performed the ritual that brought Lucien back to health. She ushered everyone else from the room and locked the door while she tried to rescue her father from the brink of death.

It was difficult. She had never studied the ancient texts that described the ritual, and she wished more than once that Charles was there to go through it with her.

After three hours she opened the door and trudged out into the apartment. Her body was covered with a film of sweat that stuck her clothes to her body and made her hair look lank and depressed.

Tom and Trey sprang up from the couch and rushed over to her like two buoyant cocker spaniels welcoming their master home at the end of the day. She looked up into their expectant faces and gave them a minuscule shrug of her shoulders.

"Now we wait," she said. "I don't know if what I did was enough. We'll have to wait and see."

Her knees gave way a little and she would have fallen if Tom had not grabbed her and helped her over to sit on the leather couch. He sat down next to her.

"I know that you've done everything you can, Alexa. And

I know that if effort counts for anything, Lucien is going to be . . ." He looked at her—she was already asleep.

Lucien woke just after nine that evening. Alexa was sitting in the chair by his bedside and it was the sound of her crying that brought Trey and Tom into the bedroom, to see Lucien sitting up against the pillows and smiling at his daughter, who was holding his hand and sobbing into the covers. His other hand stroked the back of her head.

"Thomas." Lucien nodded at his friend before turning to look at Trey with his fiery eyes. "Trey . . . you were in my dreams. You and Alexa here kept me going."

Trey nodded. "I'm glad that you're back with us again, Lucien. We missed you so very much."

Alexa looked up and turned to face them for the first time. Her red, tearstained face broke into a smile, and Trey watched her knuckles turn white as she gripped her father's hand.

The following morning Trey, Alexa, Tom, and Lucien went to see Charles. Lucien's recovery had defied all expectations and he'd waved the doctors away when they had suggested that he stay in bed for a while yet.

Charles lay in an oak coffin at the funeral home, and they stood around him, looking down at the young man who had done so much to ensure that there were four, not three, people there to mourn him.

Trey looked across at his guardian and found it almost impossible to reconcile the sight of the tall, handsome

319

creature here with him now with the pale and ancient-looking thing that had so recently laid in the hospital bed back at the apartment. The vampire's golden eyes blazed once more, the mysterious light that seemed to dwell in those fascinating globes more vibrant than ever as he stared down at the lifeless figure in front of him. Trey watched as Lucien reached down to touch Charles's cheek with the back of his hand. "Thank you," he said. "I shall do everything in my power to repay you for what you did for me and to avenge your death. I will not forget you, Charles Henstall." Then he turned on his heel and walked out of the room, leaving the remaining three people alone.

"Goodbye, lad," Tom said, placing a single white rose on Charles's chest.

Trey and Alexa held hands and let the tears flow, each of them saying goodbye to their friend in their own way.

It had been four days since they had buried Charles when Trey burst into Lucien's office without knocking. The vampire looked up from his desk, and if he was annoyed at the rude interruption there was nothing in his expression to betray the fact.

In one hand Trey held the framed photograph that Alexa had given him for his birthday, in the other the small book that the battle angel had thrown down to him at Leroth.

"Did you know about this?" Trey said, brandishing the book in the vampire's direction. "What am I saying? Of course you knew."

"Know about what?" Lucien replied, one eyebrow arching slightly. The vampire sat back in his chair, lacing his fingers before him. The light shone off his bald skull and his eyes never left those of his young ward, who stood before him, his chest rising and falling as he sought to contain his anger.

"Why didn't you tell me that I had an uncle?"

Lucien glanced toward the items in the boy's hands before returning to his face.

"I think you should sit down."

"I don't want to sit down, Lucien. I want you to tell me why you didn't let me know I have an uncle. Is this him?" Trey brandished the photograph in the vampire's direction. "This man with my mother and father. Is he my uncle?"

Lucien stood up and slowly reached out, taking the frame out of the boy's hand and studying the picture. He smiled, his eyes taking in the happy faces of the lakeside scene.

"How did you find out?"

"My father," Trey said, trying to maintain eye contact with Lucien. "Moriel wanted me to have this." He threw the book onto the desk. "It's my father's journal. I had no idea what it was—what with the funeral and everything—today was the first time that I've had a chance to open it."

"I see."

"Is he still alive?" Trey asked.

"Yes."

Trey waited, trying to keep a handle on the anger that boiled up inside him.

Lucien took a deep breath, a frown creasing his forehead as he considered how to respond.

"It wasn't my intention to keep it from you forever. But I needed to make sure that you . . . understood certain things before doing so. I'm sorry."

"Who are the LG78?"

"Ah . . ."

"They're a pack of werewolves, aren't they, Lucien? There are others like me out there, aren't there?"

"No, Trey. They are not like you. And neither is your uncle. You are unique."

Trey waited, hoping that Lucien would elaborate. When it was clear that the vampire was still not willing to talk he lost his patience.

"I have family, Lucien!" Trey shook his head in disbelief. "I thought that I had lost everyone and everything and it turns out that I have an uncle somewhere out there." He looked down at Lucien. "And I think that you know where he is, don't you?"

"Yes, I know where your uncle is. And if you would like to meet him, I'd be happy to arrange for . . ."

"No, Lucien," Trey said, unable to keep the anger from his voice. "All I want from you is for you to tell me where he is and how I can go about finding him. I have my own money. I'll make my own arrangements to meet him, thank you."

Lucien looked at the boy. He started to say something, but stopped, deciding that now was not the right time. He reached into a drawer by the side of his desk and removed a

322

sheet of paper, took his pen, and wrote down an address, folding the paper in half before handing it across the desk to the teenager standing on the other side.

"That is the address where your uncle lives. It is in Canada. If you need any help with your plans, you only have to ask."

Trey looked down at the piece of paper in his hands before nodding a surly thanks. He picked up the photograph and his father's journal and made his way to the door.

"Trey," Lucien said as the teenager was about to go, "I really would welcome the opportunity of talking with you before you go. There are things that you need to know about your uncle and the LG78. Things that could spell great danger for you if you leave without first hearing about them. In addition, I would like to ask a favor of you." He waited, but, when the boy chose not to respond, carried on anyway. "I'd ask that you do not leave right away. I'd like you to be around here for a while. We have an awful lot to catch up on, Trey."

Trey looked at Lucien and nodded. "Fine," he said. "We'll talk before I leave."

Lucien watched as the boy left the room, closing the door quietly behind him. He sighed and picked up the phone, asking for Tom to come in and join him as soon as he was free. He replaced the receiver and considered everything that had just been said. There was no stopping the boy. He would want to meet his uncle and find out what he was like and what they had in common. It was natural.

He had not wanted the boy to find out like this. He had

wanted to be the one to tell Trey about his uncle and about his group. He had won the boy's trust and now that trust had been destroyed. There were things Trey needed to know about his uncle, things that he had done to Trey's father. The uncle was poison, and the pack that called itself the LG78 could spell terrible danger for the teenager. A danger that might destroy him forever.

To be continued . . .

ACKNOWLEDGMENTS

My heartfelt thanks to all the people who have helped me to make this book possible. I'd especially like to thank:

Peter Ryder of the MRPC for his help with information on rifle clubs and shooting. Any errors and misinformation on these matters are entirely down to me.

Phil Towser for his help with all things medical. I shall no doubt continue to pester you for future books, Phil.

Catherine Pellegrino and Claire Wilson at RCW for all their hard work and help. When the going gets tough, I go to my agent.

The wonderful people at Macmillan who work so hard to make the whole "publishing thing" as painless as possible. In particular, I'd like to thank Rebecca McNally, who continues to put up with me and my ultracompetitive nature, and whose insight and wisdom made this book the best it could be; Talya Baker, for her attention to detail so that I don't look completely bungling; and Dom Kingston, for his enthusiasm in dealing with an utter scatterhead like me.

Finally, I'd like to thank the stars in my sky: Zoe, Hope, and Kyran—you are everything to me. And to all my family for their love and support and belief; I am so lucky to have you all in my universe.

WHICH NETHER-CREATURE ARE YOU?

From werewolves to djinn, vampires to Necrotrophs, all kinds of Netherworld creatures feature in the Wereling novels, but which one are you most like? Answer each question, add up the points, then find out which nether-creature you might be . . .

1. If you could have one special power, what would it be?

a) Supernatural senses of sight, hearing, and smell. *3 points*

b) Immense strength and muscularity. *2 points*

c) Everlasting youth—I want my great looks to last. *4 points*

d) Incredible speed. *1 point*

2. You have to face an enemy. What is your greatest weapon?

a) My intellect (and my fangs). *4 points*

b) Surprise (there's nothing like an ambush). *1 point*

c) Brute strength. *2 points*

d) Awesome (but controlled) aggression. *3 points*

3. It's Friday night and your best friend has offered to cook you dinner—what would be the worst food they could serve you?

a) Salad—vegetables? Yuck! *3 points*

b) Garlic bread. *4 points*

c) Roast dinner—I can't bear to wait for my food. *1 point*

d) Anything small and delicate—I've got to keep my strength up. *2 points*

4. If you could live anywhere in the world, where would it be?

a) The Canadian wilderness—I'm an outdoorsy type. *3 points*

b) Up near the Arctic Circle—those long, long nights. I'd need company though. *4 points*

c) Tokyo—for the frenetic hustle and bustle. *1 point*

d) Los Angeles—preferably near Muscle Beach. *2 points*

5. What is your favorite film?
a) The Hulk. *2 points*
b) Twilight. *4 points*
c) Harry Potter and the Half-Blood Prince. *3 points*
d) Speed. *1 point*

Now **add up your points** and see below to discover which nether-creature you could be.

0–5 points. **You are a Shadow Demon**

You are fast, cunning, and an incredibly effective killing machine. You exist within the human world by adopting a human mantle as a disguise. You like to hang out in dark places where you can hide in wait for your next victim.

6–10 points. **You are a Maug Demon**

Huge and powerful, you have a strong sense of loyalty to your friends and colleagues, making you and your kind the ideal choice as a bodyguard. Not the fastest or brightest of the nether-creatures, but you make up for this with aggression and great fighting skills.

11–15 points. **You are a Werewolf**

In wolf form, you are viciously powerful with exceptional senses of smell, hearing, and sight, far beyond those of both wolves and men. As a lyco (a hereditary werewolf, in complete control of your transformations), you combine the strength of the human mind with the physical power of a beast.

16–20 points. **You are a Vampire**

You can live for hundreds of years but often stay youthful, with pale skin and hypnotic eyes, and you have an amazing ability to heal quickly. You must live among humans to survive, but your severe allergy to the sun means that being outside can be very dangerous. You fear nothing in life, except lycos, sharp stakes . . . and garlic!

Look out for . . .

WEREling

BLOOD WOLF

STEVE FEASEY

The last hereditary werewolf has found his pack—they're vicious, bloodthirsty, and truly wild.

Trey has had enough of vampires, demons, and sorcerors. He needs to get in touch with his own kind—the ones with fur, fangs, and killer instincts.

But the wolf pack howling at the moon in Canada is not what he expected. And without the protection of defanged vampire and demon-hunter Lucien Charron, the family secret is more dangerous than he ever knew.
Trey's out of control. Can the werewolf be tamed?

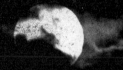